DOVER
ONE

DOVER

ONE

Joyce Porter

A Foul Play Press Book

The Countryman Press, Inc.
Woodstock, Vermont

Copyright © 1964 by Joyce Porter

This edition first published in 1989 by Foul Play Press,
an imprint of The Countryman Press, Inc.,
Woodstock, Vermont 05091

ISBN 0-88150-134-4

Printed in the United States of America

10 9 8 7 6 5 4 3

To
MY MOTHER

DOVER
ONE

Chapter One

IT was spring. The windows of the chain-stores bloomed with plastic daffodils and the first buds were beginning to burgeon through layers of London soot.

The Assistant Commissioner (C) took a deep breath and smiled happily as he detected a vernal whiff in the mingled petrol and diesel fumes. With reckless abandon he celebrated the rebirth of the year by purchasing a one-and-sixpenny pink carnation for his buttonhole. The bloom had been forced in a continental hothouse and glistened not with dew but with a mouthful of tap water which had just been spat upon it by the flowerseller, but for the Assistant Commissioner it symbolized being in England now that April was there. He strode jauntily along to his office in New Scotland Yard, casting roguish glances at the legs of such young ladies as he happened to meet.

By four o'clock in the afternoon both the pink carnation and the Assistant Commissioner were looking their age. The Assistant Commissioner had spent most of the day on one of those futile committees which bedevil the lives of our top administrators. After five hours of acrimonious bickering he had been defeated over a matter of such staggering insignificance that both sides had rapidly discarded not only common sense but even expediency, and based their arguments on matters of principle. And in matters of principle, as well as in everything else, the Assistant Commissioner liked to get his own way.

He was still resentfully chewing over his defeat when, just after four o'clock, his phone rang.

He snatched the receiver up. 'Well?' he snarled.

His secretary was unperturbed. 'The Chief Constable of Creedshire on the line for you, sir,' she said calmly, 'Mr Bartlett.'

'Hullo, Bartlett!' roared the Assistant Commissioner, who always shouted on the telephone. 'You're in the chair now, I take it?'

'Yes, I am.' Mr Bartlett's voice came tinnily over the wires. 'I took over yesterday.'

'Must be a very nice little job!' bellowed the Assistant Commissioner. 'Down there in the country at this time of the year Wouldn't mind changing places with you myself, I must say.'

'Yes, it's very ... '

'Not too much work, either, I'll bet! Bit of sheep stealing and failing to notify foot-and-mouth and that's your lot, eh?'

'Well, not quite. That's what I wanted to ... '

'I used to tell old George Turner he'd got the cushiest job in the country. God only knows, he won't have any problems adjusting to retirement! He hasn't done a stroke in the last fifteen years to my certain knowledge!' The Assistant Commissioner chuckled ruefully and prepared to launch into a well-oiled dissertation on his own unfair burden of cares and responsibilities.

Mr Bartlett cut the small talk short. 'I need your help,' he said flatly.

'Oh?' said the Assistant Commissioner. 'What's the matter?'

'A young woman's disappeared.'

'How long?'

'Her employer – she works as a kind of maid – hasn't seen her since Tuesday lunch-time.'

'But, dammit, man, it's only Thursday now!' protested the Assistant Commissioner. 'You don't want to start getting into a muck-sweat yet! She's probably only hopped off for a few days with her boy-friend!'

'There's no indication at all that she intended to go away, rather the reverse.' The Chief Constable sounded petulant. He had not expected an argument. His objections were grandly pushed aside.

'My dear chap,' said the Assistant Commissioner, only too obviously trying to be kind and helpful to the new boy, 'girls are like that, specially servant girls. Some bright young spark catches their eye and it's up with their skirts, hot foot to the nearest haystack. Figuratively speaking, of course. Happens in a flash, you know. Spring and all that!'

'Well, you may be right ... ' began Bartlett.

'Of course I'm right!' Even two hundred miles away the interruption rang with self-satisfaction.

'But I don't think you are,' Bartlett pressed on while he had the chance. 'I've got a feeling there's something fishy about this case and I'm not going to take any chances. Better be safe than sorry, that's my motto! I don't want to be caught like old George Turner was.'

'Why, what happened to him?' The Assistant Commissioner was a great one for a bit of police gossip.

'In all the twenty years he sat in this chair before me, they only had one murder in the county. Woman battered to death with an axe, blood and brains all over the kitchen floor, you know the sort of thing. Well, George turned the local boys loose on it and you've never seen such a cock-up in your life! They ended up by arresting the vicar's son on such rubbishy evidence that the public prosecutor wouldn't even let 'em bring the case before the magistrates. All the yokels were laughing themselves silly because everybody knew who'd done it, except the poor old cops. The chap got off scot-free and poor old George Turner never lived it down. They never let him forget it, I can tell you! Well, they're not going to get me tied hand and foot like that!'

'No, no, of course not!' the Assistant Commissioner chimed in with evident sympathy. 'Watch Committees can be devils, I couldn't agree more! You've got to be top dog or they'll lead you a – er – a dog's life.'

There was a pause while both men pondered over the infelicity of this metaphor.

'Well, you see, don't you?' Mr Bartlett went on. 'If my sixth sense is right and this girl hasn't just slipped off for a bit of slap and tickle with somebody else's husband, it might be a very nasty case, very nasty indeed.'

'Murder, you mean?'

'Or kidnapping.'

'Kidnapping? Now, steady on, old man, you've been seeing too much telly! We don't have kidnapping in this country, place is much too small! Besides, it's not English!'

'There's always a first time,' said Mr Bartlett darkly, 'and it'd just be my bloody luck to get clobbered with it.'

'Well, what have you done so far?'

'The local bobby's scratched around a bit. Like everybody else he thought she'd be turning up again right as rain. Bar reporting it to H.Q., I don't think he's done much. There's an outbreak of fowl pest or swine fever or something and, naturally, that's far more up his street than one of these vanishing-lady larks.'

'I suppose you've circulated the usual description?'

'Yes, we did that right away.'

'Hm. Not that it helps much. One young girl looks pretty much like another these days.'

'Not this one! She stands five foot three in stiletto heels and she turns the scales at nearly sixteen stone!'

'My God!' said the Assistant Commissioner, duly impressed at last.

'And she's got bright ginger hair! It makes a difference, doesn't it?'

'It does indeed, old man!'

'Yes, dead or alive, she's going to be difficult to hide. Now do you see why I want some help? Sixteen stone of bouncing British girlhood can't just disappear into thin air, can it?'

'No, indeed it can't, old chap. Once seen, never forgotten, by the sound of it. Yes, I'm inclined to agree with you, you should have got a line by now if she's still kicking around.'

'Then can you let me have somebody right away? Somebody good, mind, I don't want one of your old dead-beats!'

'There are no dead-beats on my staff, old man.' The Assistant Commissioner spoke with heavy reproof, but the expression had given him an idea. He still wasn't convinced that this was a case for the Yard but he didn't want to turn down a chap who was understandably being a bit wary in his new job. And, anyhow, Bartlett might just conceivably turn out to be right. Murder would be bad enough but kidnapping, from the professional point of view, could be terrible. At least in the case of murder you couldn't blame the dead body on the police, but in kidnapping whatever you did might be wrong. If you let 'em hand over the ransom money, the kidnappers might still kill their victim, and if you stopped the ransom money you were equally likely to be left with a corpse on your hands. The Assistant Commissioner shuddered gently as he thought of all the messes you could get into in a kidnapping case. It wasn't the sort of job you'd wish on a dog.

He turned back to the telephone. There was only one man for the job. 'I'll send you one of my chief inspectors,' he said. 'Good chap. Name's Dover. I'll get him down to you first thing in the morning.'

The Assistant Commissioner dropped the receiver back in place and grinned wickedly. A man in his exalted position shouldn't indulge in petty spite where his subordinates were concerned, but it was, oh, so pleasant to give way to these little human frailties, once in a while.

'I'd love to see the old bugger's face when he hears what he's got landed with this time!' The Assistant Commissioner chuckled happily to himself and picked up his phone again to send the good news down the line.

* * *

'Bloody waste of time!' snarled Chief Inspector Wilfred Dover as he sat slumped and sulky in the corner of his first-class reserved compartment.

His sergeant, sitting opposite him, sighed with resignation. He'd had nearly four hours of this and whatever sympathy he'd had at the beginning had now worn very thin.

'Yes, sir,' he said, and gazed hopelessly out of the window.

'I don't know why it is,' Dover grumbled remorselessly on, 'it always seems to be me that gets landed with these jobs. You'll see, we'll hang around there for a couple of days and then she'll turn up again, older and wiser, if you know what I mean. Holed up in Brighton, that's where she is! And when her money runs out, the boy-friend'll hop it and she'll come back home.' Dover snorted petulantly down his nose. 'Wadder say her name was?' he growled.

Sergeant MacGregor told him, wearily and for the fourth time. 'Rugg, sir, Juliet Rugg.'

Dover paused to give his little joke an appropriate build-up.

'Well, I reckon Juliet's found her Romeo!'

Sergeant MacGregor smiled bleakly. He'd heard this four times before, too.

Charles Edward MacGregor was, in fact, feeling nearly as hard done by as Dover was, though for a slightly different reason. He regarded himself, and was indeed regarded by his superiors, as one of the up-and-coming young officers at the Yard. He was intelligent, efficient, courteous and sympathetic, and extremely well dressed to boot. It seemed unfair that he should be coupled with Chief Inspector Dover, who was his exact opposite in almost everything. But the Assistant Commissioner, who kept a fatherly eye on these matters, was a great believer in baptisms of fire and salvation through suffering and he frequently used Dover to

13

provide both for young detectives whose opinion of themselves was, perhaps, a little too high. The Assistant Commissioner felt, with some justification, that if a lad could stick Dover, he could stick almost anything. It was damned good character training! He had, therefore, turned a deaf ear to the pleas of both Dover and Sergeant MacGregor that the first case* upon which they had been engaged together should be their last.

And so here they were again, already chafing in their double harness and setting out with sinking hearts and mutual ill-will to solve the apparently unmysterious disappearance of Juliet Rugg.

A police car was waiting for them at Creedon Station. The police driver saluted smartly, opened the door, packed their cases in the boot and leapt athletically into his seat. He was alert and keen. Ten minutes later, at the end of their journey, he was wondering if his brother-in-law's offer of a job in the slaughter-house was still open.

Chief Inspector Dover was a nervous passenger and he didn't care who knew it. A non-driver himself, he was none the less acutely sensitive to the hazards which beset the man at the wheel. Crouching tensely on the back seat he shared all his premonitions of impending danger with the unfortunate man who was actually driving the car. The endless stream of advice to look out for dogs, old ladies, young children, pedestrian crossings, traffic lights, bicycles, learner drivers, blind corners and one-way streets, was relieved only by pungent post-mortems on previous risky manœuvres which had already brought the three of them within kissing distance of the jaws of death.

By the grace of God, and in spite of Dover, the police driver, a man of fourteen years' unblemished experience, got the car safely to the headquarters of the Creedshire Constabulary.

Dover heaved himself out of the back and lumbered off into the building without a word. MacGregor did the honours on his behalf.

'Thank you very much, driver,' he said with a winning smile.

The driver just looked at him, not trusting himself to speak, and turned away with trembling hands to unload the baggage.

Inside the police headquarters Dover was ushered rapidly into the presence of the Chief Constable. Mr Bartlett had prepared

* 'Inspector Dover and the Spilt Milk' – this case has not been and will not be published at any price.

14

and practised a little speech of welcome, brief but covering rather neatly, he thought, all the essential points. When the two detectives were announced he glanced up distractedly from his desk. This had been rehearsed too. He was about to flash a frank, manly smile at them when his first actual sight of Dover literally took his breath away.

The chief inspector, purple in the face and with his bowler hat rammed well down over his ears, came into the room like a charging rhinoceros.

'That bloody driver of yours isn't fit to drive a toy scooter on a fairground roundabout!' he roared.

The Chief Constable's jaw dropped. Was this what the Assistant Commissioner had sent him? He gazed in helpless fascination at the figure which loomed, snorting furiously, above his desk.

Detective Chief Inspector Wilfred Dover was a big man. His six-foot-two frame was draped, none too elegantly, in seventeen and a quarter stone of flabby flesh, an excessive proportion of which had settled round his middle. Well-cut clothing can, of course, do wonders to conceal such natural defects as the spread of middle age, but Dover bought his suits ready-made, and the one he was wearing at the moment had been purchased a long time ago. It was made of shiny blue serge. Round his thick, policeman's neck he wore a blue-striped collar which was almost submerged in the folds of fat, and a thin, cheap tie was knotted under the lowest of his double chins. He wore a long, dark blue overcoat and stout black boots.

Over the whole of this unprepossessing ensemble there was, naturally enough, Dover's face. It was large and flabby like the rest of him. Only the details – nose, mouth and eyes – seemed out of scale. They were so tiny as to be almost lost in the wide expanse of flesh. Dover had two small, mean, button-like eyes, a snub little nose and a sulky rosebud of a mouth. He looked like one of those pastry men that children make on baking day out of odd scraps, with currants for eyes – an uncooked pastry man, of course. His hair was thin and black and he had a small black moustache of the type that the late Adolf Hitler did so much to depopularize.

Mr Bartlett gulped and pulled himself together.

'Chief Inspector Dover?' he asked in the faint hope that it might be somebody else.

'Yes.' The hope died. 'And this is Sergeant MacGregor.'

'Well, I'm pleased to meet you both.'

Dover grunted derisively.

'I just wanted to see you, Dover, to assure you that we'll try and – er – give you every assistance we can. Naturally we all want to get this business cleared up as soon as possible ...'

'Too right we do!' said Dover bluntly, and stared sneeringly round the room.

'Er, yes, well, I've arranged for my C.I.D. inspector to brief you and then I expect you'll be wanting to get off and have a look at the scene of the crime, eh?'

'What crime?' demanded Dover. 'Don't tell me you've actually found the body now?'

'No, no – she's still missing. I just meant where she lived and where she was last seen, and everything.' The Chief Constable had had more than enough of this and was already ringing the bell for his inspector.

Unlike Mr Bartlett, the local C.I.D. inspector hadn't bothered to prepare anything. He rummaged dejectedly among the mountain of files and odd sheets of loose paper which covered his desk.

'Judy Rudd,' he muttered, his attention momentarily caught by the sight of his football coupon. He put it carefully on one side and scrabbled around a bit more until he found the accompanying envelope. 'Judy Rudd,' he murmured again, 'I've got the file on her here somewhere.'

Sergeant MacGregor cleared his throat. 'I think the name is Rugg, sir,' he proffered, 'Juliet Rugg with a "g".'

The local man looked surprised. 'Juliet Rugg with a "g"?' he asked doubtfully. 'Are you sure?'

Dover couldn't stand it any longer. With a snort of seething impatience he strode to the desk, pushed aside three library books and a packet of sandwiches, picked up a file, glanced at the heading and slapped it down without a word in front of the inspector.

'Oh?' said the inspector. 'Oh, yes. Thank you! Well now, Juliet Rugg, that's the one you've come about, isn't it? Yes, well then, there's not much I can tell you about her case, I'm afraid.' He peered at the file. 'Oh, yes, she was reported missing by Miss Eve Counter of Irlam Old Hall on Wednesday afternoon – that's the day before yesterday, of course. Missing girl is called Juliet Rugg, age eighteen, working as a maid in the employ of Sir John Counter, also of Irlam Old Hall.' He glanced up at his visitors. 'Perhaps I should explain about Irlam Old Hall,' he suggested unenthusiastically. 'It's a bit involved. It's one of these old houses about a couple of miles outside the village of Earlam. Some time ago, before the war, I think, the family couldn't keep the place up any longer so they converted the house into flats. They sold off most of the land and they built half a dozen houses on the bit that was left – three on either side of the drive, actually. Then they did up the two small lodges by the main gates. So Irlam Old Hall these days is a kind of little housing estate, if you see what I mean. Of course, it's quite an expensive set-up, even the flats are about four or five pounds a week – unfurnished, of course, but they don't use numbers or names. Everybody puts "Irlam Old Hall" on their notepaper and the postman just has to sort out which house or flat to deliver it to by the name of the occupier. The present owner, Mrs Chubb-Smith, she is – she lives in one of the lodges now – she's had several rows with the Post Office about it but so far she's had her own way. So this gentleman who employs Juliet Rugg, Sir John Counter, he and his daughter live in one of the houses built in the grounds.'

'I see,' said Dover, and sniffed.

'Well now, where was I? Oh yes, Juliet Rugg left the Counters' house after lunch on Tuesday afternoon. It was her afternoon off and they expected her back as usual about eleven o'clock that night. Well, she didn't turn up, of course. Well, the village constable went along to see the girl's mother – she lives in the village – and – er – ascertained that the girl had called in to see her mother for about an hour on Tuesday afternoon. She didn't say anything about going away and she left to catch the three-fifteen bus into Creedon here to have a look round the shops and what have you. This was quite normal and she did it every week. The local chap – er – ascertained that she caught the bus all right. Well, at this stage in the inquiry, our chap heard that Mr Bartlett was going to call the Yard in, so he – er – didn't pursue his inquiries any further. And that's really just about all there is.

'We've booked a couple of rooms for you in the pub at Earlam. It's not much of a place but we thought you'd like to be on the spot. Oh, and we've got a car for you. You won't want a driver, will you? The file's got all the addresses in it, and there's a sketch plan of Irlam Old Hall with the names of the people living there. I don't think there's anything else you'll want at the moment, is there?' The inspector glanced anxiously at his football pools.

'No!' said Dover, and rammed his bowler hat on his head. 'Come on, Sergeant, we'd better get moving. We'll obviously have to start from the beginning again so we'll go and see this Counter woman first.'

Sergeant MacGregor accepted the file from the limp hand of the inspector, thanked him for his help, and dashed off after his superior officer. He had a feeling that this case was going to be even worse than their first one was.

Chapter Two

THEY found Irlam Old Hall quite easily and Sergeant Mac-Gregor braked gently from the cautious thirty miles an hour which was all Dover would permit, glanced in his rear mirror, changed down to third, flicked out his right trafficator, poked out his right arm to its full extent, glanced in his mirror again and with bated breath carefully turned the car across a completely deserted, dead straight country road and eased his way sedately through the entrance gates.

The two men gazed thoughtfully through the windscreen. Before them lay a wide, gravelled drive which had long ago lost its struggle with the encroaching grass and weeds. The drive ran in a series of sweeping curves, which seemed to have no functional value as the ground was perfectly flat, up to the front of a large, eighteenth-century building whose architecture was pleasing rather than distinguished. On either side of the main drive were the new houses of which the local C.I.D. inspector had spoken. They stood well back and each was separated from its neighbours by a reasonably large garden and thick clusters of trees. Four smaller paths led off from the main sweep of the drive.

On either side of the main gate were two tiny, ivy-encrusted lodges. Mrs Chubb-Smith, the present owner of the property, lived, according to the sketch plan, in the one on the left.

Sergeant MacGregor guided the shiny black police car up the drive at a docile fifteen miles an hour.

'Which is the Counters' house?' asked Dover.

'It's the top one on the left, sir. Must be that big one over there.'

'Hm,' said Dover, frowning crossly at the well-kept flower beds and trim lawns. 'Sir John or whatever-his-name-is doesn't look short of the ready, anyhow.'

The door was opened by a dark-haired, sullen-faced woman in her middle thirties. She looked anxiously at her visitors. Dover flicked the brim of his bowler hat with the index finger of his right hand.

'Good morning! Is Miss Eve Counter in? We'd like to have a word with her.'

'I'm Eve Counter.' The voice was low and pleasant but lacking in assurance. 'Are you the detectives?'

'Yes, miss. I'm Chief Inspector Dover and this is Detective Sergeant MacGregor. We've come down from Scotland Yard.'

'Well, I think you'd better come inside then.'

She led them into a large airy drawing-room decorated in a restful pastel green. Dover and MacGregor sank into the depths of a couple of huge armchairs while Miss Counter perched herself on an upright chair placed in front of a writing-desk. Just as Dover was about to begin, she shot off her seat and grabbed a cigarette box from a small table.

'Will you have a cigarette?' she asked, thrusting the box at them.

Dover accepted, as he always did, but Sergeant MacGregor refused. There was an embarrassing little moment when the table-lighter wouldn't work and MacGregor produced his, an elegant gold one, to the accompaniment of a shower of thanks and apologies from Miss Counter, who blushed slightly as she accepted a light from the tall, handsome sergeant.

Everything settled down again and Dover opened his mouth for the second time, when Miss Counter realized with another nervous start that there were no ash-trays. Once again she rushed round the room, apologizing for her forgetfulness.

Dover sighed. 'Well, now, Miss Counter,' he said at long last, 'I understand that you reported the disappearance of Miss Rugg to the police?'

'Yes, that's right! I did. My father said I was making a lot of unnecessary fuss and that she'd turn up again, but when she hadn't come back at lunch-time on Wednesday, I thought I'd better ring the police. It couldn't do any harm, could it?'

'When did you last see her?'

'Just after lunch on Tuesday. It was her afternoon off and she usually used to get back about eleven. I'd gone to bed earlier and when I came down in the morning I found that the front door was still unlocked. Then I went into the kitchen and I saw that Juliet hadn't made herself a hot drink when she came in, as she usually did. I thought it was a bit odd, but I got breakfast and took it in to my father. I asked him if Juliet had looked in last night to say good night to him and he said, no, she hadn't. Well, I got on with my work but at about eleven o'clock I thought I'd just pop up and see if she was all right. I went up to her room but she wasn't there and the bed hadn't been slept in.'

'Was anything missing from her room – a suitcase, a change of clothing?'

'No, not as far as I could see. Everything seemed to be there.'

'I understood, Mis Counter,' said Dover, 'that Miss Rugg was employed here as a maid. Wasn't she supposed to get up and get the breakfast and do the housework?'

Miss Counter stubbed her cigarette out in the ash-tray and automatically took another out of the box. Sergeant MacGregor proffered his lighter once again and Miss Counter inhaled a deep pull of smoke into her lungs. She murmured her thanks and Dover waited patiently for an answer to his question.

'Juliet wasn't exactly employed here as a housemaid, Inspector,' she said, speaking rather quickly. 'She's really a kind of, er, companion to my father. He's more or less confined to the house now, although he's not bedridden by any means. He likes to have somebody to chat to and to fetch things for him and so on. He likes somebody fresh and young around him, and that was Juliet's job – generally just to keep him amused. Usually we have a cook and a housemaid as well, but you know what it's like trying to get servants these days, even foreign ones. At the moment we haven't got anybody except a char who comes in to do the rough work a couple of days a week.' She gave a wry little laugh. 'While Juliet looks after my father, I have to turn to and look after the house.'

'What time did you expect to see Miss Rugg, then, on the Wednesday morning?'

'Well, she usually spent every morning in bed, so not much before midday, really. You see, my father stops in bed until lunch-time so there's nothing much for Juliet to do. He doesn't normally get to bed until round about midnight – he always watches the television until it closes down – so she's kept up pretty late at night. If it hadn't been for the unlocked door and no dirty cups and things in the kitchen, I shouldn't have even thought of looking for her till about half-past twelve the next day.'

'Do you know what she usually did on her afternoon off?'

'No. I never asked her and she never told me.'

Dover gazed moodily at Miss Counter as though he were trying to picture her with a hempen rope round her neck.

'How much was Miss Rugg paid as a companion to your father?'

Eve Counter frowned. 'Ten pounds a week,' she said shortly.

'All found?'

'All found.'

There was a pause while the chief inspector pondered over this interesting bit of information. He slumped back even deeper in his chair, his beady little eyes fixed unblinkingly on his hostess's face.

'Do you like Miss Rugg, madam?' he asked in a mild conversational voice.

Eve Counter jumped slightly, then her chin went up.

'No, Chief Inspector, I don't! Not much, anyhow.'

Dover accepted the implied challenge in her answer.

'Care to tell me why, madam?'

'Well, we had absolutely nothing in common. I'm very much older than she is and, well, I come from a different class of society, I have a completely different background. I don't want you to think I'm a snob, but her manners and her behaviour, well, I found them quite intolerable! For me, she just symbolized all that is so dreadful about young people today – phoney American accents, layers of make-up which are never washed off, cheap scent, nails thick with grime and looking as though they've been dipped in blood! Ugh! I thought she was quite revolting!' Eve Counter seemed to be getting quite excited. 'Of course, she looked quite awful, too! She was so fat that it was frankly unbelievable. And that terrible frizzy ginger hair, when it wasn't blonde, that is! To see her mincing along in those high-heeled shoes, well, really! And, of course, she thought she was quite the femme fatale. She was always boasting about all the boy-friends she had and hinting at the number of affairs she'd had with men! And at eighteen, too!'

'Anything else?' asked Dover.

Miss Counter shook her head as though annoyed with herself. 'She was always poking into things that didn't concern her,' she said gruffly, 'reading other people's letters and things like that. Of course, it wasn't anything serious. It was just irritating to have a girl like that in the house.'

'Then why did you, Miss Counter?'

Miss Counter looked bewildered. 'Why did I what, Inspector?'

'Why did you employ Miss Rugg?'

She took a deep breath. 'I didn't, Inspector. I told you, she's employed by my father.'

Dover eased his weight pensively from one buttock to the other. 'In that case, I think we'd better have a word with Sir John,' he said heavily.

'Oh, well, could you leave it till after lunch, Inspector?' Like most women when they are asking a favour, however small, from a man, Eve Counter smiled. The effect was devastating. Sergeant MacGregor's eyes opened wide in astonishment and even Dover, not hypersensitive to feminine charm, blinked. In repose, Eve Counter's thin face had a faintly petulant, disappointed look about it. Her mouth drooped at the corners and her forehead seemed permanently creased in a cross little frown. But when she smiled, her whole face was transformed. Her lips seemed full and red and parted delightfully over small white teeth, and her eyes, now suddenly dark and handsome, sparkled in a most bewitching manner. The lank, unkempt dark hair, the dowdy 'useful' frock she wore with such careless inelegance, the too-thin body which it covered, all this was forgotten when she smiled. Then, she suddenly became a woman of quite exceptional charm and attraction, a woman with whom a man might easily fall in love.

She seemed totally unaware of the effect she was having on the two policemen.

'You see, he's rather an old man now and he's got to harbour his strength. It's very tiring for him if his routine gets broken. I'd really rather not wake him up now, if you don't mind.'

'No, that's all right, madam,' said Dover, still rather disconcerted by the sheer beauty which had broken so unexpectedly through the habitually discontented set of Eve Counter's face. 'We've got to go and see the girl's mother in the village so it'll be quite convenient for us to come back here after lunch. Perhaps we could have a look at Miss Rugg's room at the same time?'

'Of course, Inspector.' The smile glowed briefly into life again. 'As I've told you, I don't really like Juliet, but I don't wish her any harm, naturally. I suppose you haven't found out anything yet?'

'We've only just come on the case, Miss Counter,' said Dover, 'it's a bit early in the day yet for jumping to conclusions. My own personal guess is that the girl's hiding out somewhere with some man or other. That's usually what happens in these cases. I don't doubt she'll turn up safe and sound in a day or two. However' – Dover realized that he was perhaps being a bit too off-hand about the whole thing – 'we shall pursue our inquiries, in the usual way. We've very grateful to you for your help. Good morning, madam.'

'Well,' said MacGregor as he switched on the ignition, 'that girl ought to smile more often! You'd never have thought it, would you? I wouldn't have given her a second look but, hell, when she smiled, she'd really got something! Mind you,' he added judicially, 'her legs weren't bad, either.'

'I'm sure your expert knowledge of the female sex is going to be invaluable, Sergeant,' said Dover with heavy sarcasm, 'but, perhaps, just for now, you could concentrate on your driving.'

Dover looked around as they proceeded slowly down the drive. 'Who lives in the other lodge?' he demanded.

Sergeant MacGregor thought rapidly. 'Er, Colonel Bing and a Miss McLintock.' He dug the names triumphantly out of his excellent memory. 'I suppose she's his housekeeper.'

Dover blew disapprovingly down his nose. 'Well, we all know what that means!' he commented unfairly. 'Anyhow, there's a woman standing at the front door with a dog in her arms. Must be Miss What's-her-name. Hey! Hold on a minute, Sergeant. She's waving us to stop.'

As the police car dribbled to a halt, the woman, still clutching the dog, a small white poodle, to her bosom, came up to the window on Dover's side. The chief inspector wound the glass down. The woman and the dog peered in.

'Are you the chaps from Scotland Yard?' she asked in a deep, excited voice.

'We are, madam,' responded Dover, 'and you, I take it, are Miss ... ' he nudged Sergeant MacGregor violently for his cue, 'Miss McLintock?'

The woman grinned broadly. 'Oh no, I'm not!' she chuckled, obviously enjoying her little triumph. 'I'm Colonel Bing!'

'Oh,' said Dover. There didn't seem anything else to say. He blazed a look of fury at poor Sergeant MacGregor.

'Look,' Colonel Bing went on, 'if you chaps can spare a couple of shakes, I've got a bit of information which I think you ought to have. I haven't said anything to the cops up to now because, frankly, I didn't take this absence-without-leave caper very seriously. Georgie always tells me I'm for ever poking my nose in, so this time I said to myself, Bingo, this time you're just going to mind your own bloody business! But, when we heard last night that they were bringing the big guns up, Georgie agreed with me that I ought to tell you about it and not leave you to go scratching around on your own and getting nowhere.'

'And who,' demanded Dover as he heaved himself resignedly out of the car, 'who is Georgie?'

Colonel Bing's shout of delighted laughter echoed loudly round the country-side. 'You're a witty old devil!' she bellowed. 'Why, Georgie's Miss McLintock!'

' 'Strewth!' muttered Dover sourly, and clumped heavily after her into the little lodge.

Inside the house, which really was remarkably small and unbelievably cluttered up with bits and pieces of furniture, Colonel Bing seemed to grow in stature. Her voice, which had been loud outdoors, now battered unpleasantly on the ear-drums. In reality she was only of medium height and had a no more than well-covered matronly figure, befitting her maturing years. Her hair was iron grey and cropped quite short. She was wearing a drab green woolly twinset and a pleated tartan skirt. On her legs she had a pair of sensible, ribbed lisle stockings and her feet were shod in a pair of highly-polished brogues which looked stout enough to kick the heart out of a highlander.

'Come along, you chaps!' she rallied them. 'Squat yourselves down and take a load off your minds!'

Dover, lumbering clumsily across the threshold of the sitting-room, stumbled slightly as he caught his foot in a small rug. He lurched forward, his hand automatically stretched out to help regain his balance, just as Colonel Bing bent down to release the poodle. Dover saw the straining expanse of Hunting Stewart, but not in time.

Colonel Bing straightened up smartly and cut through the chief inspector's muttered apologies.

'Just watch it, old chap!' she warned him grimly. 'Just watch it!'

Dover backed nervously away as far as he could, which was not more than three inches, and collapsed heavily into a chair. Colonel Bing, keeping a wary eye on Dover in case his bestial instincts got the better of him again, sat down too, and this left just enough room for Sergeant MacGregor to squeeze in. With his knees almost touching those of Colonel Bing, he managed to drag out his notebook and pencil and waited, hardly daring to breathe, for the revelations to begin.

'Right,' said Colonel Bing, 'everybody settled? Well, I'll kick off, shall I? Now, as I understand it, this is as far as you chaps have got: you know Juliet Rugg left the Counters' house after lunch on Tuesday and then went down to the village to see her mother. Right? And then you know she caught the three-fifteen bus into Creedon. Right? But after that it's a complete blank.'

'I wouldn't say that,' objected Dover in a half-hearted attempt to regain control of the situation, 'we've barely started our investigations.'

'My source of intelligence' – Colonel Bing crushed him without mercy – 'is Police Constable Robson, on whose report your briefing was based this morning. The police, so far, have not traced that girl's movements after the bus dropped her in Creedon.'

Colonel Bing's emphatic statement of the facts brooked no argument, and Dover didn't attempt any.

'All right,' he said sulkily, 'I suppose you saw her later than that?'

'Indeed I did! Very much later! I saw her just before eleven o'clock on the Tuesday night!'

Dover sat up slightly. 'You did, did you? Where was this?'

'I'm telling this in my own way,' said Colonel Bing flatly. She nodded to Sergeant MacGregor. 'You take this down, young man, and stop me if I go too fast for you. Right?

'Well, Georgie, that's Miss McLintock – m, small c, capital l, i, n, t, o, c, k – got it? – Georgie and I went across on Tuesday evening to play bridge with the Freels – f, r, e, e, l, s. They're a brother and sister, Amy and Basil – you can spell those all right, can you? – a brother and sister who live in the first house next to the lodge opposite. We arrived at about half-past seven and got back here at a quarter to, or maybe ten to eleven. Now, I'd had to leave the hell-hound here by himself because the Freels have got a cat, and naturally the poor brute wanted a breath of fresh air and a walk round the garden before heading for the pit. Georgie went in to make the cocoa and I stood outside with Peregrine, that's the dog, while he had a sniff around. He's rather a highly-strung beast and he doesn't like being out by himself after dark.

'Well, while we were both outside there in the garden, a car drew up at the entrance gates. They're closed at nights, you know, because we've had a lot of trouble with courting couples driving in to do their snogging off the main road – damned disgusting but you know what they're like these days. Well, naturally, having nothing else to look at, really, I moved across to the hedge and had a squint at the car. After a minute or two the passenger door opened and this girl, Juliet Rugg, got out. I expect you've had a description of her so you'll know she was a pretty unmistakable figure. Disgustingly overweight for a girl of her age, but far too lazy and stupid to do anything about it! Anyhow, I could see quite clearly because the car had stopped directly under the lamp. She was giggling, as usual, and exchanged a bit of repartee, which I didn't catch, thank God, with whoever was driving the car.

'Then she went through the small gate in the big gates, which is always unlocked, and started walking up the drive in the direction of the Counters' house.

'Well, by now Peregrine had done what he was supposed to do and wanted to go back inside – hates the cold, that dog – so in we went. Just as I was closing the door I heard the car drive off down the road towards Earlam. So, you see, as late as about five to eleven on Tuesday night that girl was safe and sound, walking up the drive to get home.'

'Hm,' said Dover thoughtfully.

'Useful bit of information, eh?' demanded the colonel.

'Hm,' said Dover non-committally. 'Did you notice anybody else about at that time?'

'No, place was as quiet the grave.'

'You didn't get any glimpse of whoever was driving the car, Miss Bing?'

'Don't you call me "Miss"!' she snapped belligerently. 'You expect to be called "Chief Inspector", don't you? Well, I expect to be addressed as "Colonel"! I did twenty-two years in the army and I'm entitled to be called by my rank, same as any other retired officer.'

Dover yielded happily to the ignoble temptation. 'Which army was that?' he asked politely. 'The Salvation?'

Colonel Bing's eyes bulged ominously for a moment, but then she let rip a guffaw of hearty laughter which made Sergeant MacGregor wince. She leaned across and slapped Dover playfully on the knee, leaving a bruise which lingered on long after the case was closed.

'You naughty old devil!' she howled, wiping away the tears of mirth with the back of a large, capable-looking hand. 'It's a damned good thing for you I've got a sense of humour!' She turned to Sergeant MacGregor. 'Does he always go on like this?' she demanded. 'He must be a riot to work with!'

Sergeant MacGregor gave one of his bleak little smiles and primly turned over the page of his notebook.

Dover repeated his original question, rather disappointed that she had taken his unkind and catty remark so well.

'Did you see the driver of the car?'

'No, not a glimpse.'

'You don't know if it was a man or a woman?'

'Knowing Juliet Rugg, I should say it was bloody well beyond the bounds of any probability that she was driving around late at night with a woman. That girl was man-mad, if you ask me!'

Dover lapsed into a moody silence. It looked impressive – the Great Detective mulling over his case – but all it meant was that he had run out of questions. Sergeant MacGregor decided to take it upon himself to ask the obvious one.

'You didn't by any chance, madam, get the number of the car, or its make or colour, or anything?'

Colonel Bing smirked triumphantly. 'Indeed I did!' she said happily. 'It was a blue and cream 1957 Hillman Minx saloon, registration number UGK 823.'

Sergeant MacGregor looked up in surprise.

'Thought that'd shake you, young man!' she laughed happily. 'However, I'm not an old Fanny for nothing, you know!'

Sergeant MacGregor gulped and tried, unsuccessfully, to stop the grin cracking across his face.

Colonel Bing was not amused. 'That stands for First Aid and Nursing Yeomanry!' she sniffed crossly. 'We formed the nucleus of motor transport in the A.T.S. at the beginning of the war.' She swung back to Dover. 'Well, is there anything else you want to know?'

'No, I don't think so,' said Dover, jumping nervously as the poodle shot out from under his chair and rushed yelping hysterically out of the room.

Colonel Bing consulted her watch, a sensible man's model which she wore with the face on the inside of her wrist. 'That'll be Georgie!' she announced.

The poodle tore back into the room and leapt, panting with excitement, on to Dover's knees. For a second they glared balefully into each other's eyes, their noses not more than a couple of inches apart.

'Here!' said Dover, startled not only by the dog's sudden appearance but by the undisguised contempt which he read in its shrewd, calculating eyes. 'Get off!' He pushed it. Peregrine bit his hand. Dover screamed in anguish and the poodle looked smugly at his mistress.

'Naughty Peregrine,' she said without much interest.

'That blasted dog's bitten me!' howled Dover, waving a hand decorated with Peregrine's teeth-marks in the air.

'Rubbish!' said Colonel Bing. 'It was only a nip and, anyhow, it *is* his chair.'

At that moment Miss McLintock appeared. Sergeant Mac-Gregor rose politely half-way from his chair but found that further movement would land him in Colonel Bing's lap, so he flopped back again. Dover now had the poodle firmly and growlingly ensconced on his knees and acknowledged his introduction to Miss McLintock by a curt and restrained nod.

Miss McLintock beamed at him. 'Ah, I can see you're a dog lover, too!' she cooed. 'Dear little Peregrine can always tell, can't you, darling? I think dogs have an instinct about these things, don't you?'

Dover raised his eyes to heaven.

'Get everything, Georgie?' demanded Colonel Bing.

'Yes, I think so, dear,' Miss McLintock answered placidly. She looked several years older than the colonel and had a pale, vague face with kindly, faded blue eyes. Her hair was almost white and crammed untidily into a hair-net. 'I managed to get the new Ian Fleming at the library. You know, the one the Sunday paper critic called "a sadistic wallowing in pain and sex". Are you a James Bond fan, Inspector?'

'No, I'm not!' snarled Dover, who hadn't read a book right through for twenty years. He made a tentative move to get to his feet. Peregrine turned to look at him and bared his teeth.

Colonel Bing playfully wagged a reproving finger and continued her interrogation.

'Did you get the stamps, Georgie?'

'Yes, dear.'

'And posted Tommy's parcel?'

'Yes, dear. The girl was most unpleasant about it. She didn't want to register it because it rattled. I told her it was only that tube of toothpaste in its box but she started saying it was against the regulations or something. I was getting really flustered. I knew the parcel had to go off today and I knew you wanted it registered and I was trying to work out if I'd time to bring it back and repack it and there was a queue and everybody was fidgeting about and that young man, Boris What's-his-name, was waiting just behind me – oh, it was so embarrassing!'

'But you got it posted in the end, I trust?'

'Oh yes, dear.'

'And registered?'

'And registered, dear.'

'And what was this Boris man doing in the post office?'

'He was posting a parcel too, dear. Poor young man, I felt so sorry for him. He looks so thin and haggard.'

'Fiddlesticks!' snorted Colonel Bing. 'He looks dissipated, that's what he looks!' She turned to Dover. 'If it does turn out that somebody's done away with Juliet Rugg, you want to put this chap at the top of your list, Inspector! He'd murder his own grandmother, soon as look at her!'

'Oh, Bingo!' protested Miss McLintock.

'Don't be a fool, Georgie!' snapped the colonel. 'His sort want booting back where they came from. Wouldn't surprise me if he wasn't a Communist spy or something.' She addressed Dover again. 'I'll tell you something very odd about him,' she said, reducing her voice to a deafening conspiratorial whisper. 'Georgie here, she's a schoolteacher. Taught French and German in a girls' high school for thirty-eight years. All right, what happens? This Bogolepov fellow's supposed to be a German. Well, Georgie's a soft-hearted old idiot and one day she thinks she'll make him feel at home and have a bit of a chat with him, in German. And what happens?' Colonel Bing leaned forward to drive the point home. 'Not only does he not understand a bloody word she says, but she couldn't understand a bloody word he said either! Now, what do you make of that, eh?'

Miss McLintock gave an embarrassed laugh. 'Oh, it wasn't as bad as that, Bingo!' she protested.

'Rubbish!' retorted Colonel Bing, 'if the fellow's a German, he ought to know the lingo! I've been out there, Georgie, you haven't.' She nodded curtly at Sergeant MacGregor's notebook. 'You'd better take his name down, young man. Boris Bogolepov – *b, o, g, o, l, e, p, o, v* – got it? He lives in the top house on this side, well, it's a bungalow really, not a house. He's some sort of refugee, you know, or so he says. God alone knows why they always finish up in this country!'

'But, Bingo, the poor boy suffered terribly during the war. He was in a concentration camp!'

'So he says!' repeated Colonel Bing darkly. 'That's what they all say! And whatever he may or may not have done during the war, I know what he's doing now. Damn all! He's been here, what? Two years? And never done a day's work since he came. Where does he get his money from, that's what I'd like to know!'

'Well, I think he's a very nice kind boy,' retorted Miss McLintock firmly.

'Kind!' exploded the colonel. 'You're getting senile, Georgie!'

'That's as maybe,' said her friend huffily, 'but I happened to notice in the post office that he was sending quite a large parcel to one of those refugee organizations in London. And in my view, that is a *kind* action.'

'Pooh!' scoffed the colonel. 'Pile of old clothes he didn't want, I expect!'

Miss McLintock didn't answer and there was a rather uncomfortable silence. With the quiet assurance of one who knows that she is right and doesn't need to argue about it, Miss McLintock placidly opened her library book and began carefully turning over the pages one by one. The other three watched her and sought frantically for some new topic of conversation. Miss McLintock with a forgiving smile provided it.

'Have you offered a glass of sherry to these gentlemen, dear?' she asked sweetly.

'Of course not, Georgie!' Colonel Bing snubbed her friend. 'You know they're not allowed to drink on duty!'

Dover glared at her. He'd never been known to refuse a drink, even from the hands of a man he was on the point of arresting for murder. And at the moment he could do with one.

'For God's sake, Georgie,' Colonel Bing spoke with exasperation, 'stop turning over those blasted pages! You're really getting quite neurotic about library books. If you must do it, why don't you do it in the library?'

'I didn't have time, dear,' said Miss McLintock mildly. She smiled cosily at Dover. 'I have quite a thing about library books,' she confided with a little giggle. 'I always look through them very carefully. You'd be surprised at what people use as book-marks! I've got quite a little collection of things that I've found over the years – bus tickets, an old suspender, half a regimental tie, a hundred-franc note – that was very exciting. I've got them all in a box with a label giving the name of the book I found them in and the date. Of course, I don't keep all the things I find, naturally. Pieces of bacon and things like that I have to throw away. And the pension book, naturally I sent that back. Oh, and the letters, all stamped and addressed, I always pop those in the pillar box for them. But everything else I keep in my little museum.'

Dover sighed. 'Sounds a very interesting hobby,' he commented impatiently. 'But now, Colonel Bing, if you'd just call this dog off, I think it's time we were on our way.'

'Peregrine!' bawled Colonel Bing in a voice which rattled the windows. 'Get down, sir!'

The poodle regarded her with lazy insolence but, deliberately taking his time about it, eventually jumped down obediently from Dover's lap.

Colonel Bing accompanied the police officers back to the drive, pausing only to demonstrate that the spot where the car had parked on Tuesday night was clearly visible from her garden. Dover peered grumpily across the bushes and then, with a speed of reaction which was far from typical of him, side-stepped neatly as Peregrine tried to spend a penny on his leg.

Colonel Bing laughed heartily and even Sergeant MacGregor's face twitched momentarily into a smirk. Chief Inspector Dover had very little sense of humour where his own dignity and importance were concerned. He stumped away snorting furiously down his nose.

'The Two Fiddlers!' he snarled viciously to Sergeant Mac-Gregor as he slammed the car door. 'And check up whether she's got a licence for that blasted dog!'

Chapter Three

THE village of Earlam lay in a shallow hollow about two miles from Irlam Old Hall. It was a small, rather uninteresting place, containing one or two pleasant-looking houses, the pub in which Dover and MacGregor were quartered, two scruffy multi-purpose shops plastered with advertisements for cigarettes and detergents, and a house which the representative of Lloyds bank visited for one and a half hours each week. Standing back a little from the village proper was the church. Next door to it was a large empty vicarage and nowadays Earlam had to share its vicar with three other neighbouring parishes.

Mrs Rugg, the mother of the missing Juliet, lived in a council house. A small estate of them had been built at the north end of the village and while, architecturally, they were really no worse than the older houses lining the main street, for some unfair reason, they looked it. The raw red brick, the gaudy modernistic paintwork, the unmatured naked-looking gardens added up to a rather unattractive vista. Sergeant MacGregor edged the car carefully along the road which was littered with sheets of dirty old cardboard, battered toy motor-cars, dogs of dubious parentage and children. At the same time he searched among the welter of Balmorals and Sandringhams, Elms and Holly Views for Ingoldisthorpe which was where, according to his notes, Juliet's mother lived.

Dover looked up casually. 'There it is!' he snapped, a split second ahead of Sergeant MacGregor, who had swerved to avoid a large eyeless Teddy bear abandoned in the middle of the road. 'You want to get your eyes seen to, my lad!' he said patronizingly as he climbed out of the car.

Sergeant MacGregor carefully repeated the same rude word to himself ten times as he followed his chief up the path to the front door. He could only hope that the chief inspector's petty little success would put him in a better frame of mind than he had been so far.

Lunch at the village pub had not been an entirely happy affair.

34

Dover's amour propre was still quivering from its encounter with Colonel Bing, or rather with Colonel Bing's revolting dog, and he continued to harp fretfully on his favourite theme: there was no case here, there never had been a case and there never would be a case. At any moment the blasted girl would turn up safe and sound and everybody would blame everybody else for making a lot of fuss and palaver about nothing. It was disgraceful that the time of an experienced senior police officer like himself should be wasted on such trivialities. He'd a good mind to put in a formal complaint about it. But, nevertheless, if Sergeant Mac-Gregor wanted to waste his own time and that of other over-worked branches of the police organization, he could get them to trace the owner of the car which Colonel Bing was purported to have seen parked outside on the road. For all he, Dover, cared, Sergeant MacGregor could stand on his hands and wiggle his toes in the air. He, Dover, for his part, was hungry and was now going to have his lunch, to which he had been looking forward ever since he had eaten that abortion of a breakfast which to his amazement British Railways had had the nerve not only to serve, but to charge for as well.

The village pub was called The Two Fiddlers, a name which was not inappropriate when the character of the landlord and his wife were taken into consideration. The landlord, Mr Jelly, had complacently assured Dover that his house knew its limitations. There was none of that fancy foreign muck, all written in French, here. Good plain English cooking at its best, that's what they offered.

Dover sat down with a glass of beer and high hopes.

After a repast of tinned tomato soup, congealed shoulder of New Zealand lamb, which might well have been cooked and carved in that distant country, soggy potatoes and bright green cabbage, his face had sunk even deeper into its habitual, sullen scowl and his stomach was rumbling ominously. Through gritted teeth he refused the lump of off-white ice-cream which it was proposed to inflict on him as a sweet, and finished off his meal with a slab of unripe Danish blue cheese and two limp water-biscuits. The coffee was quite undrinkable.

Dover rose from the luncheon table with a face like thunder, and Sergeant MacGregor sighed miserably. All the signs were set for a stormy afternoon.

Dover was, in fact, looking at his most boot-faced and terrible as he ignored with a sneer the small bell-push adorning the front door of Ingoldisthorpe. He raised a large meaty fist and crashed it three times into the top left-hand panel. The row was satisfying. He stood, with Sergeant MacGregor close behind him, glowering balefully at the door. Nothing happened. Dover cursed and thumped again, even more energetically. Neighbours four houses away peeped curiously out from behind their curtains.

'Fer Gawd's sake,' came a weary, lacklustre voice, 'I wonder yer don't use yer boots on it! Gawd knows, they look big enough.'

A small thin woman with stringy, peroxide blonde hair had appeared from the back of the house. She was wearing a faded grubby overall and a pair of down-at-heel shoes. A cigarette dangled permanently out of the side of her mouth.

Dover glared at her. 'Mrs Rugg?' he queried.

She looked him contemptuously up and down. 'Y'll have to come round the back,' she said, 'that door's stuck.'

Dover and MacGregor followed her meekly round the corner of the house and into the kitchen. Mrs Rugg resumed her ironing, pausing only to blow the ash off the end of her cigarette, a feat which she performed without removing it from her mouth.

Sergeant MacGregor rapidly cleared a couple of chairs of a mixed collection of toys, articles of clothing, a pile of nappies and an old newspaper, and he and Dover sat down by the kitchen table. Dover's nose wrinkled in distaste as he looked around the room. Mrs Rugg was a slut. The room had a most unpleasant smell which he squeamishly refrained from trying to identify, and the table was covered with the unwashed crockery of several meals. A squadron of corpulent bluebottles hovered like miniature helicopters over an uncovered dish of crumb-bespeckled butter. He turned his eyes back to Mrs Rugg as the lesser of the two evils.

Mrs Rugg was not a very enthusiastic witness, but she confirmed what Dover had already gathered about her daughter's movements on the day of her disappearance.

'Did she come and visit you every week on her day off?' he asked, his one thought now being to get outside and draw some clean air into his lungs.

'Usually,' said Mrs Rugg without much interest. 'Her ladyship used to bring me her washing to do.' She jerked her head at a vast, unidentifiable article which was draped over her ironing board. 'This is hers.' She got another cigarette out of a packet in her overall pocket, lit it from the one which by now must have been burning her lip, and dropped the mangled-looking stub into the sink. She picked up her iron again, spat experimentally on it, and added in a grudging afterthought, ''Course, she come to see the baby as well.'

'Oh, you've got a baby, have you?' said Dover, now concentrating on trying not to breathe.

'Not me!' replied Mrs Rugg shortly. 'Her!'

'Her?' yelped Dover. 'Wadderyemean, her?'

'It's her baby, not mine,' explained Mrs Rugg impatiently.

'Her baby? Do you mean your daughter, Juliet, has had a *baby*?'

''Sright!' agreed Mrs Rugg coyly. 'Wouldn't think I was a grannie, would yer?'

'But nobody told *me* she had a baby!' howled Dover, glaring at Sergeant MacGregor.

'Well, p'raps yer didn't ask. Yer can take it from me, it's no secret round here, though I must say, she didn't hardly show at all, with her being so fat, you know.'

Dover was spluttering with fury. 'And how old is this child?'

''Bout seven months or so. She had it just before she went to work up at Irlam Old Hall.'

'But, is your daughter married then?' demanded Dover, promising himself a good old dust-up with the local boys about this one.

''Course not!' Mrs Rugg gave him a sardonic look out of eyes screwed up against the cigarette smoke. 'Yer don't have to be married to have a baby, yer know.'

'But, who's the father?'

'Search me, mate!' Mrs Rugg shrugged her shoulders and went on with her ironing.

'Now look here, Mrs Rugg,' Dover got a grip on himself, 'let's just get this straight. Seven months ago your daughter had a baby and then she went to work for Sir John Counter. What was she doing before that?'

'Oh, she's tried several things since she left school. She worked in a shop for a bit in Creedon, then she had a job with a hairdresser. Then she helped out at The Two Fiddlers, serving lunches and things. But none of them suited her, really. She couldn't do with a lot of standing, not with her legs and being such a size, yer know, and, of course, she always had to wear them damned high-heel shoes which didn't make it any better.'

'She was living at home during this time?'

'Oh yes, and that was a bit of a nuisance, too, having a girl of that age hanging round the place all the time.'

'I see,' said Dover, who wasn't in fact seeing much at this stage. 'And what about Juliet's father, Mr Rugg?'

Mrs Rugg removed her cigarette from her lips and elaborately flicked the ash on the floor.

'Well, which one do yer want to know about?'

'They aren't the same person?'

'Fred Rugg and me got married in 1946. Juliet was about two then. Her dad was a corporal in the army and I never did know his surname, so when I got married I just called Juliet "Rugg" like the rest of us. I thought it looked better, like. Well, Fred Rugg hopped it about a year after we'd got married, when the twins was getting on for six months, and I haven't seen hide or hair of him since. Nor ever likely to.'

'The twins?' repeated Dover.

'Yes, I packed 'em both off into the army soon as they was old enough. Couldn't do with two grown lads hanging round the place.'

It was at this moment in the conversation that the kitchen door opened and a child about four years old toddled into the room. He stared unblinkingly at Dover and MacGregor who each did a swift calculation, based on the date at which Fred Rugg had abandoned his wife and family to the care of the Welfare State.

'Gimme some choc, mum!' demanded the child in an ear-piercing voice.

'No!' The maternal reply was short and to the point.

'Aw, mum, gimme some choc!' The child's voice rose to a whine.

'No, I shan't! I haven't got any. And you go and put yer trousers on – coming in here like that, showing all you've got! Go on, hop it!'

She speeded the child on its reluctant way with a resounding slap on its bare bottom.

'That's Barry,' she said as he disappeared back through the door.

'Well,' said Dover, 'we were hardly likely to think it was Gwendoline!'

Mrs Rugg looked blankly at him.

The chief inspector sighed deeply. He was getting very bored with the whole thing. 'I take it, Mrs Rugg,' he went on with an effort, 'that your daughter left her child here with you to look after?'

' 'Sright!' said Mrs Rugg. 'She had it all worked out, she had. She was going to pay me so much a week for looking after the kid, only, of course, everything went wrong and I've hardly seen a penny piece for all me trouble. I told our Juliet, there's many a slip, I said, but, of course, she knew better.'

'She was going to make you a weekly payment out of her wages?' suggested Dover, who was beginning to flounder.

'No!' said Mrs Rugg impatiently. 'She thought Mrs Chubb-Smith would go on footing the bill!'

'Mrs Chubb-Smith? What the devil has Mrs Chubb-Smith got to do with it?'

'She was very good to our Juliet when the baby was coming, paid for her to go to a proper hospital and everything. 'Course, our Juliet counted on her going on helping after the kid was born but, naturally, she didn't, like. Not, mind you, that our Juliet is one to lose heart! She's a trier, I will say that for her. Only on Tuesday she was saying that everything was going to be all right again. Who she was going to touch for a bit of the ready this time I don't know. Mrs Chubb-Smith again, far as I could gather, but I don't hardly think that can be right, do you? 'Course, she'd been very good to her before but ... '

'Now, just a minute,' roared Dover, 'this Mrs Chubb-Smith – is she the one up at Irlam Old Hall?'

' 'Sright,' agreed Mrs Rugg. 'She's the lah-di-dah old cow that runs the place.'

Dover breathed deeply through his nose. 'And why should she help your daughter?'

Mrs Rugg smiled shrewdly. 'Search me,' she said, 'p'raps she's got more money than sense.'

'And why did she stop helping after the baby was born?'

Mrs Rugg looked at Dover with a mixture of exasperation and pity. With an irritable gesture, she slammed her iron down on its stand. 'I can see I'm going to have you two here all bloody day!'

she muttered crossly. She eyed the two policemen up and down. 'And they say crime doesn't pay!' she snorted scornfully. 'You'd better come outside and have a look at the kid. P'raps you'll be able to answer yer own damn-fool questions then.'

The baby was fast asleep in its pram in the back garden. Dover and Sergeant MacGregor bent down cautiously to examine it. It looked like any other sleeping baby except, perhaps, for the fact that it was coal black.

'Oh,' said Dover in a somewhat inadequate comment.

Mrs Rugg stalked silently back to her ironing.

The two policemen trailed after her.

'Have you got any questions?' Dover hissed at MacGregor. 'If you have, ask 'em and let's get the hell out of here!'

'Mrs Rugg,' said the sergeant with a friendly smile designed to differentiate his technique from the surly, growling approach favoured by the chief inspector, 'did Juliet have any boy-friends?'

Mrs Rugg slowly placed her hands on her hips. 'Are you kidding?' she demanded wearily. 'How the hell do yer think she got that out there?' She jerked her head in the direction of the garden. 'By correspondence course?'

Sergeant MacGregor blushed in discomfort and Dover smirked.

'I meant any special boy-friends,' the sergeant tried again, 'anybody she'd be likely to run away with, for example?'

Mrs Rugg laughed shortly. 'If you'd seen our Juliet you wouldn't talk about running away, sonnie! She could hardly walk a hundred yards without stopping for half an hour's rest. Something the matter with her glands, the doctor said, but I used to tell her, if she didn't spend so much time flat on her back she might lose a bit of weight. 'Course she'd got gentlemen friends, dozens of 'em, I shouldn't wonder. Our Juliet was a great one for anything in trousers. She liked having a good time and you're only young once, I always say.'

'But you don't know the names of any of them?'

'No,' said Mrs Rugg enigmatically, 'I've got enough troubles of me own!'

Chapter Four

HALF an hour later Dover collapsed exhausted into one of the leather armchairs in Sir John Counter's study and sulkily prepared himself to ask another lot of damn-fool questions about nothing.

Everybody was swamping him with information, every item of which, he was sure, would turn out to be a complete waste of time. All sixteen stone of Juliet Rugg would appear on the scene again at any moment and he, Dover, would thankfully catch the next train back to civilization. Chief Inspector Wilfred Dover of New Scotland Yard wasn't, however, a complete fool. He was only pig-headed. So far he had managed to shut out a niggling doubt as to the correctness of his theory about Juliet Rugg's disappearance. He still clung obstinately to his original views on the subject, but he was uneasily aware that none of the evidence, if you could call it that, which he had so far received gave him much support.

Juliet Rugg had been last seen at eleven o'clock at night, making her way, on foot, up the drive to the Counters' house. But, she'd never arrived there. If she'd left the grounds of Irlam Old Hall – and, of course, she must have done – how had she managed it? She obviously wasn't capable of walking far, certainly not the two miles into the village, and it wouldn't have done any good if she had. All the buses had stopped hours ago and the last train from Creedon, which was another six miles away, left at 10.10 p.m. The railway staff were quite convinced that nobody of her description had left by any of the early morning trains the next day, and they would certainly not have overlooked a girl whose appearance was as bizarre as Juliet's was.

That left a car as the only solution. But if the Hall gates were locked at night, presumably no car could get in or out of the grounds. Blast it – he'd have to check about those gates! Of course, she could have walked back to the road after Colonel Bing had gone inside again, but why should she? All the signs seemed to indicate that she'd had her evening out and was just going back, quite normally, home to bed. Oh dear, and then there was that black baby! Dover wondered fretfully if that was a clue to anything. He'd certainly have to look into this Mrs Chubb-Smith business, not that it wasn't pretty obvious why she'd stopped playing Lady Bountiful as soon as the baby was born. Oh blast the whole damned case! He could think, without trying, of a dozen explanations for everything, and he contemplated all the tedious work of checking which was the right one without any enthusiasm at all.

The chief inspector was brought back to his surroundings by the sound of Sir John Counter's voice. He was addressing his daughter. He spoke in a tone far curter than Colonel Bing would ever have thought of using to her dog.

'We shan't want you! I'll ring when they're ready to leave.'

Eve Counter shrugged her shoulders faintly and left the room.

'Insipid specimen, isn't she?' Sir John addressed the question to the company at large. 'Fancy being practically confined to your room, like I am, and seeing nothing but that walking zombie day in and day out! I wish to God you people would get a move on and find Juliet before I go stark raving mad through sheer boredom!'

Dover sniffed. He didn't care much for Sir John's manner of speaking. He sounded like a captain of industry addressing a shareholders' meeting, polite enough but with a thinly concealed contempt for all those not lucky enough to have been born Sir John Counter. If Dover hadn't been feeling quite so lethargic he might have tried a bit of heavy-handed bullying himself, but at the moment listlessness and boredom had settled on him like a black cloud, and his stomach didn't feel too good either. Must have been the cheese.

'I understand, Sir John,' he began, 'that you and your daughter live here alone?'

'That is quite correct,' said Sir John briskly in his sharp, clipped, old man's voice. 'Now that Juliet's not here, we have no servants living in at all. My daughter, Eve, claims that you can't get 'em these days, a statement which I find hard to believe.'

'And Miss Eve Counter is your only child?'

'My only *legitimate* child, yes. However, I flatter myself that there are a goodly number of what we might call Fitz-Counters scattered around, don't you know.' Sir John bared his artificial teeth in a well satisfied grin and helped himself to a sweet from a large bag which lay on a table by his elbow. 'Toffee, Inspector? Constable?'

Dover shook his head and resumed his questioning.

'And Lady Counter?'

'Lady Counter, I am glad to say, is dead, and has been these many years. She was an even more colourless woman than her daughter, if you can bring yourself to imagine such a thing. I have made very few mistakes in my life, Inspector, but marrying that woman came dangerously near to being one of them. I was nearly fifty when I married. Up till then I had always avoided matrimony like the plague, going on the principle that there is no need to throw yourself into the river to get a drink of water. But in 1926, I shall never forget the year, my valet, who'd been with me for over a quarter of a century, had the base ingratitude to leave me to go and keep a public house in some godforsaken backwater or other. I found him impossible to replace and, after some ghastly experiences with which I won't bore you, I finally decided that the only solution was to get married.

'The girl whom I selected was the daughter of an old friend of mine. She was a sickly, unattractive, dowdy individual who hadn't enough spirit to say boo to a gosling. Her sole virtue was that she was a very wealthy woman in her own right, with large expectations from her father. I wasn't exactly a pauper myself, but it is a common fallacy to believe that only the poor want money.

'She died, rather to my surprise, I must admit, a year after we were married and left me with that.' He jerked his head at the door through which his daughter had just gone. 'I inherited all my wife's money so I suppose I shouldn't complain about the inconvenience she caused me. I got my sister to come and look after the girl until she was old enough to be packed off to school. I have, of course, never remarried. For the most part I have availed myself of the services of the maids. Whenever I hire a new girl, I make it quite clear to her what is expected. I flatter myself that I have never had one who turned the job down. Juliet Rugg is the latest in a not inconsiderable line.' He popped another sweet into his mouth and crunched it loudly.

Dover gaped in astonishment at the old man in front of him, sitting bolt upright with a rug over his knees. You might call Sir John wonderful for his age, marvellously active and surprisingly

43

well preserved, but, none the less, he was still a very old man. Dover gazed blankly at the wrinkled parchment skin drawn tautly over the skull, at the eyes sunk deep under bushy white eyebrows, at the thin body lost in clothes which had been cut to fit a more robust frame, and at the thick knotted veins on the slightly trembling hands. He calculated rapidly. Good grief ! The old roué must be well over eighty !

'So Juliet Rugg was your mistress, Sir John?' he asked in a non-committal voice.

'She was, Inspector. Do I gather from your question that my daughter had not informed you of this fact? She, of course, neither approves nor understands. Having no sex life of her own she naturally considers herself well qualified to criticize that of others.'

Dover groped for a moment, wondering how best to phrase his next question.

'We have reason to believe, Sir John,' he said, 'that this girl, Juliet Rugg, has other men-friends. You yourself must know that she was the mother of an illegitimate child.'

Sir John shrugged his shoulders. 'I am a realist, Inspector, I always have been. Juliet is a lusty young wench with a rather insatiable appetite. I am no longer a young man. Obviously I couldn't hope to satisfy *all* her demands. Of course she was having affairs with other men. She used to amuse me for hours telling me all about them.'

'Did she give you any hint that she might run away with one of them?'

'No, that would seem to imply love and I doubt if Juliet is capable of love – if, indeed, it exists at all. She is quite simply a nymphomaniac, Inspector, of a rather plebeian sort. One man is pretty much the same as another from her point of view. Besides, her life here is very comfortable. She is living a life of luxury with ten pounds a week pocket money. It would have to be a very attractive offer to lure her away from that.'

'You know of no reason, then, why she should run off at this stage?'

'No, rather the reverse. She had been trying for some time to get me to marry her. She rather fancied herself as the second Lady Counter.'

Dover exchanged glances with Sergeant MacGregor, whose unobtrusive note-taking had been going on all through the interview.

'Did you intend to marry her?' asked Dover.

Sir John placed his finger-tips judiciously together. 'I was thinking about it,' he said. 'It was a suggestion which merited thinking about. Juliet's a common little tart, of course, but since I have virtually ceased going out in society nowadays, that wouldn't matter all that much. My daughter,' he glanced slyly at the chief inspector, 'my daughter, however, didn't like the idea at all. To be fair, Juliet as a stepmother would be hard for anybody to swallow. And, at the present moment, Eve is my sole heir, but if I married again and if I fathered another child – which is not beyond the realms of possibility – then her position would be very different.'

'Yes,' agreed Dover and sighed. He decided to try another line of questioning.

'According to our investigations, Sir John,' he said, 'Juliet Rugg was last seen at about five to eleven on Tuesday night. She was walking up the drive in the direction of this house. According to Miss Counter's statement, she doesn't appear to have got here. I take it, you didn't see her that night?'

'No, the last time I saw her was at lunch before she went off.'

'Where were you at eleven o'clock, Sir John?'

'I was in bed watching television. I have a second set in my bedroom. When the programme ended I switched off my light and went to sleep.'

'Would you have heard her if she had come into the house?'

Sir John thought for a minute. 'I doubt it,' he said. 'My room is quite a distance from the front door and, of course, my hearing is not so acute as it was. By the way, who saw Juliet at that time?'

'It was Colonel Bing.'

'Ah, the Irlam Amazon! Well, the woman's a fool, but I've no doubt she can see straight enough.'

'Had Miss Rugg any friends or contacts among the people who live up here? Was she perhaps – er – friendly with any of the men?'

'Not as far as I know, Inspector, though if she were having an affair with any man up here I think she'd be shrewd enough not to tell me about it.'

'Why not?'

45

'I should not' – Sir John paused to pop another toffee in his mouth' – I should not be quite so complaisant at finding her carrying on with somebody in my own social set as I was about her amorous adventures with farm labourers and shop assistants. It is illogical, I admit, but I wouldn't tolerate her sleeping with one of my neighbours. However, I am sure my daughter would have been very quick to tell me if something of that sort had been going on. As far as the women up here are concerned' – he shook his head – 'I doubt if any of them ever passed more than the time of day with her. She is a servant, you know, and not an over-savoury one at that. In fact, I can't see her popping in to pay a social call at eleven o'clock at night with anybody in Irlam Old Hall – if that's what you're getting at.'

'Are there any single men in the houses or flats?'

'Two, I believe – that's not counting Freel who lives with his sister. There's Bondy, a retired soldier, who does the caretaking in the Old Hall itself. He's about sixty, I suppose, and I don't think he'd touch Juliet with gloves on, if you see what I mean. Then there's this foreigner chap, Bogolepov. Now, he's a different kettle of fish. He's one of these gaunt, hungry-looking young men – the sort that women are supposed to want to mother. Jew he is, and they're an oversexed lot, if you like. I've caught him looking at Juliet once or twice with those big dark eyes. Looked as though he could eat her – you know, practically slavering at the lips.

'Yes, if anything has happened to Juliet, he's your man ! Might be well worth your while to go and give him a bit of third degree – it's all these damned foreigners understand. If I were ten years younger, he'd have had the toe of my boot up his backside, I can tell you ! I don't hold any brief for Hitler, Inspector, obviously he went much too far, but he was on the right lines where the Jews were concerned. I can never understand why Kitty Chubb-Smith ever let him have that house in the first place. I told her she was lowering the tone of the whole set-up. Lazy young whelp wanders about half the day in his pyjamas, shaves about once a week and doesn't look as if he'd had a wash since he came here.'

'Well, sir,' said Dover, who'd had enough of Sir John but who was loath to leave the comfort of his armchair, 'I think that's about all for the moment. Thank you very much for your help, sir.'

'Not at all, Inspector. I miss Juliet – for obvious reasons – and

I'm only too pleased to do anything I can to help get her back. Sure you won't have a toffee before you go? They're very good. I have them specially sent down from London.'

'No thank you, sir,' said Dover, and rose reluctantly to his feet. 'Oh, there is one thing, sir. You don't by any chance happen to have a photograph of Miss Rugg?'

Sir John had the grace to be, just a little, put off his stride. 'Well, as a matter of fact, I – er – have, Inspector. Constable!' He waved a hand at MacGregor. 'Could you go into that top left-hand drawer over there – yes, that's the one – you'll find a card-board box. Just bring it over here, please!'

Sir John opened the box and took out about six or seven half-plate photographs. He looked at them for a moment with pursed lips, and then handed them to Dover.

'I don't know if these will be much use to you, Inspector, but perhaps you've got an artist or somebody who could – er – paint the clothes in … '

Dover looked at the photographs with a carefully blank face. They were all of Juliet Rugg, taken in the nude in the sort of poses which generally land the photographer up in court.

'Hm,' he said, raising his eyebrows slightly, 'unfortunately, the faces are a little blurred.'

'Well, you may be right.' Sir John, who had taken the photo-graphs himself, sounded a little offended at this lack of appreci-ation. 'But, I can assure you, otherwise they are an excellent likeness.'

'I shall have to take your word for that, Sir John,' said Dover, tucking them away in his wallet.

Eve Counter, summoned by an imperious ring from her father, came to conduct them up to Juliet's bedroom. They followed her up the wide staircase to the first floor.

'We gave Juliet one of the main bedrooms,' she explained, 'nobody ever stays here and my father didn't want her too far away.'

Juliet's room was spacious and well furnished, with her own private bathroom leading off. Like her mother, she was clearly extremely untidy and slovenly in her habits. Bits and pieces of clothing were littered round the room, the bed had been straight-ened rather than made, and the bedside table bore a number of disfiguring cigarette burns. The top of the dressing-table was

47

covered with sticky-looking bottles and jars of cream, most of them with the lids left off. There were a couple of dirty broken combs, several lipsticks, a large box of face powder, bits of soiled cotton wool, orange sticks and a pile of plastic hair-curlers. The whole sordid mess was covered with a fine film of pink powder and more lay scattered around on the carpet.

Dover eyed a row of nail-varnish bottles ranging through all possible shades of red with a shudder of disgust.

'Just have a search round, Sergeant,' he said, determined not to grub about in this lot with his own hands. 'See if you can find anything.'

'Very good, sir,' replied MacGregor, for once not displaying his usual enthusiasm.

The inspector sat gingerly on the edge of the bed and waited. Eve Counter started to fiddle restlessly with the shade on the bedside lamp.

'Inspector,' she began abruptly.

'Yes, madam,' said Dover resignedly. It had been too much to expect that he would be allowed to enjoy a few minutes' peace and quiet.

'I suppose my father told you that Juliet was his mistress? Well, it's not true! He's just boasting, like a little boy. He tells everybody the same thing – and it's just too stupid for words! He's just not capable of that sort of thing any longer.' Her face was bright scarlet.

Dover sighed. What the hell did it matter anyhow?

'I know what I'm talking about, Inspector,' Miss Counter went doggedly on, determined to make her point. 'His doctor told me. He's just too old.'

Dover shrugged his shoulders. 'He was apparently toying with the idea of getting married again,' he observed, and watched Eve Counter's face.

She turned away and gave the lamp-shade a few more pokes. 'That's quite ridiculous,' she said in a strangled voice, 'he's eighty-five and Juliet's eighteen. What on earth would everybody say?'

'It's been done before, madam.'

'I know, but not by men like my father.' She turned with a jerk to face Dover, her chin up. 'My father, Inspector, has had plenty of opportunities to re-marry, but he's remained faithful all these years to the memory of my mother. She died after they'd been married only a year and I don't think my father has ever got over it. He doesn't love me very much – I suppose you've noticed that – but that's because my mother died when I was born and it's quite natural, in a way, that he should blame me for it.'

It was a gallant effort, but it didn't convince Dover. Eve Counter didn't look as though it had convinced her either.

Sergeant MacGregor emerged from the bathroom, fastidiously wiping his hands on his handkerchief.

'Find anything?'

'Only this, sir.' MacGregor reopened a drawer in the dressing-table. Under a pile of voluminous underwear lay an envelope containing fifty-four one-pound notes. 'She'd have hardly left this lot behind, would she, sir?'

To say that Dover was annoyed would be an unfair under-statement. Scowling heavily, he stamped out of the house with the fury of an enraged bull elephant. He flung himself petulantly into the car and the springs sagged with the shock. Sergeant Mac-Gregor followed him apprehensively. The two men sat in silence, gazing vacantly through the windscreen.

After a few minutes Dover broke the impasse.

'What time is it?' he growled.

'Getting on for half-past five, sir.'

Dover's habit of always asking somebody else what the time was and never bothering to look at his own watch was one of those irritating little things which before now have led to violent physical assault, and even murder.

Dover grunted sulkily. 'Let's have a cigarette,' he said.

Sergeant MacGregor took a conscious grip on himself, other-wise he might have fallen to screaming and foaming at the mouth. With a restrained sigh, he meekly produced his cigarette-case. The chief inspector was a heavy smoker, but since he was rarely known to buy a packet, he depended on his sergeants to keep him supplied. He wasn't too pleased if he was offered filter-tips either.

When he had lit both their cigarettes Sergeant MacGregor judged that the atmosphere had eased enough to make conversation possible. He appreciated Dover's frame of mind. Ever since he had first heard of the case, the chief inspector had been squealing loudly that it was a complete waste of time. But now, even after the little they had learned so far, it was becoming increasingly unlikely that Juliet Rugg had just skipped off quietly of her own free will to enjoy a honeymoon unsanctified by church or state. Dover now found himself in the uncomfortable situation of having to admit that, possibly, his original view of the case was, to put it bluntly, wrong.

This was, however, not a particularly novel experience for Chief Inspector Dover. His judgment had frequently been at fault, not only in the initial stages of a case but, occasionally, right up to the end as well. The fact that his career as a detective had endured, and even flourished in a mild way, was almost entirely due to the fact that most criminals, incredible as it may seem, were even more stupid and inept than he was.

Sergeant MacGregor, who was really quite a nice young man, tried to be tactful about it.

'I'm afraid it's beginning to look as though something really has happened to that girl, isn't it, sir?'

Dover grunted and stretched his legs out as far as they would go. 'Yes,' he agreed complacently. 'Of course, it was obvious from the start that there was something fishy going on.'

This was a bit too rapid a volte-face even for Sergeant Mac-Gregor's loyalty. 'But, sir,' he protested, 'you ... '

'The trouble with you young men' – Dover steamrollered on, ignoring the interruption – 'is that you always start formulating theories and jumping to conclusions before you've got the facts. It's a very dangerous habit to get into, Sergeant, prejudices your whole attitude to a case. A good detective's got to keep an open mind until he's got real evidence in his hands – then you don't have to make up theories, the facts speak for themselves.'

The chief inspector paused to flick a chunk of cigarette ash off his waistcoat.

Sergeant MacGregor was beyond arguing. 'Yes, sir,' he said in an expressionless voice. Life was easier that way.

'Now, just let's have a look at what we've got,' Dover continued with the air of a kindly sage speaking to an idiot child. 'The girl was seen, alive and well, here on this very drive late on Tuesday night, going, apparently, straight home. She never got there. So she must have gone, willingly or unwillingly, somewhere else. Right? Now, let's assume that she's gone off somewhere under her own steam – your original theory, Sergeant. We've got three points to take into account here. One, she didn't hint either to her mother or to her employer that she was going to skip, though, when you consider the terms she was on with the pair of 'em, it doesn't seem very likely that either would have batted an eyelid if they knew she was off for a dirty week-end somewhere.

'Two, she left over fifty pounds in ready cash behind, and according to Eve Counter, none of her belongings are missing. Of course, it's possible that her departure was voluntary but unpremeditated, though it's a bit hard to stomach that she made her mind up in the depths of the country after eleven o'clock at night.

'And that brings us to the third point – how did she get away from Irlam Old Hall? Having seen those shoes of hers in her bedroom, I think we can rule out that all sixteen stone of her went on foot. I don't see her hiking through the countryside, do you? We can rule out public transport because there isn't any and I reckon we'd have had a report by now if she'd boarded a bus or train anywhere in the country. So now, Sergeant, what's the only alternative?'

'A private car, sir,' said Sergeant MacGregor obediently.

'Yes, but there's a snag there too. Those damned wrought-iron gates! If it was a car already in the grounds, how did it get out? And if it was a car outside the grounds, why was she walking *away* from the entrance?'

'Somebody might have arrived by car, left it outside the gates, run after her and persuaded her to go off with him.'

'Yes,' said Dover grudgingly, 'I suppose that's possible.'

'Or,' Sergeant MacGregor pointed out, 'she may have stayed the night in somebody else's house or flat up here and left the next day by car when the gates were open.'

'Hm,' said Dover frowning – he hadn't thought of that – 'but that would mean she'd run off with somebody from up here. We can check if anybody's missing but, surely to goodness, we'd have heard by now. There are still lots of points that need clearing up, but everything we've discovered so far seems to indicate that something or somebody prevented her return home on Tuesday night. Question now is, what happened to her?'

'Well, it's likely to be one of two things, isn't it, sir? I think we can rule suicide out, because where's the body? So it must be either kidnapping or murder.'

Dover blew crossly down his nose. 'Well, we can scrub kidnapping right away! It's inconceivable that anybody kidnapped a girl of her weight and size, and anyhow there's virtually no kidnapping in this country. Besides, who's going to pay the ransom? Her mother?'

'What about Sir John Counter?'

'Well, it's possible, but I don't think so. He's more likely to engage another maid. No, let's use our common sense on this, Sergeant, kidnapping is out!'

'Then you think it's murder, sir?'

Dover nodded. 'Yes, my money's on murder.'

'But where's the body?'

'How the hell do I know? If I knew where the body was, why in God's name should I be sitting here discussing with you what might have happened to her?'

'The local police have had a pretty good look round the district, sir, and if she's been taken further afield, we come up against this transport business, don't we? And when you think of trying to get rid of a sixteen-stone corpse, well, the mind boggles a bit, doesn't it?'

'Yours might,' commented Dover nastily, 'personally, I can think of half a dozen ways.' He was careful not to enumerate them. 'Anyhow, we've got to have a theory to work on, otherwise we'll be running round in circles. I've told you before, Sergeant, when you're dealing with crime, ninety-nine times out of a hundred the obvious explanation is the right one. I don't think this girl committed suicide and I'm damned well sure she's not been kidnapped, and it doesn't look as though she's just run away. Therefore she must have been murdered, and we shall work from now on that assumption.'

As a piece of deductive reasoning this had more flaws in it than Sergeant MacGregor dared to contemplate, but he had learned from bitter experience that it was no good arguing when the chief inspector was in this frame of mind. All you could hope for was that the blundering old fool would, even by accident, uncover the true facts of the case in the course of his so-called investigations. Sergeant MacGregor fell into his favourite day-dream in which he composed his umpteenth letter to Higher Authority requesting a transfer. Before he had actually got it signed and posted he was brought down to reality by Dover demanding yet another cigarette.

'What about motive, sir?' he asked as he flicked his lighter.

'Could be dozens,' said Dover grandly. 'She might have been insured and her mother's croaked her for the money. Sir John might have done it in a fit of senile jealousy – that man struck me as being capable of anything, supercilious old devil. Or his daughter might have done it to stop the marriage.'

'Yes.' MacGregor sounded doubtful. 'And then there's this Mrs Chubb-Smith business.'

'What Mrs Chubb-Smith business?'

'Well, her subsidizing Juliet before the baby was born.'

'Oh yes,' said Dover vaguely. 'Well, while we're up here, I suppose we might as well go and have a word with her. Get moving!'

Chapter Five

MRS CHUBB-SMITH was a very good example of a mid-twentieth-century decayed gentlewoman, though she would have been very offended at the decayed part. The fact that she was a greengrocer's daughter, who getting on for thirty years before had had the incredible luck to marry into the minor aristocracy, had been buried in the sands of time under layers of carefully acquired gentility.

Her story had not, however, had the happy ending which she had been led to expect. Her husband was the well-born master of Irlam Old Hall but that was all he was master of. There was no money. But he was an ingenious man, if not very business-like. He decided to convert the Old Hall into flats and to build a select number of residences in the grounds. People, he argued, were always wanting to live in the country, but they didn't want the complete isolation from their own kind which such retirement often involved. He intended to keep his prices high and envisaged Irlam Old Hall becoming a little colony of *nice* people, 'from our own class'.

It was, on the whole, a very good scheme, and it worked. Just before his death – his health had never been robust – the whole project had been completed. He, his wife and small son had moved into the largest of the new houses, the one now occupied by Sir John Counter, and all the flats plus the five other new houses and the two converted lodges were let to acceptable tenants on enormously long leases. Mr Chubb-Smith died happy in the knowledge that his widow and son were well-cared for. No one could blame him for not foreseeing all the consequences of the Second World War which broke out some twelve months later.

Mrs Chubb-Smith, in telling the story of her life and hard times, took nearly twenty minutes to reach the outbreak of the Second World War, and both Dover and Sergeant MacGregor were looking a bit glassy-eyed as she gabbled inexorably on.

She was very bitter, and long-winded, about the Second World

War itself which she evidently regarded as a bit of personal spite directed against her by Almighty Providence. Her grievance was, briefly, that property values, especially in safe country areas, shot up to heights beyond the dreams of the late Mr Chubb-Smith. The leases of Mrs Chubb-Smith's highly desirable houses and flats changed hands at fantastic profits, all of which unfortunately went into the pockets of the leaseholders. The current tenants were more than content to pay her the originally agreed rents which, though they had seemed pretty hefty in 1938, were ludicrously small by 1945, and pitifully minute now. And, of course, Mrs Chubb-Smith was still, as landlord, responsible for the upkeep of the property, and costs here had proved that the sky was not the limit.

'Would you believe it,' exclaimed Mrs Chubb-Smith, throwing up her hands in far from mock despair, 'some of the leases won't expire until 2037! And most of the others are nearly as bad. Of course, Michael and I had to get out of the house Sir John has now. Luckily we were able to make a little profit on that deal, but I had to pay a fantastic sum to buy back the lease of this place. It's really been too ridiculous for words! And then, about a year ago, the first lease on one of the houses expired – the middle one on the other side. I was having a lovely time planning how to spend the money – I thought of going to the South of France for the winter or, perhaps, taking a cruise – and what happens? Michael comes in and announces that he's going to get married! Well, what could I do? I didn't want Maxine's father to think we were *paupers*! He's frightfully rich and just doesn't understand that not everybody's made of money these days.

'So there it was! I had to give Michael and his wife the house. And now, just when another lease has expired – the Prentice's place – and I've at last got an empty house of my very own to dispose of, this wretched girl has to disappear and I have policemen swarming all over the place. How can I impress people who come to look at it with all this going on? You can't expect our sort of people to take a house with girls vanishing into thin air every five minutes, can you?'

She paused, mercifully, for breath and looked appealingly at Chief Inspector Dover. Kitty Chubb-Smith had been in her youth very pretty in a chocolate-box way, and she was, thirty years on, still fighting to preserve the wide-eyed, girlish innocence which had stood her in such good stead. Naturally the line of the chin was no longer so clear cut, the brow was not so smooth, the cheeks were not so unlined, the waist was not so trim, but, at the very least, she could be awarded high marks for trying. Her clothes were good and expensive, and only a trifle too young for her. And she was liberally drenched in the very latest Parisian perfume. In fact, Dover was finding the whole thing a bit overwhelming. The room was small and a large electric fire pumped out heat on both bars. There were huge vases of flowers everywhere and their scent fought valiantly with whatever seductive preparation Mrs Chubb-Smith was currently paying fifteen guineas an ounce for.

Dover grimly took out his handkerchief and wiped not only his brow but the back of his neck as well. Mrs Chubb-Smith's smile grew a little stiff. Her first doubts looked like being confirmed. The fat one wasn't a gentleman – not one of nature's sort nor any other kind.

Dover belched, softly but audibly, and frowned. His stomach really did feel a bit queer. Perhaps he was going to be ill. They'd have to take him off the blasted case if he was sick. He brightened up at the thought and even managed a flaccid smile. Mrs Chubb-Smith acknowledged it with a gracious flash of brilliant white teeth.

'We were wondering, madam,' Dover began, 'if you could perhaps give us a little help – some general information about the set-up here. For example, the main gates. I understand they are closed at nights?'

'Yes, Bondy – he's my caretaker up at the flats – he locks them every night, usually about ten o'clock, not before, anyhow.'

'And he opens them again? At what time?'

'At seven o'clock in the morning. The trouble was, er ... Sergeant?'

'Chief Inspector!' snarled Dover.

'Oh, Chief Inspector – the trouble was that on several occasions last year we had people – couples, you know – driving their cars into the grounds and staying all night. Well, naturally, we couldn't have that sort of thing going on here so we've had to lock the gates at night. Some people have complained about it and I admit it is a little inconvenient, but, as I said to them, "Which do you want?" Anyhow, it's most unusual for anybody to be coming back after ten o'clock and they can always leave their cars outside and walk up the drive. Michael and Maxine always do that if they're out late.'

'Bondy keeps the key, then?'

'Oh yes, he keeps the key.'

'Hm.' Dover digested this moodily and tried another line. 'Do you know this girl Juliet Rugg well? I mean, are you on friendly terms with her at all?'

'Friendly terms!' Mrs Chubb-Smith made a fair shot at an insulted-grande-dame pose and then, because even aristocrats these days have to watch their step, she switched to a sweet, more-in-sorrow-than-in-anger smile. 'My dear Inspector, I don't want to appear a snob but she was, or is – it's so difficult, isn't it – she is only a servant girl.'

'But you did know her?'

'I knew her by sight, naturally, everybody did, and I made a point of saying good morning or whatever it was when I met her. But that was, I'm afraid, the extent of our relationship.'

'I see,' said Dover mildly and, much to Sergeant MacGregor's surprise, left the matter there. From time to time the chief inspector rather fancied a bit of subtlety – it made a change any-how. He moved on to another line of questioning, skilfully designed to lull poor Mrs Chubb-Smith into a fragile sense of security.

'I suppose, as ultimate landlord here, madam, you have the right to approve a new tenant when there's a sub-let or when a lease changes hands?'

'I have indeed, and I'm very particular, I may tell you.'

'I wonder if you could just tell us something about the people here. We've got the names, but if you could just fill in a bit of background ... '

'Well, I don't know very much about the people in the flats. They had very good references, of course, but they're all rather elderly, dull people, you know. They seem to live very quiet, decent lives, retired civil servants and people like that. Bondy would be able to tell you much more about them than I could.'

'What about the people in the houses? We've already met Sir John Counter and his daughter, and Colonel What's-her-name in the other lodge.'

'Colonel Bing? Yes, a delightful person, isn't she? Her bark's much worse than her bite, I always say.' Mrs Chubb-Smith tossed this off politely without much conviction. 'Well, next to her, the first new house up on the other side from here, lives our celebrity, Miss Eulalia Hoppold. She's borrowed the house for six months to write her next book. She says it's completely hopeless trying to get peace and quiet in town.'

'Eulalia Hoppold?' repeated Dover scratching his head in a most unpleasant manner. 'What does she do?'

Mrs Chubb-Smith watched the dandruff fall gently on to the shoulders of his overcoat, and shivered fastidiously.

Her voice was rather chilly. 'She's the world-famous explorer and anthropologist.'

'Oh,' said Dover, deliberately unimpressed. 'Does she live alone?'

'Yes,' said Mrs Chubb-Smith.

'Has she got a car?'

'She has one of these tiny little two-seater sports cars. Very chic, of course, but rather noisy.'

'Who lives next to her?'

'My son, Michael, and his wife.'

'And what does your son do for a living?'

'Well, he's not actually doing anything at the moment. He's got several openings in view but he's still not sure that he's found just the right thing for him, you know. Maxine's father is coming back from abroad in a couple of months and we're hoping he may be able to suggest something. All these large organizations are very keen to get public-school boys working for them, aren't they? Meanwhile Michael helps me out running the business side of things up here – more as a hobby, really, than as a job. He's not very robust, poor boy, and he can't just take any job that comes along.'

'I see. And how old is he?'

'He's twenty-six.'

Dover sniffed but offered no additional comment.

'And the house next to his, the last one on that side?'

'Oh, that's this Bogolepov man. I'm afraid he's been rather a disappointment.'

'Yes' – Dover cut this short – 'we've heard about him. Has he got a car?'

'No, he's far too er, nervous to drive, I'm sure.'

'Has your son got a car, by the way?'

'Oh yes, they've got a Jaguar.'

'Does it belong to your son or to his wife?'

'Well, it's Maxine's, actually, but naturally they both use it. It was a present from her father.'

'Now, opposite this foreign chap is Sir John Counter's house, has Sir John got a car?'

'Yes, a very old Rolls – but then a Rolls is a Rolls, isn't it, even when it's very old? Bondy usually drives it for them, but they don't use it often.'

'Does Miss Counter drive?'

'I don't really know, I'm afraid. I rather think she does, but I'm not sure.'

'And who's in the house next to Sir John?'

'That's the one that's empty at the moment.'

'Did the local police look in there? When Juliet Rugg was reported missing?'

'Yes, I took the policeman in myself. He found nothing, of course. The place was locked up just as I'd left it.'

'And the last house, the one here next door to you?'

'Oh, that belongs to the Freels, Amy and Basil. They're brother and sister. He's a retired clergyman.'

'They're quite an elderly pair, then?'

'No, middle fifties, I should think. He must have retired early, health perhaps. He spends his time marking exam papers, or something like that.'

'Have the Freels got a car?'

'Yes, but they only use it in summer. Basil props it up on bricks and takes the wheels off and things like that in winter. Why all this interest in cars, Inspector?'

'Just something that may help us, madam,' said Dover suavely. 'Have you got one, by the way?'

'Good heavens, no!' Mrs Chubb-Smith laughed a silvery laugh. 'Poor me, I can't even afford a bicycle!'

'Hm,' said Dover, looking for no particular reason highly sceptical. His gaze was fixed, quite unconsciously, on Mrs Chubb-Smith's plunging neckline. Although it was intended to attract roving masculine eyes, Mrs Chubb-Smith had not quite had a man like Dover in mind when she put it on. She raised a protective hand and fiddled idly with her string of pearls.

'Oh well' – Dover rose reluctantly to his feet – 'I don't think we need bother you any more, Mrs Chubb-Smith, at the moment. Thank you for being so helpful.'

'It's been a pleasure,' responded Mrs Chubb-Smith, not seeking to detain them. 'I'm only too glad to be able to do what I can to get this dreadful business cleared up – for the girl's sake, of course, as well as everything else.'

'Quite, quite,' said Dover, and moved towards the door. Mrs Chubb-Smith surged thankfully after him and Sergeant Mac-Gregor, with a disloyal shrug of his shoulders, closed his notebook and prepared to follow.

Dover had his hand actually on the doorknob (hand-painted porcelain) when he stopped. Mrs Chubb-Smith stopped too and Sergeant MacGregor hovered uncertainly. Dover swung round.

'How much money did Juliet Rugg get out of you before the baby was born?' he asked with the air of a genuine inquirer.

The effect was dramatic, just like the films. Dover felt rather pleased with himself. Mrs Chubb-Smith had started to smile politely when Dover began speaking, then her jaw had dropped with a jerk which almost dislocated her false teeth when the import of his words sank in. Her face went quite white beneath her pancake make-up, her eyes bulged out in horror, her hand flew to her throat and she took an involuntary step backwards.

'I don't know what you mean!' she floundered, unconsciously playing her part in the melodrama.

'I think you do, madam,' said Dover ponderously. 'Suppose we sit down again and get this little matter straightened out? Get your notebook out, Sergeant, I think we'll get the truth this time. Won't we, Mrs Smith?'

Mrs Chubb-Smith was too shocked even to bridle at Dover's spiteful little abbreviation of her name. She groped behind her for a chair and collapsed into it, still staring at Dover like a person anxious not to miss whatever's going to happen next on TV.

'Now, don't let's waste any more of my time!' Dover scowled unpleasantly. 'We have evidence that you paid a considerable sum of money to Juliet Rugg before the birth of her baby. Why?'

'Who told you?' asked Mrs Chubb-Smith faintly.

'Never mind who told me!' snarled Dover viciously. 'You're here to answer questions, not to ask 'em! And I'll remind you, there are very heavy penalties for lying to the police. Now, get on with it!'

Mrs Chubb-Smith resorted to her only defence. She burst into tears. Dover, completely unmoved, watched sourly as she carefully dabbed at her eyes with a tiny lace-edged handkerchief. He hadn't been a policeman for over twenty years to be put off his stroke by a snivelling woman. She could scream and chew the carpet for all he cared.

Mrs Chubb-Smith shot him an oblique look, and sighed.

'Oh well, I suppose I'd better tell you the whole thing,' she snapped crossly, 'though it's nothing at all to do with this wretched girl's disappearance.

'The thing is, Inspector, that I had every reason to believe that the baby was Michael's – my son's. She came to see me one day, it must have been almost as soon as she knew she was pregnant, and told me that she was "in trouble" as she put it. She said my son was responsible.'

'And you believed her?' asked Dover.

'It was not beyond the realms of possibility,' replied Mrs Chubb-Smith grimly. 'Michael has been rather naughty where some of the local girls have been concerned, and this dreadful Rugg girl has quite a reputation in the district for, well, for being rather loose in her ways. Michael is, I'm afraid, rather highly sexed – like his dear father – though, of course, he's never got a girl into trouble before. In any case, these modern girls are just as much to blame as the men are. More, really. After all, it is up to them to set the standards.'

'Anyhow, you accepted her statement that your son was the putative father?'

'After I'd had a little talk with Michael, yes, I did.'

'Then what?'

'She wanted money, naturally.'

'Blackmail?'

'I suppose you could call it that. But what could I do? I had to keep her quiet. It was just about the time that Michael was getting engaged to Maxine and, of course, neither she nor her father would have tolerated a scandal like that! I just couldn't afford to take the risk.'

'So you paid up?'

'Yes.'

Dover scratched his stomach pensively. 'Why didn't she go to your son?'

'Oh, she knew he'd no money!' Mrs Chubb-Smith gave a short, scathing laugh.

'And when the baby was born?'

'Well, it was obvious it wasn't Michael's, and she couldn't even pretend for a moment it was. You can imagine how relieved I was when I heard!'

'And you stopped the payments?'

'Naturally. The whole thing was over. There was no point in continuing them, was there?'

'Did Juliet Rugg start the same little game again, just recently?' asked Dover.

Mrs Chubb-Smith tossed him a look of loathing and started to shake her head.

'I wouldn't bother lying if I were you,' advised Dover, 'we've other sources of information.'

Mrs Chubb-Smith uttered a short, rude word not usually found in the vocabulary of gentlewomen, however decayed.

'I met her about a week ago,' she snapped. 'She said something about some letters she had, from Michael. She kept simpering like a great fat cow and saying she wondered what his wife would think about them. She didn't actually ask me for money, but I gathered that was what the filthy little bitch was leading up to.'

'Has she approached you since?'

'No. I've been expecting her every day. I don't mind telling you that I've been nearly at my wits' end. I can't go on paying money out for ever!'

'Did you discuss what Juliet had said to you with your son?'

'Oh yes!' Mrs Chubb-Smith laughed bitterly. 'You can imagine what a tower of strength he was! He admitted that he'd written some letters to Juliet, the damned fool, and they certainly weren't the sort he wanted Maxine to see. All he could suggest was that I should go on paying through the nose to keep Juliet Rugg's mouth shut.'

'You didn't consider calling her bluff? After all, this business took place before your daughter-in-law was married, didn't it? Perhaps she wouldn't be quite so upset as you seem to fear.'

'In the first place,' said Mrs Chubb-Smith, 'I'm not absolutely sure that Michael hasn't been seeing this Rugg girl since his marriage. He won't admit it, but I'm not quite so stupid as you may think, Inspector. Maxine is a rather, well, shall we say she's not a submissive wife. At times Michael may have turned else-where for – er – consolation.

'And in the second place, Maxine is not the kind of girl to forgive and forget. I'm very fond of her, naturally, but she's been very spoilt and she's rather used to having her own way. Modern girls, Inspector, especially those with rich fathers, have one eye on the divorce courts when they're walking up the aisle. In my day a woman accepted a little infidelity on the part of her husband as regrettable, even painful perhaps, but not disastrous. But a girl like Maxine doesn't marry for a home and children and security. She marries for her own pleasure. And I can assure you that, devoted as she is to Michael, Maxine would break that marriage up without a qualm if she thought Michael has as much as looked twice at a girl like Juliet. Young people, I find, are very selfish and self-centred these days.'

'Hm,' said Dover with a deep grunt of agreement. He was second to none in his disapproval of the younger generation. 'So, Juliet's disappearance must have come as quite a relief to you?'

'When I heard she was missing, it was one of the happiest days of my life!' Mrs Chubb-Smith spoke with weary frankness. 'I suppose it's a dreadful thing to say, but if she's dead ... '

She couldn't finish the phrase and shrugged her shoulders helplessly.

Chapter Six

CHIEF INSPECTOR DOVER was never, as his wife well knew, at his brightest and best first thing in the morning. But when he appeared in the dining-room of The Two Fiddlers on the Saturday, even the landlord's wife, a woman of considerable experience, was a bit taken aback at the air of gloom, despondency and sheer bad temper which shrouded him. His face had acquired a most repulsive grey tinge, his eyes were sunken and bloodshot and his efforts at shaving had been far from successful.

He joined Sergeant MacGregor at the breakfast table, casting a jaundiced eye at that, as ever, immaculate young man and at the enormous greasy plateful of bacon and eggs which he was demolishing with the unthinking abandon of youth. Dover's stomach heaved, warningly.

'Coffee and toast!' he growled sourly.

Sergeant MacGregor looked up in surprise because Dover, given half a chance, normally munched his way through everything on the menu.

'Did *you* sleep well?' The question was flung at MacGregor in a sulky growl.

'Well, yes – thank you, sir.' Sergeant MacGregor was astonished at being asked. After a pause he returned the courtesy. 'Did you, sir?'

'No, I did not!' Dover's heavy jowl sagged miserably. 'I spent more time in the bathroom last night than I did in bed. Must have been something I ate. My stomach feels as though all the policemen in the Metropolitan area have been trampling on it with hobnail boots.' He took a tentative mouthful of dry toast. 'God only knows what effect this'll have on it!'

Friday night had been pretty disastrous all round, apart from the fact that it had upset Dover's stomach. When the two detectives had left the still sniffing Mrs Chubb-Smith, Sergeant MacGregor was all for going on and tackling her son, Michael, right away. Dover however, had had enough of interviews for one day and, anyhow, he wanted his dinner. He'd been looking forward for some time to a bit of peace and quiet and, in his opinion, Michael Chubb-Smith could well wait till the morning.

Dinner at The Two Fiddlers was no better than lunch. Indeed it was almost identical. The tomato soup, the ice-cream and the cheese appeared once again, but instead of the New Zealand lamb they were presented with an unappetizing, painfully thin slice of Argentinian beef, submerged in a thick grey gravy. They retired to the bar.

It is generally believed that strangers invading the privacy of some remote rural pub are treated by the locals with frigid in-difference and even antagonism. This was not the case with the regular clientele of The Two Fiddlers. Fortified by their know-ledge of police procedure, culled from detective stories and im-ported television serials, they flung themselves with gusto at the chance of contact with the real thing. Dover and MacGregor soon found themselves hemmed in by a crowd of sweating, grin-ning faces whose owners insistently plied them with questions and pint tankards of the locally brewed beer. This thick, fruity bever-age, a deep mahogany red in colour, was known as Long Herbert and was guaranteed by one revolting old boozer as being strong enough to rot the socks off you.

The ringleader of this bucolic gang was an elderly man who had clearly drawn his own deductions about the perennial popu-larity of 'The Archers'. He gave such a well-studied and accurate impersonation of Walter Gabriel that strangers, on meeting him for the first time, were inclined to consult their watches to see if it wasn't really a quarter to seven.

In spite of some pretty stout opposition, the Walter Gabriel character succeeded in hogging the show. He treated Dover to a long-winded, village-eye view of Irlam Old Hall which contained so many mock dialect words and deliberate mispronunciations as to be wellnigh unintelligible.

'Lot of glormy parishites they be up there,' he concluded. 'Bain't one of 'em what's done an honest day's work in their life. Coming down here and boppiting around as though they was lords of the manority or something ! You mark my words, mister, if anything's happened to poor Juliet Rugg, it's one of them bloody capitalists up there what's done it ! Me old dear, me old beauty !'

'Really?' said Dover.

a   65

'Yah' – the old man nodded emphatically – 'nobody down here'd have touched a ginger hair of that poor girl's noddle! Right popular lass she was down here. General favourite, you might say.'

' 'Cept with t'other women, p'raps!' came a slow sardonic comment from the back.

The old man ignored it.

'She used to work here, you know, me old dear, me old beauty, here in this very bar. Fine figure of a girl she was, too. I dunno whether the constipation of beer went up but, by Gordy, my bloody-pressure did! I allus used to say' – he nearly choked with anticipatory mirth – 'I allus used to say she ought to go on the stage!' Sniggers from those who'd heard this many times before. 'She ought to go in the theater, I allus used to say. 'Cause why? 'Cause she'd be the only Juliet with her own balcony!'

There was a flattering roar of laughter and the old man turned dangerously red in the face as tears of senile joy streamed from his eyes. Dover didn't move a muscle. He made a point of never laughing at other people's jokes. He tried, not with much hope, to turn the conversation to more useful channels.

'I understand Juliet Rugg had a number of boy-friends?'

Old 'Walter Gabriel' nodded happily. 'Aye, that she did! She were a lusty-busty wench, she were.'

'Do you know the names of any of them?'

'The problem bain't naming 'em, it be remembering 'em. Fact is, I'd be hard put to name a chap for twenty miles around, what was in full possession of his facilities, what hadn't taken a walk with her up to the churchyard.'

'That's the local spot for courting, is it?'

'Ah, nice and quiet up there, it be. Nobody don't go up there 'cept to be laid under the ground, or on it, if you follow me, me old dear, me old beauty.'

Dover blew down his nose. He was getting fed up with this.

'Do any of the people from Irlam Old Hall come down here at all?'

'No, not so's you'd notice.' The Walter Gabriel type pursed his lips in thought. 'That cansy lad, Chubb-Smith, used to come down sometimes afore he bedded that rich, moppity young wife of his. But that was when Juliet were behind the bar. And he didn't come for the beer, neither! That writer woman comes in sometimes, what's her name – Hoppit or som'at.'

'Eulalia Hoppold?' suggested Sergeant MacGregor.

'That be her! Drinks neat gin, she does. Doubles too.'

A youth, incongruously sporting both a cowlick and Elvis Presley side whiskers, leaned towards Dover across the old man's shoulder.

'I read one of her books once,' he announced, not without pride. 'It weren't half hot stuff! Some of the things them blacks got up to out there – cor!'

'Walter Gabriel' elbowed the village intellectual back out of the limelight. 'Well, we know what some of them blacks round here get up to, don't we? I'd have given two loads of horse manure to see our Juliet's face when she saw that babby for the first time!'

Dover broke through the laughter which greeted this witticism.

'Do you know who the father was, by the way?'

'No, no more than she does, I reckon. They say all cats looks grey in the dark, don't they? We had some of these 'ere West Indians working on the motor-way t'other side of Creedon round about that time. Must've been one of they heathens.'

Dover had endured another hour of this sort of thing and then thankfully retired to bed at closing time, his head buzzing with the local accent and his stomach awash with the local beer. His night had not been a peaceful one, and thanks no doubt to the peculiar qualities of Long Herbert, he greeted the start of a new day with a lacklustre eye and flaming bad temper. The thought of spending another stretch of dismal hours asking endless questions about this dratted girl almost made him groan aloud. If only they'd some idea whether she was dead or alive there might be a bit more point to all this, though Dover doubted if he could work up much enthusiasm either way.

When they got back to Irlam Old Hall after breakfast, for no reason at all, except perhaps to annoy and confuse Sergeant MacGregor, Dover decided to call on Eulalia Hoppold first, instead of tackling Michael Chubb-Smith.

Miss Hoppold showed her visitors into her study, or perhaps 'den' would be a better word for it. It was certainly full of wild animals. They were there, stuffed, skinned or in photographs, wherever the eye was turned. In the odd spaces unoccupied by the animals or bits of them were other trophies of Miss Hoppold's apparently fruitful travels. There were bunches of wicked-looking spears, there were primitive bows and arrows with nasty brown marks on their tips, there were native drums and tomahawks, samples of African beadwork and a collection of nose bones from fourteen different tribes. There were iron cooking-pots and gaudily painted clay bowls. There was even, in a little glass case all of their own, a couple of doll-sized, shrunken human heads, the pièce de résistance of the collection.

Dover moved an elephant-hide whip and a boomerang to one side and sat down. He gazed slowly round the packed room, not so much fascinated as stupefied. He noted the four shelves devoted to copies of Miss Hoppold's literary endeavours (translated into eight languages). He read some of the titles: *Lone White Woman, Initiation Rites in the Dark Continent, My Hosts were Cannibals, The Silent Killers of the Upper Amazon, Zulu Bride*. He vaguely remembered having read somewhere that Eulalia Hoppold's books were certainly exciting and sold like the proverbial hot cakes but, in some quarters, her scholarship as an anthropologist was, not to put too fine a point on it, suspect.

He had a look at the photographs which crowded in on him. They had been taken in innumerable foreign climes but they all had one thing in common, the central figure was invariably Miss Eulalia Hoppold, dressed in a khaki shirt and slacks and grinning broadly into the camera. She was everywhere, towering over sheepish-looking pygmies or being dwarfed by gigantic, satin-skinned Zulu warriors. She was portrayed draped in boa constrictors, nursing tiger cubs and cuddling chimpanzees. The photographs also revealed her as a huntress of no mean achievement, and she appeared time and again standing in dramatic poses over the dead bodies of every kind of rare and exotic animal. Were there tigers, Miss Hoppold had shot one. Were there gazelle, Miss Hoppold could be seen skinning one with her own strong, brown hands. Were there elephants, Miss Hoppold had just hit this poor tusked brute plumb between the eyes, or wherever it is that the real experts shoot elephants.

Dover turned from his inspection to stare poutingly at Eulalia Hoppold herself, in the flesh. He was a little disconcerted to find that she was already gazing avidly at him, as though she were mentally drawing a bead on an interesting specimen of a hitherto unknown species. Dover's stomach rumbled loudly, and Miss Hoppold, with a slight shake of her head, relaxed behind her desk.

She was a small, tough, wiry woman in her early forties. She looked rather like an engaging monkey with sharp, pale blue eyes. A mop of short, ruffled, straw-coloured hair framed her brown, finely wrinkled face. She wore no make-up at all. She was a very intense woman with a positive greed for life. As an anthropologist, one would expect her to be interested in her fellow men, and she was, rather overpoweringly so. 'I love people,' she had declared in one of her books, 'people are meat and drink to me!' It was to be hoped that Dover wouldn't give her indigestion.

But on the subject of Juliet Rugg, Miss Hoppold wasn't very helpful. She knew the girl by sight, of course, but then – who didn't? 'Great overweight slob,' was Miss Hoppold's forthright pronouncement. 'Looked like a cow hippopotamus in calf and had, I imagine, about the same I.Q. rating. How Eve could tolerate her in the same house for more than five minutes, I really don't know! Oh I know she was supposed to be a companion to Sir John, whatever that may mean – but if I'd been Eve, I'd have booted her out of the place before you could say Gilbert and Ellice Islands. The girl was an immoral slut and that's the long and short of it. She was whoring around with every available man in the district. When Eve told me she was going to report her disappearance to the police I told her not to be such a damned fool. "Be thankful you've got rid of her," I said, "for God's sake don't go looking for her! What with black babies, green nail varnish and stiletto heels, you're well shot of her! Never mind your father," I told her, "he's got his television and that's more than enough at his age." Disgusting old scoundrel he is, too. Of course, Eve's too damned spineless to do anything about him. I'd have had him shut up in a home twenty years ago if I'd been in her shoes.'

'Yes,' said Dover sadly. He wished he could get hold of one of these taciturn witnesses some time, the sort that just said 'yes' and 'no'. All the people in this case were too damned articulate for words.

'Miss Hoppold,' he went on, 'we have reason to believe that Miss Rugg was safe and unharmed as late as eleven o'clock on Tuesday night.'

'Yes, so I've heard. Colonel Bing saw her, didn't she?'

'So she says,' agreed Dover darkly. 'Did you, by any chance?'

'See her? Good God, no!' Eulalia Hoppold gave a short laugh. 'I'm always in bed by ten. Get used to keeping early hours in my line of business, you know.'

'You're alone in the house?'

'Yes, and I was alone in bed too, if that's going to be your next question.'

'Yes,' said Dover, 'of course.'

'What do the police think has happened?' asked Miss Hoppold, her eyes boring deeply into Dover's.

'Well, it's early days yet,' said Dover, feeling he'd said it so many times before, 'but it's beginning to look as though she didn't go off of her own free will.'

'Hm,' said Miss Hoppold, 'and what does that leave?'

'Murder, possibly.'

'What about kidnapping? I've heard that mentioned as a possibility?'

'In the police view,' said Dover firmly, 'kidnapping is quite out of the question.'

* * *

After leaving Miss Hoppold's lair the natural thing would have been for Dover and MacGregor to call next door to see the young Chubb-Smith couple, but Dover still wasn't in the mood to do what he thought his sergeant expected, however logical and obvious it might be. With his head sunk well down in his shoulders and his thoughts concentrated on his still tender stomach, Dover plodded on until he came to the bungalow occupied by the foreigner, Boris Bogolepov. He rammed his finger viciously into the doorbell and was furious to find that it was the sort which played a tinkling, insipid tune. Dover didn't feel that this was a fitting herald of his menacing appearance on a prime suspect's doorstep. Dover didn't approve of foreigners, mainly on the irrefutable grounds that they were un-English, and he was looking forward to giving Boris Bogolepov, guilty or not, a rough old time just for the sheer hell of it.

After a few moments the door was opened by a strikingly handsome young man dressed in the top half only of a pair of pyjamas.

The young man had rather bright, staring eyes which peered desperately out of a drawn and haggard face. His dark hair was uncombed and his chin carried at least two days' growth of beard. He didn't look any too clean either, but there was no denying his attractiveness in a Byronic-beatnik way.

'Ah, the Gestapo!' he said with a slight Teutonic accent of the kind favoured by film stars when playing swinish German officers in war pictures. 'Come in, gentlemen, but please leave your rubber truncheons in the hall. You will not need them. You have only to shout to me and I confess everything.'

He led the two detectives into the kitchen. 'I am just consuming my breakfast,' he said, sitting down at the table, 'cornflakes and whisky. Perhaps you will join me?'

Dover scowled blackly. He suspected that he was having the mickey taken.

The kitchen looked just like you would expect from a man who breakfasted, half naked, at eleven o'clock in the morning off cornflakes and whisky. The garish cereal packet flaunted its free offers by the side of a three-quarters-full bottle of Black and White.

'You wish to ask me questions about the disappearance of Miss Rugg? I can tell you all very quickly. I know nothing. Now you can go and interrogate somebody else.'

'Where were you on Tuesday night at eleven o'clock?' asked Dover curtly.

Bogolepov shrugged his shoulders. 'Here.'

'Alone?'

'We are all alone, sir, in spite of your John Donne. Each man *is* an island.'

Much to Sergeant MacGregor's relief Dover didn't bother to ask who John Donne was, and not because he knew either. Charles Edward MacGregor eyed Boris Bogolepov curiously. The interest was mutual. The two equally attractive and handsome men examined each other critically. One had the charm of exuberant health, but his rival was equally fascinating with his air of sickness and neglect. Their instant antagonism and jealousy was ridiculous but it was almost tangible. The fat, middle-aged chief inspector didn't, of course, enter into this masculine beauty contest.

'Were you in bed?' Dover plodded on.

'I cannot remember. I may have been in this room. Does it matter?'

'What nationality are you, sir?'

'Oh, I am British, Inspector. So you will not be able to kick me about too much. Only naturalized, of course! I am not a dyed-through-the-wool Englishman.'

'How long have you been in this country?'

'I came here first in 1947. Before that I had been in the States for some months. And before that I had been in Germany.'

'You were in Germany during the war?'

'Yes' – Bogolepov waved his index finger loosely in the air – 'but not, my dear sir, as a soldier. I was in a concentration camp, as a prisoner, you understand.' He took a drink of whisky. 'I have had a very interesting life, Inspector. I will tell you of it. I have told it so often to so many officials that, now, it is easy. Now it is no longer real. It is just a story – to them and to me.'

Dover didn't answer. He just kept his eyes fixed on Bogolepov, noting the slight tremble in his hands and recording the increasing bitterness in his gestures and voice.

'My father was a Russian – my surname is Russian, of course – but I was born in Germany in 1927. My father was a refugee, too, you see. He left Russia after the Revolution and eventually he went to Germany. He was a doctor, a good doctor, but it is difficult to make a new start in a foreign country. However, he was lucky. He married my mother and her family helped him. They were very kind and good, but there was one thing wrong with them. They were Jews. That was a stupid thing to be in Germany when the Nazis came to power, Inspector, a very stupid thing to be.

'Well, you can imagine what happened. It is a very common story. Things got worse and worse for us. I was sent away to a private school, high in the mountains, where my little friends did not spit at me and beat me up and cover me with filth. Then, in 1937, my father was warned by a grateful patient that the Gestapo were going to arrest him. There was, as you say, no time to lose. My father and my mother and my two sisters got out of the country within twelve hours. They left me behind. There was not time to get a message to me. You find it hard to believe, eh? That a family could leave their only son behind like that, a little, half-Jewish boy of ten alone in Germany? Oh, of course, I was to join them later but, unfortunately, it was too late.'

Boris Bogolepov gave a bitter, sardonic laugh and slopped more whisky into his glass.

'So there I was! The only people I could turn to for help were the family of my mother. But they were dirty Jews, too. When the war broke out they were all shipped off like silly cows to the concentration camps, and I was shipped off as well.

'But I was one of the lucky ones! As you see, I survived. And the big joke is that my mother and father and my two sisters – they are all dead! Isn't it funny? They were all killed in an air raid in London in 1940 while I was safe and sound in my little concentration camp. Sometimes I wake up at night and laugh until the tears run down my face at the wonderful irony of it.

'I spent six years in concentration camps. I lived because I was young and strong and ruthless. I am only half a Jew, you see. I was not resigned to the extermination of my race, I did not deliver myself up passively into the hands of God! No, I made up my mind to live at any cost! And I did! Do you know what my dream was all those dreary years, Inspector, the fantasy I hugged to myself when I went to sleep? I wanted to be a Nazi! I wanted to wear that uniform, to flourish that twisted cross on my arm, to have a dagger at my waist and those wonderful jackboots on my feet! I did not hate them! I admired them, their arrogance, their power, their superb contempt for human life and suffering. I did not blame them for what they were doing to the Jews. I admired and envied them. If only I could have become one of them, I would have done twice as much!'

Bogolepov's eyes were blazing fanatically and his voice was hoarse and excited. Dover stirred uneasily in his seat. This chap must be a nut case, all right.

Bogolepov apparently guessed his thoughts because he grinned and said: 'Oh, do not worry, Inspector. I am not mad. Most boys go through a stage of this kind. I was lucky to be so normal. In fact, you could say I have been lucky all my life, in a way. I was a very handsome boy, and that was lucky. If I had been ugly I would surely have been dead by now. One of the camp commanders saw me and took a fancy to me. You know what I mean. I did not understand at first, but when I did I was wonderfully

73

happy. At last, for the first time in my life, I had some power, however small it was, on my side. This great and important man in his beautiful colonel's uniform wanted something that only I could give him. It was a marvellous feeling. And when he was sent away, I found another "protector" and I soon learned to market my talents where they did the most good.

'Not that my "friends" overwhelmed me with their generosity. I was not suddenly transported to a life of ease and luxury. But a little extra food here, one of the better jobs there – these are the things which make the difference between life and death in those camps. I used to try and get on the burial squad. We carried the bodies out of the gas chambers to the pits near by. Sometimes you were lucky, you found some old Jew had a gold ring or a piece of bread still clutched in his hand – the bread was the bigger treasure, of course.'

Bogolepov paused and shrugged his shoulders. 'Well, I am probably boring you,' he said with heavy sarcasm, 'all this happened a long time ago, and who cares, anyhow? My cousins in America felt much the same. They got me out of Germany when the war was over and, at first, they nearly stifled me with compassion and sympathy. You know what Jews are like. They are a very emotional people. They felt obscurely guilty because they had not suffered as we in Europe had suffered. They felt that they had missed something! But they got bored with it, too. I was eighteen. They could not understand why, now it was all over, I did not settle down and became a regular, all-American boy. They tried hard but it just did not work. I embarrassed them. After six years in concentration camps, I embarrassed them. In the end I said I wanted to come to England – it was just to get out of an impossible situation. They were delighted. They made me an allowance and booked my ticket. I went to live in London. I was supposed to be a student. I did not need to work, which is lucky because there is nothing I can do. I made many friends, misfits like myself. I drank. I got arrested by the police. My cousin came rushing across the Atlantic Ocean and they put me in a home for a cure. It did not make any difference, but the next time I was arrested for something else, and so was my boy-friend. My cousin paid for psychiatric treatment. Then I started taking drugs. Did you guess I was a junky, Inspector? There is no degradation to which I have not sunk. But Cousin Reuben is always there. He always talks about me being sick, but he is a good man and he tries hard – the bloody fool!

'And that is how I am living here in Irlam Old Hall. Cousin Reuben fixed it all up. I am well away from the evil company which was leading me astray in London, I am enjoying the fresh country air and, as a properly registered drug addict, I get not quite enough of the stuff to keep me going, under the National Health Service. Every Wednesday morning I go into Creedon and collect a little white packet from the chemist. The Welfare State provides for everything, security from conception to the crematorium. Now I am all right. I do not drink more than a bottle of whisky a day and I have not got a single boy-friend. So, are you satisfied? Because if you are, you can clear out!'

Dover was still gazing moodily at Bogolepov. Talk, talk, talk, he thought crossly to himself, I must spend three-quarters of my life listening to other people yapping away. He sighed wearily once again.

'Why have you told me all this, sir?' He made no attempt to keep the exasperation out of his voice.

'Just to prove to you, my dear Inspector, that if you are looking for the murderer of Juliet Rugg, it is no good looking at me. I no longer have enough interest in the human race even to kill one of them.'

'What makes you think Juliet Rugg has been murdered?' pounced Dover sharply. 'We haven't said she was.'

'My dear Inspector, do not try to spring your little traps on me! It is logical enough to suppose that Juliet Rugg may have been murdered, otherwise why are two such distinguished, high officers from New Scotland Yard spending so much time here at Irlam Old Hall? I was merely putting, as you say, two and two together, not confessing my guilt.'

Dover grunted. 'When did you last see Juliet Rugg?'

'I do not remember. I see her passing by sometimes, but I do not make a note of when. A man or a woman walks by. As long as they do not come near me, I can endure it. And Juliet Rugg, all that fat and bouncing flesh – it was revolting! Nature at her most nauseatingly generous! And such sagging, lifeless flesh it was too. She looked like an enormous Egyptian mummy – the body tightly wrapped in corsets and brassieres to stop the flesh disintegrating, and the face painted into a grotesque semblance

75

of life, the green eye-shadow, the red lips, the pink cheeks, the black eyebrows, the hair stiffened into formalized designs. Only a resolute necrophile could have had any interest in her! And that is a little variation which, as yet, I have not tried.'

'You weren't on friendly terms with Miss Rugg, then?'

'My dear Inspector, the thought of touching a woman, any woman, makes me physically sick! Apart from what we may call my early "training", it is generally recognized by those who know about these things, that it is beyond the masculine capabilities to cope with both women and drink and drugs. I would have thought that you in your profession would have been aware of this. Of all men, I am the least likely to have lusted after that colossus of a girl. And I understand, from the gossip, that her attraction lay in the body alone. I do not think anyone loved her for the qualities of her mind. No, my dear Inspector, you will have to look somewhere else. I did not kill Juliet Rugg.'

'Well, that's very reassuring, sir, I must say,' growled Dover, annoyed at being reduced to cheap sarcasm but using it none the less.

'Ah, but I do not want you to think that I am not capable of destroying human life,' Bogolepov went on in a mocking voice. 'I have fought frail old men, old enough to be my grandfather, for a leaf of cabbage and I have tried to kill myself more than once. It is only that I would not be bothered with murder on such a trivial scale. One fat girl with red hair – there would be no satisfaction, no point in that. When I decide to deal with humanity, my dear sir, I shall use a machine-gun, or a bottle of prussic acid in the local reservoir. Murder does not interest me, but a massacre, to wipe out a whole village, a whole town – that is an idea which might attract me!' He laughed, and with a defiant gesture tipped the remains of his whisky down his throat.

Dover didn't find this kind of childish cynicism either amusing or useful and he stared suspiciously round the kitchen to save himself the trouble of finding a reply. The room seemed to be crammed with a surprisingly large number of status symbols. There was an enormous electric cooker with an infra-red grill, a washing machine, a spin dryer, a large refrigerator and an even larger deep freeze, a complicated waste disposal unit mounted on a stainless-steel sink and several other shiny, sleek appliances whose purpose Dover couldn't even guess at.

Bogolepov saw him looking. 'All presents from my cousin in America,' he explained with a contemptuous wave of his hand. 'Most useful for a man who lives almost exclusively on whisky and dope, don't you think? Of course, Cousin Reuben is in the trade so he gets them at cost price. When I get a little short of money I sell a piece or two of American culture to my neighbours. I sold Sir John Counter the very latest electric shaver only the other day. Would you believe it, it has six separate speeds! Who in God's name wants to be able to shave at six different speeds? But then, I think our civilization is wonderful, don't you?'

Dover reached for his bowler hat.

'My dear Inspector, must you leave so soon? I was hoping you and your charming assistant would stay for lunch. I've got another bottle of whisky cooling in the fridge.'

'I'm afraid we've got to get on, sir,' said Dover with a dead-pan face.

'Well, then, I can only wish you success in your work – I believe that is the right phrase. You must forgive me if I do not take your researches too seriously. I have seen five hundred people killed in a day and, after that, what does one Juliet Rugg more or less in the world matter?'

'She matters in this country, sir,' said Dover stiffly.

Bogolepov smiled charmingly and shook his head. 'Ah, you English! We poor foreigners will never understand, will we?'

'Apparently not, sir,' said Dover.

Chapter Seven

''STREWTH!' said Dover when they got outside. 'Well, if I was his American cousin I'd get him certified pretty damned quick! Remind me to warn the Chief Constable to keep an eye on him.'

'Do you think he was telling the truth, sir?' asked MacGregor.

'God only knows!' replied Dover, shaking his head in despair. 'I've heard enough bloody twaddle in the last thirty-six hours to do me for a lifetime. Anyhow, he's right about one thing, if you're a dipso *and* a junky, you aren't likely to be chasing women as well – that's for sure. Apart from the fact that his inclinations seem to lie in another direction.'

Sergeant MacGregor looked disappointed. 'Do you think it's a sex crime then, sir?'

'Well, I'm damned if I can see what else it can be, can you? From what everybody says the only thing that girl had was sex.'

'Then, we're looking for a man?'

Dover wrinkled his nose thoughtfully. 'I dunno we can go as far as that. Might be a woman. Jealousy, you know. And then there's this blackmail business. That might be mixed up in it somewhere. But I'm not really bothered about who did it at the moment. I'd just like to know where the flaming body is! We still haven't got a single line on that at all. I don't understand it, you can't just sweep a girl that size under the carpet, dead or alive. She must be somewhere, blast her!'

'What are we going to do now, sir?'

Dover looked at Sergeant MacGregor in blank astonishment.

'We're going to go and see this Chubb-Smith fellow and his wife. What did you think we were going to do – go to Brighton for the week-end? You'll never make a successful detective, Sergeant, if you can't sort your priorities out. Once you get yourself bogged down under a lot of useless information, you'll never be able to see the wood for the trees. Get yourself a working hypothesis, soon as you can, work out a plan and stick to it! It's no good going round with an open mind like a vacuum cleaner because all you'll finish up with is ... ' Dover paused to work this one out ' ... is fluff !' he concluded triumphantly.

'Yes, sir,' said Sergeant MacGregor, poker-faced.

Michael Chubb-Smith was understandably embarrassed when he showed the two detectives into the drawing-room.

'I'm afraid,' he apologized, snatching up a couple of dusters and tucking an apron behind a cushion, 'that the place is a bit upset.' He trundled a carpet-sweeper rapidly out of the room. 'I was just giving my wife a hand with the housework.'

Dover sniffed. 'Very commendable,' he said with a marked lack of approval. He held very strong views about husbands undertaking domestic chores and in his own house things were arranged differently. Michael Chubb-Smith hurriedly pulled the furniture back into its proper place.

'I suppose your mother has told you about the conversation she had with me yesterday, sir?'

'Well, yes, she has.' Michael Chubb-Smith smiled hopefully. 'I do hope there'll be no need to mention all this little business to my wife, Inspector? It would only upset her and really the whole thing's just a lot of fuss about nothing.'

'Oh? You didn't take Miss Rugg's threats of exposure seriously, then?'

'Well, in a way. She was quite capable of letting the cat out of the bag to Maxine all right. She was a spiteful little bitch in many ways, you know. What I meant was that my mother would have kept her mouth shut when it came to the point. She always makes a hell of a fuss about money, but she'd have paid up in the end. She always does. We shall probably be moving from here soon, my wife and I. I shall be going in with my father-in-law; we may even be going abroad. Once we were out of the way Juliet would be stumped and she'd have to let it all drop. She wouldn't have enough energy or intelligence to go on making threats long distance.'

'You weren't expecting to be blackmailed for the rest of your life, then?'

'Good heavens, no, Inspector!' Michael Chubb-Smith regarded his questioner with wide-eyed surprise. 'She was only a village girl, you know. She just saw her chance of making a spot of extra cash and took it, that's all. It was only a matter of a few measly quid. There was nothing sinister about it.'

'I see,' said Dover. 'By the way, sir, can you tell me where you were round about eleven o'clock on Tuesday night?'

'Oh, Maxine and I were both in bed. We didn't see or hear anything.'

'You and your wife share the same room, I take it?'

'When I let him!' came a drawling voice from the open doorway.

The three men turned round and MacGregor and Michael Chubb-Smith rose with alacrity to their feet. Dover contented himself with a vague grunt and a half-hearted attempt at rising a couple of inches from his chair.

'This is my wife,' said Michael Chubb-Smith. 'Darling, these are the detectives from Scotland Yard.'

'I can see that, darling, I'm not blind.' Maxine Chubb-Smith, the cynosure of three pairs of interested masculine eyes, undulated across the room and propped herself on one arm in a reclining position on a chaise-longue upholstered in white leather.

She was a small, exquisitely shaped girl with large dark eyes which she directed with frank curiosity at Sergeant MacGregor. He gazed appreciatively back at her. In skin-tight scarlet matador pants and an extremely revealing, close-fitting black blouse, she was well worth the sergeant's contemplation.

'I was just telling Inspector Dover, darling, that we were in bed on Tuesday night at eleven. You remember, that was when Colonel Bing saw this girl walking up the drive.'

Maxine turned her head slowly and looked at him. 'What a bloody liar you are, darling,' she said in a bored, languid voice. 'You know damned well I'd locked you out of the bedroom! For all I know you may have been out murdering this fat girl for hours.' She turned back to smile bewitchingly at Sergeant MacGregor.

Michael Chubb-Smith blushed furiously and avoided Dover's eyes.

'Is this true, sir?' asked the chief inspector in pained surprise.

'I suppose so,' muttered the young man.

'I hope you realize, sir, that giving false information to the police is a very serious offence.'

'Oh hell, what does it matter?' Chubb-Smith shot an irate look at his wife who was now eyeing Sergeant MacGregor up and down with patent admiration. 'Maxine and I had a bit of an argument. It's nothing to do with anybody else.'

'It wasn't an argument, darling, it was an ultimatum,' corrected his wife, not bothering to look at him.

'Well, anyhow, it's nothing to do with the police. And it makes no difference, Inspector, neither of us saw or heard anything which could be of the slightest help to you.'

'You speak for yourself, darling' – Maxine smiled sweetly at Sergeant MacGregor – 'I saw something which might very well interest these gentlemen.'

'Did you indeed, madam.' Dover turned towards her. 'Sergeant!' he snapped. 'I thought you were supposed to be taking notes!'

'Oh, sorry, sir!' Sergeant MacGregor flicked the pages over with a belated show of efficiency.

'Sergeant?' Maxine was disappointed. 'Does that mean you're not commissioned?'

'Detective Sergeant MacGregor's in the police, madam,' retorted Dover on his subordinate's behalf, 'not the army. We work on an entirely different system.'

'Oh,' said Maxine, not really sure whether this did or did not make Charles Edward MacGregor more or less of an 'other rank' than she had thought.

'Mrs Chubb-Smith!' thundered Dover in an only partially successful attempt to win her attention. 'Would you mind telling us what it was you saw on Tuesday night?'

Maxine looked without much interest at the chief inspector, whose temper was beginning to fray. 'Well, I don't know about that, darling,' she said. 'Daddy always warned me never to talk to the police without a solicitor. He always says that if people would only have enough sense to keep their mouths shut, they'd never be where they are today.'

Dover's fists clenched and a rather frightening purple tinge spread inexorably over his face and neck. Maxine's husband intervened before the inspector reached his never very high flash-point.

'For God's sake, Maxine,' he pleaded, 'tell them what you know and let's get rid of them. They'll be here for the rest of the day if you don't. Your father wasn't talking about this kind of thing.'

'All right, darling,' said his wife after staring at him with critical calculation for a few moments, 'if you say so. I'm sure

81

you've had more experience of these things than Daddy has. But just don't blame me if things go wrong. I'm only telling them because you told me to.'

'Telling us what, madam?' demanded Dover through clenched teeth.

'Only that I saw Eulalia Hoppold going to Boris's bungalow at about ten o'clock on Tuesday night. She went along the bottom of our garden, at the back. Of course, she always does. She thinks people won't see her that way.'

There was a moment's silent anticlimax and Dover's eyes rose heavenwards.

'I see,' he said with heavy patience. 'You saw Miss Hoppold going to Mr Bogolepov's house at ten o'clock on Tuesday night?'

'Going secretly,' Maxine pointed out.

'But that's all?'

'That's all I saw on Tuesday night,' Maxine agreed amiably.

'But you did see something else, later perhaps?'

Maxine rolled over on to her back, placed her arms behind her head and crossed one scarlet-cased leg over the other. She looked even better from this angle.

'Yes, I did see something later. I saw Eulalia Hoppold coming back again from Boris's, by the same route, at six o'clock on Wednesday morning.'

'Oh, really, Maxine, don't be childish! This isn't a game! She's just making it up, Inspector.'

'Really, sir,' said Dover, 'what makes you think that?'

'Because she's jealous, that's what! She's been making a play for Boris for months and he's just not having any. He's made that perfectly plain. Maxine just can't accept the fact that he prefers Eulalia's company to hers. She's making the whole thing up out of spite!'

'Oh, am I?' Maxine swung round on him, her eyes blazing with anger. 'You're such a damned fool that you can't see what's going on in front of your eyes! And how dare you say that I'm lying?'

'Because you've never got up at six o'clock in your entire bloody life, that's why! And our bedroom's at the front, so you couldn't possibly have seen Eulalia!'

Maxine replied with ice-cold dignity. 'I got up to go to the bathroom,' she stated, 'and the bathroom is at the back of the house.'

Michael Chubb-Smith got up angrily and poured himself out a drink.

'Are you implying, madam,' asked Dover, 'that Miss Hoppold and Mr Bogolepov spent the night together?'

'Of course they did! It's absolutely disgusting. She must be more than twice his age. And they'd had a fine old time, too. She was so exhausted she could hardly walk – filthy old cow – she looked as though she'd been pulled through a hedge backwards. And those great staring eyes! Ugh, it's enough to make you sick.'

'I see,' said Dover, who didn't by any means.

Half an hour later he was pounding wearily up the path to Boris Bogolepov's front door once again. Neither Maxine Chubb-Smith nor her husband had been able to throw any more light on the disappearance of Juliet Rugg. Maxine knew of the girl's existence, but was frankly surprised that Dover should even have expected her to have had any further connection with her. Dover toyed with the idea of giving Michael Chubb-Smith a really good grilling, and leaving him to sort out the consequences afterwards with his wife, but, masculine solidarity in these matters being what it is, he nobly restrained himself.

In any case the chief inspector felt he had got enough bits and pieces of useless information without going out of his way to collect any more. Michael Chubb-Smith would keep. No doubt the whole perishing lot of the Irlam Old Hall tenants would keep too, but Dover was only too well aware of the consequences of appearing to do nothing. Nasty, unsympathetic messages came shooting down from his superiors, and unkind remarks were made and old skeletons were taken out of dusty cupboards and rattled menacingly. But as long as Dover kept on interviewing people, however pointless and confusing it all was, nice full reports could be written (by Sergeant MacGregor) and everybody was kept more or less happy. Dover was, to put the matter bluntly, just filling in time until the body was found. As far as he could see, the only hope of solving Juliet Rugg's disappearance lay in the clues which the discovery of her corpse would no doubt reveal. Everything was in such a glorious muddle that, unless a miracle of forensic medicine came to his aid, Dover was quite prepared to leave the whole damned case unsolved and get back to London as quickly as he could. For the moment, however, he would just have to plod doggedly on.

Boris Bogolepov was clearly not pleased to see him. The feeling was reciprocated.

As soon as the front door was opened Dover shoved his way in uninvited and thumped down the hall into the kitchen. He was not surprised to find Miss Eulalia Hoppold there. She closed the lid of the deep freeze into which she had been peering and smiled politely at the chief inspector.

'Hullo, are you back again? I thought you'd finished with Boris. I was just looking around to see if the poor devil's got anything for lunch.' She grinned ruefully. 'Apparently he hasn't. The cupboard's bare.' She turned to Bogolepov who was still dressed in his pyjama jacket. 'Next time you invite me to lunch, my lad, just think on to get some food in, will you? I'll pop across to my place and bring something back with me.'

'You'll stay here,' said Dover firmly. 'I've a few questions I want to put to the pair of you.' He sat down at the kitchen table.

His two victims exchanged glances and then stared doubtfully at the chief inspector as he worked himself up into quite a passable state of righteous indignation about the iniquity of lying to the police. It was a subject about which he felt quite strongly. Lies meant more work for poor old Wilfred Dover who was already carrying more than his fair share of the burden.

'Now,' he snarled, having exhausted both himself and the theme, 'let's have the bloody truth this time! You' – he waggled a fat, admonitory finger at Boris – 'you told me that you spent Tuesday night here alone. And you' – the finger waved at Eulalia – 'you told me that you were alone in *your* house.'

There was a dramatice pause.

'So what?' said Boris, and shrugged his shoulders. The pyjama jacket rose alarmingly. Luckily Miss Hoppold's eyes were riveted on Dover's pouting countenance. She stared intently at the chief inspector with the air of one well versed in assessing the potential of animals of uncertain temper.

'It's no good, Boris,' she said with decision. 'We might as well come clean. Who told you?' she asked Dover, still not moving her eyes from his in case he decided to spring.

Dover wrinkled his nose. 'I am not at liberty to reveal my sources of information,' he proclaimed pompously.

Eulalia snorted contemptuously and bared her gleaming white

teeth in a humourless grin. 'Such chivalry can only mean dear Maxine. Blast her eyes! Well, what do you want to know?'

'Just the truth,' said Dover.

'By God!' Boris flung himself on to a chair in disgust. 'Just the truth, that is all he wants! " 'What is truth?' asked jesting Pilate; and would not stay for an answer." '

'Oh shut up, Boris! There's a good chap! All right, Inspector, Boris and I weren't alone in our respective houses on Tuesday night. We were here, together.'

'All night?'

'All night.'

'Doing what?'

'My dear Inspector' – Eulalia's tone bore little affection – 'surely we don't have to draw diagrams for you, do we? What in heaven's name do you think we were doing?'

Dover was unperturbed. 'Am I to take it that you were sleeping together, madam?'

'Oh my God!' said Boris sarcastically. 'Let us call a spade a spade! We were copulating.'

'Really, sir.' Dover turned to Boris who was pouring himself out another tumblerful of whisky. 'That isn't quite the story you gave me at our first interview, is it?'

Boris gave a short bark of a laugh. 'No, I am afraid I led you softly up the garden path, my dear sir, but you must admit I did it rather well.'

'Why didn't you tell me the truth?' snapped Dover viciously.

Boris looked steadily at him, his lips twitching into a faint smile. 'Chivalry, my dear sir,' he said grandly. 'I was protecting the good name of a lady.'

Dover emitted a sceptical grunt and swung back again to Eulalia who was still avidly watching him. 'And you, Miss Hoppold, why did you lie to me?'

'Well, it's not the sort of thing you shout from the house-tops, you know.'

'A confidential interview with the police is hardly shouting from the house-tops.'

'Well, I just didn't want anybody to know about Boris and me. You see, I'm married, Inspector. My readers don't know this because naturally it makes a better story if they think I do all my trips alone – you know, one helpless female surrounded by naked savages – but in actual fact my husband and I have always worked together. He takes all the photographs.

'I've come up here to get some peace and quiet while I get my next book finished and my husband's tied up in London making the arrangements for our next trip. There's nothing serious between Boris and me, but I'd simply rather my husband remained in ignorance about it. What the eye doesn't see, you know … '

'I see,' said Dover. 'And how long has this liaison between you and Mr Bogolepov been going on?'

'Oh, month or so.'

'And you've kept it completely secret?'

'Well, we thought we had.'

'Did Juliet Rugg know about it?'

Eulalia's eyes opened wide and she exchanged a quick glance with Boris. 'No, not as far as I know. Why should she?'

'It's very hard to keep a thing like this quiet, you know, madam,' Dover pointed out patiently. 'Neighbours can often put two and two together and arrive at the right answer. We've got every reason to believe that Juliet Rugg was not above a bit of gentle blackmail when she had the chance. You would appear to be an ideal victim. Did she ever try to blackmail you?'

'No, she certainly didn't!' Eulalia's jaw set in a pugnacious line. 'Just what are you getting at, Inspector? Are you hinting that we'd something to do with Juliet Rugg's disappearance?'

'It's a possibility, madam, isn't it? It wouldn't be the first time that a blackmailer's been bumped off by one of his victims.'

'And no doubt it will not be the last,' Boris commented helpfully into his glass of whisky. 'Do you want me to accompany you as I am, my dear sir, or will you permit me to put on a pair of trousers?'

'Oh Boris, do for God's sake shut up! This isn't a parlour game.'

'My dear Eulalia,' said Boris solemnly, 'I have never suggested it was.'

Eulalia turned impatiently to Dover. 'Now, look here, Inspector, let's just get this straight. Juliet Rugg did *not* know of my association with Boris and she was *not* blackmailing me. Why on earth should she? Apart from the fact that I should just have told her to go to hell, I think it extremely unlikely that she even knew I was married. Why, even Boris didn't know at first.'

86

'Nobody,' Boris chimed in plaintively, 'ever tells me anything.'

'And I can assure you, Inspector,' she continued after an irritated glance at Bogolepov, 'that whatever has happened to Juliet Rugg, I had nothing to do with it at all.'

'Nor,' said Boris, finishing off his whisky, 'had I.'

'Well,' said Dover, reaching for his bowler hat, 'we shall have to look into all this a bit further. Are there any other parts of your earlier statements that you would like to revise – just in case somebody else knows a bit more than you think they do?'

Eulalia and Boris shook their heads. 'No, my dear sir,' said the German in a voice which was becoming slightly slurred, 'now you have the truth, the whole truth and nothing but the truth. So help me God!'

'Hm,' said Dover sceptically, 'I hope you're right.'

'But there is one small point which you may have overlooked,' Boris squinted carefully into his empty glass.

'Really?' asked Dover with heavy sarcasm.

'Oh, yes. Don't forget that both Eulalia and I now have an alibi.'

Chapter Eight

'CHEEKY young bastard!' commented Dover grumpily when they found themselves once more standing on the drive of Irlam Old Hall.

'It was a rather fishy story, wasn't it, sir?' ventured Sergeant MacGregor. 'I mean, it doesn't sound very likely, does it?'

'The truth rarely does,' Dover observed with a deep sigh.

'But what about all this drink and dope business, sir? You said ...'

'Oh, never mind what I said!' snapped Dover, who couldn't stand people quoting his own words back at him. 'We can't stand here all day discussing things. Who've we got left to see up here?'

The sergeant was understandably somewhat flabbergasted at this apparent thirst for work on the part of his chief inspector. 'But, it's getting on for two o'clock, sir,' he pointed out, 'and we haven't had any lunch yet.'

Dover thought this over for a moment. His stomach appeared to have settled down fairly well, but he squirmed slightly at the prospect of what lunch at The Two Fiddlers would do to it. No, better not risk it.

'You young coppers are all the same,' he said blisteringly, 'never thinking about anything else except your stomachs! If you wanted a regular nine to five job, my lad, you shouldn't have joined the police. Crooks won't wait while you sit down and stuff yourself with meat and two veg, you know. We haven't time for lunch. Now, who've we got to see up here?'

'The Freels,' replied Sergeant MacGregor sulkily – he was hungry – 'and all the people in the flats.'

'Oh, hell!' said Dover. 'Well, let's start with the Freels. Maybe one of 'em'll up and confess and then we can all go home.'

The Freel's front door had two bells on it, marked A and B. With a muttered curse Dover stuck his finger into B and kept it there.

After a long wait the door was opened a grudging crack and a man's face peered out at them. With great reluctance he admitted that he was Basil Freel and allowed his visitors to cross the threshold.

'Kindly keep to the left of the line,' he begged them, indicating a thin piece of white tape which had been laid down the centre of the hall carpet. He led them to a room at the back of the house. 'This is my study,' he observed. 'I was working.' He paused for a moment. 'I'm very busy,' he added.

'We shan't keep you a moment, sir,' said Dover, hoping it was true.

'Good,' said Mr Freel bleakly and sat down gingerly on the edge of his chair. He was a tall thin man with a greyish but impressively strong face. Unfortunately, behind Basil Freel's beaked nose and eagle eye, there lurked only a bird's brain and he was inclined to fuss and cluck like an old hen.

He knew nothing, he protested with feeble fretfulness, about Juliet Rugg or her disappearance. He admitted that Colonel Bing and Miss McLintock had spent last Tuesday evening playing bridge with him and his sister.

'They came *after* supper,' he pointed out anxiously. 'They come to us on Tuesdays and we go to them on Fridays, but always *after* supper. It comes so expensive if you have to provide a meal every time and, frankly, you don't get enough to keep a sparrow going at their place, so it isn't worth it.'

'What time did Colonel Bing and Miss McLintock leave?'

'Rather early, I remember. About a quarter to eleven. They were winning. They always leave early when they're winning, just so that their luck doesn't change. Not quite the behaviour you'd expect from gentlemen, but there you are, aren't you?'

'Where were you playing, sir?'

'In here,' said Mr Freel with a sigh. '*She* said it was my turn but I don't think it was. I'm going to keep a notebook in future. Whoever's host has to give 'em a hot drink, you know. I always make Ovaltine. They don't like Ovaltine much so they generally leave quite a lot. I warm it up for myself the next day. Sometimes they leave nearly a whole cupful. The only trouble is,' he sighed again, 'I don't like Ovaltine much either.'

'What did you do when they left, sir?' said Dover, who was beginning to feel he'd caught a ripe one here.

'Oh, I went to bed straight away. The electric light had been on all evening, and the fire. I leave the clearing up till morning, when it's daylight.'

'And is your bedroom at the front of the house, sir?'

Mr Freel looked longingly at the pile of papers on his desk and sighed yet again. 'Yes,' he said reluctantly, 'I sleep in the front room downstairs. My sister has the top floor for her quarters and I live down here.'

Dover's next question was postponed by a loud, persistent miaowing outside the door.

'Oh, dear,' complained Mr Freel distractedly, and got up to let a large, bad-tempered-looking and very pregnant cat into the room. She stalked around with a deliberate, sneering gait while Mr Freel hovered anxiously over her.

'For God's sake, don't frighten her!' he hissed at Dover. 'If she has the kittens down here I shall have to dispose of them, and it's not fair. It'll be the third time. *She* shoos her downstairs, you know,' he added spitefully.

Mr Freel's anxiety was catching. Dover and Sergeant Mac-Gregor watched the mother-to-be with bated breath as she made a leisurely tour of inspection. There was an audible sigh of relief as she finally waddled insolently out of the door by which she had entered. Freel collapsed into his chair and wiped a grubby-looking handkerchief over his face.

Dover resumed his questioning, but Mr Freel had neither seen nor heard anything on Tuesday night which had struck him in the slightest as suspicious or unusual. He always slept with the windows closed and the curtains drawn, and a dozen Juliet Ruggs could have walked up and down the drive without his being aware of it. Yes, he knew who Juliet Rugg was but he couldn't ever recall having even spoken to her. He lived a very retired life nowadays and his few social contacts did not include the missing girl.

'I understand,' said Dover, 'that you are a retired clergyman?'

'Yes,' said Mr Freel with his habitual sigh, 'you can put it that way if you like. I lost my faith, you know. It was very awkward. Of course, one had always had minor doubts and reservations here and there, but to lose all one's faith all at once was a bit of a blow. In the prime of life, too, I was. Had a brilliant career ahead of me in the Church. Everybody said so. I might,' he offered abjectly, 'I might have been a bishop by now, or even had my own programme on television. But, there it is. You can't go on if you've lost your faith, can you?'

'No,' said Dover, 'I suppose not. And what do you do now?'

Mr Freel waved a long bony hand vaguely in the direction of his desk. 'Mark correspondence course papers, mostly,' he said. 'Not very satisfying work, really. Most of 'em never last beyond the first lesson. I mark exam papers, too, sometimes. It's all very depressing. Doesn't pay all that well either. I have to live very modestly these days. Still, I don't suppose you can expect to become a millionaire when you've lost your faith, can you?'

Dover and Mr Freel achieved a joint sigh in unison and there was a short pause while both men silently contemplated the unhappiness of their lot and the general unfairness of life itself. Sergeant MacGregor stared abstractedly at the almost blank pages of his notebook and tried to control the peevish rumbling of his empty stomach.

'Well, thank you very much, Mr Freel. We won't keep you any longer. Perhaps, however, we could have a word with your sister before we leave?'

'Glad to have been some help to you,' said Mr Freel, rising to his feet. 'Perhaps you'll follow me.' He led them out into the hall again, indicating that they should keep to his side of the white line down the carpet. Somewhat to their surprise he opened the front door and ushered them out.

'That's her bell,' he said, pointing to the one marked A. 'She'll come if you ring that. I haven't,' he added, 'spoken to her for fifteen years and I don't intend to start now. Good afternoon.' And with that he closed the front door in their faces.

'Oh, ring the bloody bell, Sergeant,' growled Dover, 'and let's get on with it. I've never met so many nuts on one case in my entire life. Wouldn't surprise me if his blasted sister came down on a broomstick!'

When Amy Freel, however, eventually opened the door she looked surprisingly normal. She was a plumpish, untidy-looking woman wearing a shapeless flowered dress and gold-rimmed spectacles. Dover guessed her to be in her middle fifties and possibly a year or two younger than her brother.

She was obviously delighted to see the two detectives and gushingly conducted them upstairs, smilingly requesting them in the hall to keep to her side of the white line. They were shown

91

into her sitting-room in which every visible item of furniture seemed to have been covered with chintz. What looked like a very substantial afternoon tea lay waiting for them on a low table by the fire.

'I saw you coming,' she explained, 'so I'd time to get it ready for you. I knew you wouldn't get anything from *him*. And you haven't had any lunch either, have you, you poor things! What did you go back to see Mr Bogolepov for? Was it something the Chubb-Smiths told you?'

Amy Freel's sandwiches were excellent, and very welcome, but Dover had no intention of paying for them by satisfying his hostess's startlingly well-based curiosity. He plunged once more into the old routine, alternating mouthfuls of food with his tatty stock questions. He got, once again, tatty stock answers. Although Amy Freel clearly spent most of her days peeping out at her neighbours' doings from behind her sitting-room curtains, she was, regrettably, not indulging in her hobby late on Tuesday night. She was as sorry about this as Dover was.

'If only I'd known,' she wailed, 'that something like this was going to happen! I'd have sat up all night for you. It's really most frustrating to have Bingo getting all the excitement. And detective stories are *my* hobby, you know, not hers! She's more interested in dogs and war memoirs, but I'm the recognized crime expert. Of course Georgie reads a lot of thrillers, but I don't think those count, really, do you? Besides, she never remembers what she's read and what she hasn't. She doesn't read *constructively*, like I do.'

'Did you know Juliet Rugg well?' asked Dover.

'No.' Miss Freel shook her head in regret and passed a plate of cakes around. 'I doubt if I've said more than "good morning" to the girl more than twice in my life. Of course I know all about her reputation, that's common knowledge. She was very friendly with Michael Chubb-Smith at one stage, you know. His mother was very worried about it. Juliet used to call at her house quite often before the baby was born.' She cocked an inquiring eye at the chief inspector, who, munching away placidly, didn't rise to the bait. 'And, of course, I shudder to think what's been going on at the Counters' place. I know Sir John's as old as the hills but I always say, you know what men are like. I mean, why on earth should he employ a girl with an illegitimate black baby if it wasn't for something like *that*? I feel so sorry for Eve. Sir John may be a baronet and he may have lots of money, but in my opinion he's a disgusting old man, and I don't care who knows it. Some of the things he's said in my presence – well, I just wouldn't dare to repeat them.'

'Good,' said Dover without thinking, and passed his cup over for a refill.

'Mind you,' Miss Freel went happily on, 'if I'd known Juliet was going to disappear like this I'd have taken much more interest in her. I'd have invited her to tea and had a nice long chat with her. I might have been able to help you then,' she said with a kindly smile. 'However, it's no good crying over spilt milk, is it?' She leaned forward eagerly in her chair. 'Now, tell me, what do you really think has happened to her? As I see it, it must be either murder or kidnapping. We can rule suicide out, I'm quite sure of that. She wasn't the type. And if she'd just run off with some man or other, I'm sure somebody would have reported her whereabouts by now. No, what puzzles me is – where's the body? She was such a big girl, you know. If something happened to her after Bingo saw her on Tuesday night and before she got back to the Counters – where's the body? You couldn't just pick her up in your arms and walk out with her and you couldn't drive her out in a car because the gates were locked.'

'Somebody might have taken her out next morning when the gates were open,' said Dover.

Miss Freel shook her head triumphantly. 'Nobody did,' she said firmly. 'I checked! Not one of the cars in Irlam Old Hall left here on the Wednesday. And no tradesmen's vans or anything like that called either, because I checked that too.'

'Oh,' said Dover.

'Bit of a facer, isn't it?' asked Miss Freel cheerfully. 'But I've got one or two theories of my own which might interest you. They'll probably strike you as a bit far-fetched at first, but they do give us a lead. Now, if we could all work together on this, I'm sure we'll be able to get it solved in no time. I could be a sort of unofficial collaborator, you know, like the amateur detectives in the books, and you could ... '

'No!' Dover had finished his tea and saw no point in wasting any more of his time. Amateur middle-aged lady detectives! My God, the things he had to suffer! 'I'm very sorry, madam,' he said shortly, 'but things don't work like that in real life, you know. This is a job for the professionals,' he smiled smugly. 'We shall get to the bottom of it, never fear!'

'But, Inspector, this book I was reading ... '

Dover raised a lordly hand with a gesture which he had used many times as a young constable on traffic duty. He could stop a London bus with it in those days and he stopped Miss Freel now.

'No!' he said again. 'We really haven't time to discuss wild theories at this stage, madam. Sergeant MacGregor and I have got a lot of work to do. Perhaps later on...' he concluded vaguely.

Miss Freel's crestfallen face brightened a little. 'Well, I'll go on working on it independently,' she suggested, 'and if I get anything concrete I'll let you know, eh? But I really think this book I was reading ... '

'Yes, that'll be fine, madam,' said Dover, heading rapidly for the door. 'Come on, Sergeant!'

Miss Freel followed them downstairs.

'I don't suppose you got much help from *him*?' she said in a loud whisper, jerking her head at her brother's portion of the house. 'He wouldn't notice a body if he fell over it. He cheats at bridge, too, you know, if you don't watch him.'

'Really?' said Dover.

'I suppose,' Miss Freel whispered on, putting a restraining hand on Dover's arm, 'I suppose you know he was once a clergyman?'

'Yes,' said Dover, 'he told us. Said he'd lost his faith or something.'

'You didn't believe that cock-and-bull story, did you?'

'Why?' asked Dover with slightly more interest. 'Isn't it true?'

Miss Freel sniffed scornfully. 'Loss of faith, my eye! Choirboys! That's what his trouble was! Disgusting beast! Lucky not to finish up in prison. If Juliet Rugg had been a choirboy, now, you wouldn't have had far to look for the guilty party, I can tell you.' Miss Freel shook her head regretfully at this lost opportunity and reluctantly let her visitors out of the house.

Outside Dover took a long, deep breath. He was beginning to wonder how much more of this he could stand before qualifying for a strait-jacket himself. But, with Miss Freel's fortifying tea resting peacefully inside him, he felt strong enough to tackle one more interview before calling it a day. Just one more, he promised

94

himself, and then he was heading straight back to the hotel for a 'quiet think' before dinner.

He set off once more up the drive, every stone and weed of which he felt he now knew intimately. He'd have a word with the caretaker at the Hall and that was his lot for the day.

William Bondy was a refreshing change from some of the other people who lived at Irlam Old Hall. He was a well-made man, getting on for sixty but still bearing himself with the upright, alert carriage of the professional soldier. He'd spent nearly forty years in the army, progressing from boy's service to regimental sergeant-major of a crack infantry regiment, and naturally such an experience had left its mark on him. He was a man of comparatively few words and he answered Dover's questions clearly and intelligently.

He dismissed Juliet Rugg flatly as 'white trash'.

'She should never have been allowed to set foot inside the gates,' he stated. 'I told Mrs Chubb-Smith so on several occasions but, of course, I've given up expecting anything from her. She tried giving me the glad eye once or twice – Miss Rugg, I mean, not Mrs Chubb-Smith – but I told her I'd seen better specimens crawling out of the cracks in a Cairo whorehouse, and she seemed to take offence at the remark. Anyhow, she gave me a wide berth after that.

'Tuesday night, sir? I was in here watching telly till about eleven and then I went to bed.'

'What about closing the gates?'

'I went out and closed them at about half-past nine – same as I always do this time of year. Then I came back here, locked the front door of the Hall and switched all the lights out, except the emergency ones on the stairs.'

'So that any of the flat tenants who came in after that would have to knock you up?'

'That's right, sir, except they were all in anyhow. Most of 'em are pretty old and rickety and I don't encourage 'em to go gadding about late at night.'

'What about one of them leaving the Hall, say at eleven o'clock – would you have seen them?'

Sergeant-Major Bondy permitted himself a rich chuckle.

'If you're thinking that one of my tenants had a rendezvous with Juliet Rugg at any time, never mind in the middle of the night, you can put it straight out of your head right away, sir. In the first place, there's not one of 'em that isn't well past it, if you see what I mean, and in the second place, not only were all the doors locked and bolted, but I keep the keys.' He nodded at a large bunch hanging on a nail. 'If any of 'em had wanted to get out after say twenty-one forty-five hours on Tuesday evening, they'd have had to find me to let 'em out, and I should have wanted to know where the hell they thought they was going.'

'I see,' said Dover thoughtfully. 'What about climbing out of a window?'

'Not a hope, sir! All the ground-floor windows have got bars on 'em and I check 'em every week when I'm doing my inspection. Nobody could get out that way. I don't think you need bother about my little squad in here, sir. I'm prepared to bet that not one of 'em as much as opened their flat door after I'd locked up on Tuesday night. They used to trip around for hours, visiting each other, when I first came here, but I soon put a stop to that. I didn't issue an order or anything – you can't do that with civilians, can you? – but all the floors are laid with lino, 'cept the hall and that's parquet. I soon got the cleaners to put a good shine on it – come up a real treat it has. Well, naturally, the old dears don't like it. Scared of slipping and breaking their poor old necks. They're hardly likely to go wandering around after I've put all the main lights out, are they? It'd be suicide! Beside, I keep my own door ajar so I can hear if any of 'em are creeping about. I always go up and ask 'em what they're doing if I catch one of 'em. They don't try it on often these days and nobody as much as moved a muscle on Tuesday night.'

'I see.' Dover contemplated Bondy with no little respect. 'Have you been here long, Mr Bondy?'

'Oh, getting on for five years now, sir. I came here straight after I left the army. It took me a bit to get things licked into shape, but everything's running very smoothly now. Lots of people told me I'd never settle to civilian life after all that time in the army, but I can't say I've had much difficulty. The job's much the same whether you do it in uniform or in civvies in my experience. A recruit training school or a houseful of retired gentry – it's all human nature, isn't it, sir? I use the same technique and I get the same results.'

'I'm sure you do,' murmured Dover.

''Course, I've had my little difficulties,' said Bondy, anxious to be fair. 'Mrs Chubb-Smith's a very nice woman, I'm sure, but no backbone, you know. You've got to keep prodding her to get anything done. D'you know it took me six months to get her to see sense about dogs and children?'

'Dogs and children?' repeated Dover.

'Yes, sir. She used to let the flats to anybody, anybody at all. Place was swarming with kids and animals.' Bondy pursed his lips in a self-satisfied smile. 'But we've put a stop to that now. I let 'em keep a tank of tropical fish if they want a pet. Dogs and cats is out! So's kids! I've got a very nice class of tenants here now, quiet and well behaved. But that's only because I put my foot down with Mrs Chubb-Smith. You can see what she does when she's left on her own.'

'You mean the people living in the houses?'

'I do indeed, sir. They're as fine a collection of layabouts as you'll find anywhere, most of 'em. There's that Bogolepov chap – bloody pansy if you ask me! My word, I'd like to have him as a recruit for a couple of months. Not that young Michael Chubb-Smith's all that much better, but he does shave regular, I'll say that for him. And then there's that writer woman, Miss Hoppold. Have you read any of her books? Enough to make your hair stand on end. I saw a few dicey things when I was seconded to the Commandos during the war, but it was nothing to some of the things she describes. Not nice, that sort of thing, in a woman.'

'What about Colonel Bing?' asked Dover maliciously.

'Barmy,' said Bondy shortly. 'Makes you wonder what the army's coming to, doesn't it? But I like her, mind, always calls me "Sergeant-Major" and speaks respectful like. And come to think of it, she's no barmier than plenty of men I've known with red tabs on their lapels.'

'And Sir John Counter?'

'Oh, he's an old devil, he is! But he's a gentleman and that makes a difference somehow, doesn't it? He'd have made a good officer, he would. Absolute swine but a professional, if you know what I mean. I do quite a lot of odd jobs for him and to hear him going on, it takes me back twenty years or more. I served under a major just like him. He was a real pig, he was. First time his mob saw action in the war, he got it! In the back and I'll stake my pension it wasn't a German bullet.'

Dover blinked slightly at this jovial reminiscence but pressed on. 'What about the Freels, do you know them?'

'Not really, sir. Hardly ever see him. You know they never speak to each other, I suppose? Write each other little notes, so I've heard. But they always partner each other at bridge. Gawd only knows how they manage then. Still, it takes all sorts, doesn't it, sir?'

And on this happy note of soldierly tolerance the interview came to an end.

Dover and Sergeant MacGregor got back into their car.

'That's a relief, sir, isn't it?' asked Sergeant MacGregor. 'Looks as though we needn't bother about all those people in the flats.'

'Hm,' said Dover, who had just been thanking his lucky stars for the same thing. 'Of course,' he pointed out grumpily, 'we don't know that Bondy was telling the truth.'

'But surely those old crocks can't have had anything to do with it?'

'I shouldn't think so,' said Dover grudgingly, 'but what about Bondy himself? We've only his word for it that he was in his room all night. As I see it, he was the one person inside the Hall who could have got out without being spotted.'

'Well, yes.' Sergeant MacGregor pondered this over doubtfully. 'But do you think a chap with his record ... ?'

'It's his record that set me wondering,' said Dover crossly. 'My God, doesn't anything ever penetrate that thick skull of yours? You were there, you heard what he said! He served in the Commandos! You know what they were trained to do, don't you? They were trained to kill, silently!'

Chapter Nine

WHEN Dover arrived back at The Two Fiddlers he found a message asking him to ring police headquarters in Creedon. He left Sergeant MacGregor to deal with it and headed resolutely upstairs to his room. He had just removed his boots, dropping them one by one in grateful relief on the floor, and was loosening the waistband of his trousers when MacGregor came bursting in to report.

'They've traced the owner of that car, sir!' he announced excitedly. 'You know, the one Colonel Bing saw Juliet get out of on Tuesday night.'

Dover wiggled his toes and removed his collar and tie, revealing a thin red mark round his beefy, policeman's neck. He grunted interrogatively. MacGregor took this as meaning he could continue.

'It belongs to a fellow called Pilley, sir, Gordon Pilley. He lives in a place called Coleton Garden City. It's about forty miles from here. The inspector says he's a commercial traveller and do you want to go over and see him or shall they cope with it?'

'Not bloody likely!' snorted Dover. 'Tell him to keep his paws off my case! You can drive me over there tomorrow morning.'

'O.K., sir,' said Sergeant MacGregor brightly, 'I'll ring him back.' He looked pointedly at the chief inspector who was now flat on his back on the bed and happily pulling the eiderdown up to his chin. 'Will you want me for a bit, sir?'

'No,' said Dover, settling his head more comfortably into the pillows. 'You can go off and get the reports written. And make 'em nice and long. That way nobody'll ever bother to read 'em. People always read short reports and then they start bothering you. Put down everything every blithering idiot we've seen so far has said.' Dover closed his eyes. 'You never know, it might prove useful, though I doubt it. Give me a knock when it's time for dinner.'

'Yes, sir,' said Sergeant MacGregor with evident disapproval.

Dover opened one eye. 'I'm just going to have a quiet little think,' he explained huffily. 'I want to clarify my ideas about the case.'

* * *

Whether or not the chief inspector succeeded in clarifying his ideas, the world will never know. Certainly he made no effort to share his enlightenment, if any, with Sergeant MacGregor on the following morning as they proceeded with the dispatch of a hearse along the roads to Coleton Garden City. Dover was his usual glum, early-morning self and he gazed sullenly out of the window, only occasionally glancing at the speedometer to check that the needle had not insidiously crept above thirty. He noted with sulky satisfaction that the little lambs in the fields on either side of the road were now sufficiently grown up to pass their sunny days bashing each other violently on the head. Somehow, it confirmed Dover's views on human nature.

Coleton Garden City consisted of acres upon acres of small semi-detached houses set in scruffy unkempt gardens. Everywhere had a raw, unfinished look about it. Reddish-brown soil showed clearly through the wispy green of nascent lawns, and small, leafless hedges marked lines of demarcation but as yet offered no privacy or protection. By dint of much asking of the way they eventually reached the address they had been given – a small semi-detached house in a scruffy unkempt garden.

Dover walked moodily up the path and gave the little brass gnome affixed to the door a good belting. He was rewarded by a sound of scuffling and whispering from inside and somebody peeped round the curtains of the front room to have a look at him.

Eventually the front door was opened by a youngish woman wearing a grubby pink housecoat and a pair of bedraggled mules on her bare feet. Under a crumpled silk head-scarf it was evident that her hair was still imprisoned in a ferocious-looking cluster of curlers.

'Good morning.' She spoke with a cautious gentility which was painful to hear. 'Ken ay help yew?'

'We'd like to speak to Mr Gordon Pilley, madam,' said Dover, wrinkling his nose in a disconcerting manner. 'Is he in?'

'Well,' said the woman doubtfully, 'ay reelly don't know. Ay'll just see.' She turned back into the house, pulling the door to behind her.

Dover stuck a timely, heavy-shod boot forward. 'Just get him,' he said briefly, 'we're from the police!' Followed by Sergeant MacGregor, he pushed his way into the hall.

Mr Gordon Pilley hadn't quite time to duck out of sight. The presence of a small child clinging to his left leg no doubt impeded him.

'Mr Pilley?' demanded Dover in one of his voices of doom. 'We'd like a few words with you, sir. We're from Scotland Yard.'

There was a moment's confusion while Mr Pilley picked up the child, which immediately started bawling, handed it to his wife and then squeezed past her in the narrow hall-way. With many 'excuse mes' and 'pardons' and much to-ing and fro-ing the two policemen eventually found themselves ushered into what Mr Pilley referred to as the 'lounge'. Whatever else may have taken place in this room, the door of which was kept locked against possible depredations by young Pilley, lounging almost certainly didn't. This was a room in which you sat, careful not to crease either your best trousers or your hostess's loose covers, and sipped tea out of the best teacups while everybody tried to outdo everybody else in good manners and delicate breeding.

Dover flopped exhausted into an armchair and let his head drop back on a garishly embroidered antimacassar. His feet, in their dirty great boots, were planted firmly on Mrs Pilley's pink flowered hearth-rug. Mr Pilley averted his eyes and sat nervously on one corner of the settee, wondering fretfully whether or not he ought to switch on the electric fire with the imitation logs which gave the room, according to his wife, such a cheery look. Sergeant MacGregor, without so much as a by-your-leave, had removed the hideous black statuette of a nude woman from a small occasional table and calmly planked his notebook on the polished surface. Mrs Pilley, thought Mr Pilley, would throw a fit if she knew. Mrs Pilley, thought Mr Pilley feeling slightly sick, would throw fifty fits if she ever got a whiff of what these policemen had come about.

With a desperation shown only by the timid, Mr Pilley took the plunge.

'I suppose you've come about Juliet?' he began, grinning stupidly through sheer nervousness.

'Oh, what makes you think that?' demanded Dover aggressively, employing the policeman's favourite trick of answering one question with another.

Mr Pilley licked his lips and fingered his unshaven chin. He wasn't looking his best, no collar and an old pair of carpet slippers on his feet.

'Well, I read about her being missing in the papers ... ' he ventured gingerly.

Dover pounced, metaphorically speaking. 'Oh, so you admit that you knew Juliet Rugg?'

Mr Pilley gulped and glanced anxiously at Sergeant Mac-Gregor. Sergeant MacGregor stared impassively back, waiting to write down his reply. Mr Pilley, not knowing what else to do, decided to tell the truth.

'Well, yes, I knew her all right, have done for about six months. We were friends, like.'

'Friends?' repeated Dover with a sneer which nearly twisted the moustache off his face.

'Well, you know ... ' Mr Pilley wriggled uncomfortably.

'Oh yes,' said Dover, laughing shortly, 'I know all right! Now, my lad, I want the whole story of your association with this girl – right from the beginning! And don't try any fancy business. I want the truth and if I don't get it things may be very unpleasant for you!'

Mr Pilley leaned forward and spoke in a hoarse whisper. 'Listen, I'll tell you the truth, honest. I've nothing to do with Jule's disappearance, nothing at all, but it's my wife, you see. She's a bit – well, you know what women are like, and my old woman's the same only more so. If we could keep our little talk confidential, like ... ?'

Dover pondered dramatically, just to keep Mr Pilley on edge. 'Well,' he said at last, 'we shan't go out of our way to give Mrs Pilley any information about what you tell us, but, of course, when the case comes to trial all relevant evidence will naturally have to be disclosed. Still' – he leered encouragingly – 'if your neck's in danger of being stretched, I don't suppose you'll worry over much about your wife finding out one or two things you'd rather she didn't, will you?'

'No,' agreed Mr Pilley unhappily, 'but I told you, I didn't ... '

'Just answer my questions!' Dover broke impatiently through

the protestations of innocence. 'And speak slowly so the sergeant here can get it all down.'

'Yes, sir,' said Mr Pilley miserably.

'How long have you known Juliet Rugg?'

'About six months. We met quite casual like when I was in Creedon. I'm a commercial traveller, you see, and I travel in ladies' underwear.' Mr Pilley laughed ingratiatingly. 'Er – that's a little joke I always make, see?'

'Very funny,' said Dover without a flicker. 'Go on!'

'Well, Jule was having quite a job getting undies – bras and panties and things – to fit her, with her being so big, like, and naturally when she heard about my job she asked me if I could help her, me being in the trade, like. Well, naturally I was only too pleased to help out if I could and after that she used to tell me what she wanted and the size and everything and I used to get the things for her. And it wasn't all that easy, I can tell you, not even with my contacts. Why, one of my suppliers thought I was pulling his leg at first, straight he did! He says to me ... '

'You met Miss Rugg fairly frequently?'

'Er – yes, about once a fortnight. Whenever I was in Creedon.'

'And did she pay you for the goods you supplied her with?'

Poor Mr Pilley licked his lips again and passed a hand over his thinning hair. 'Well, not in money, if you see what I mean.'

Dover stared gloomily at him and sighed. 'Yes,' he said, 'I see what you mean. You were on terms of fairly close intimacy with Miss Rugg?'

'Er – yes,' agreed Mr Pilley doubtfully.

'And where did your meetings take place?'

Mr Pilley grinned sheepishly. 'Well, in the back of my car, as a matter of fact. You see, the lady I stay with in Creedon's a friend of the wife's, so ... Anyhow, Jule didn't seem to mind.'

'All right. Let's turn to last Tuesday, the day she disappeared. You were with her then?'

'Yes, we met as usual, like. It was her day off from this place she worked and when I'd finished my business I met her about five o'clock in the café at the Regal cinema. We had some tea and then we went to the pictures. We came out about nine o'clock, I suppose, and went and had a quick one in The Fading Rose.'

'What did Miss Rugg drink?'

'Jule? Oh, cherry brandy, same as always. She only had one. I had half a pint of bitter.'

'Then what did you do?'

'Well, then I took her home, like.' Even Mr Pilley didn't expect this innocent statement to go unchallenged.

'It doesn't,' observed Dover in a bored voice, 'take an hour and a half to get from Creedon to Irlam Old Hall by car.'

'No, well,' said Mr Pilley with another foolish grin, 'we sat and talked for a bit and, er ... '

'You had sexual intercourse with Miss Rugg on the back seat of your car.' It was a statement, not a question.

'Well, yes, if you want to put it like that.' Mr Pilley appeared shocked at such frankness.

'When you got to Irlam Old Hall, what did you do?'

'I parked the car outside them iron gates, like, and we said good night. Then Jule got out and went through that little gate what's in the middle of the big ones, and I drove back to my digs in Creedon. I was in bed by half past eleven, straight I was! You can ask Mrs Clayton.'

'Why?' asked Dover, never one to miss a chance of cheap sarcasm. 'Was she there with you?'

'Here, there's no need to be coarse!' objected Mr Pilley. 'I only meant ... '

'Oh, never mind,' snapped Dover crossly. He couldn't stand people who couldn't take his jokes. 'Now, when you were with Miss Rugg, did she last Tuesday evening, or any other time for that matter, say or do anything to indicate that she intended to run away from home or commit suicide, or anything?'

Mr Pilley thought for a moment. 'No, I can't say she did. She behaved just like normal. She asked me to get her a couple of petticoats – tangerine colour, she wanted them, it's this year's colour, you know – and I said I'd try and have them for Tuesday week – that's when I was going to be in Creedon again.'

'Did you have any quarrel or argument with her?'

'No.' Gordon Pilley shook his head. 'Well, I was a bit short with her when I found her painting her finger-nails all over the tea table. I mean, the Regal's a very respectable place with proper table-cloths and waitresses and everything. It's not one of these crummy help-yourself joints, you know. I know Jule's rather common, like, but I thought that was going a bit too far. She was painting 'em green, too.' Mr Pilley shuddered fastidiously. 'Fairly put me off my tea, it did. Looked blooming awful, I thought, like a vampire, but it seems she'd just bought the stuff and couldn't wait to try it. She must have spent a fortune on cosmetics, that girl. Still, it wasn't a row or anything serious like.'

'Just a lovers' tiff, no doubt,' said Dover, indulging in a bit of elephantine irony.

The questioning went on. Dover took Mr Pilley through his story again and succeeded in getting nothing more of interest. Mr Pilley, not surprisingly perhaps in view of everything, was able to supply the chief inspector with a highly detailed account of every single item of clothing which Juliet was wearing that night. For the underwear he gave, with a superb air of professional detachment, not only the colour but the make, style, size and cost as well. Sergeant MacGregor dutifully wrote down all the details.

At long last Dover gave a disgruntled sigh and looked as though he was about to take his leave. Mr Pilley was sweating slightly and now, seeing an end to his ordeal, relaxed understandably with relief. Dover noted this and fired, as he always did, a parting shot aimed at the solar plexus, or even lower.

'How much did Juliet Rugg blackmail you for?' he demanded abruptly with a terrible, menacing scowl.

'Eh?' yelped Mr Pilley.

'You heard me!' snarled Dover. 'How much were you paying her to keep her mouth shut?'

'I wasn't paying her nothing!' howled Mr Pilley. 'Here, what are you getting at? There was no question of payment between Jule and me. I give her a few presents now and again but that's all. What the hell do you think I am?' He bridled at the implied slur on his manhood. 'I don't have to pay for it, you know!'

'I'm suggesting,' repeated Dover doggedly, 'that Juliet Rugg was blackmailing you. I want to know how much she got out of you in return for not spilling the beans to your wife!'

'Oh no,' wailed Mr Pilley, 'you've got it all wrong, straight you have. Jule never even mentioned my wife. I'm not saying she wasn't a bit on the greedy side and she certainly stung me a packet on all these suspender belts and things – course I got 'em at cost, but even so. But Jule wasn't a fool – give credit where it's due, I say. She knew I'd no money to spare! What do you think I am, a bleeding millionaire? What with the kid and the payments on the furniture and Marge wanting a holiday at Butlin's this year! God help me, I can hardly keep me head above water as it is! And I've got to spend a lot on my clothes, you know, you've got to dress snappy in my line of business.'

Dover blew crossly down his nose and scowled at Gordon Pilley, who was now quite pink with indignation.

'So you deny that Juliet Rugg was blackmailing you?'

'I do indeed. Definitely!' said Mr Pilley with dignity.

'Make a note of that, Sergeant, just in case!' This was Dover being nasty. His shock tactics hadn't worked quite so successfully as he'd hoped, but that was no reason for letting Gordon Pilley think he'd got away with it.

There was a long pause while Sergeant MacGregor wrote up his notes, during which Dover stared unblinkingly and ferociously at Mr Pilley. Mr Pilley fidgeted uneasily. He was feeling terribly guilty and knew that he looked it. If only he'd known that they were coming he could have smartened himself up a bit, but getting caught like this, unshaven and in his shirt-sleeves, well, it gave rather a bad impression.

At long last he had his statement read over to him and listened anxiously to Dover's warning that if it wasn't the truth he'd better say so now, otherwise it would be the worse for him. With a trembling hand he signed his name, failing miserably to produce his usual flourish.

Then the two detectives, as unsmiling and menacing as when they arrived, took their leave.

The drive back was not enlivened by the fact that Dover was sulking. When he put himself to the trouble of bullying a possible suspect, he liked some concrete results for his efforts – a nice 'voluntary' confession, for example. He was extremely peeved that Gordon Pilley had, so to speak, let him down. Dover had heard, of course, of the Judges' Rules, had probably even read them at some stage in his career, but his detailed knowledge of their contents had become a little blurred with the passage of time. He found that, on the whole, he managed quite well without them. There was trouble sometimes. Prisoners in the dock often started whining to the judge about tricks and promises and threats, and sometimes the judge believed them. This invariably enraged Dover but, philosophically, he took it as one of the occupational hazards of his chosen profession, like getting flat feet.

'Bit of a dirty dog, our Gordon Pilley,' said Sergeant Mac-Gregor with a smirk. 'Wife looked a bit of a shrew. I reckon she'll half kill him if this comes out.'

'In that case she's probably swinging the hatchet now,' observed Dover glumly, his eyes resting on the speedometer.

'Why? You don't think he's up and confessed all, do you, sir?' asked MacGregor in astonishment. 'I thought he looked fly enough to cook up some cock-and-bull story to explain us away.'

'Won't do him any good,' said the chief inspector with bleak relish. 'She was listening at the door.'

* * *

The rest of Sunday passed uneventfully. Dover 'thought' all afternoon, flat on his back and snoring gently. Sergeant Mac-Gregor was packed off on a lot of not very important missions, checking this and counterchecking that. Dover didn't really mind very much how the sergeant occupied his time as long as he got out from under his, Dover's, feet.

As far as Dover was concerned the whole case had ground to an unimpressive halt, if you could use such a phrase about an undertaking which had never got moving in the first place. It was obvious that Juliet Rugg was not a particularly nice girl. There were a number of rather woolly motives which, in the continuing absence of the body, didn't amount to all that much. Sir John Counter might have murdered her because she was two-timing him with one of his social equals, though there was no evidence that she was. Eve Counter might have murdered her to stop her marrying her father. Michael Chubb-Smith and/or his mother might have done the girl in to put a stop to her blackmailing game. Maxine Chubb-Smith might have finished her off in a fit of wild jealousy. Gordon Pilley might have ... Oh, what the hell, thought Dover crossly, if pigs could fly, anybody in the entire country could have done the dratted girl in! All he'd got so far was a lot of airy-fairy speculation. He hadn't enough factual evidence to cover a sixpence. He'd no proof that Juliet was even dead, although, he told himself pompously, and not risking all that much, he'd stake his professional reputation that she was.

As the chief inspector slipped gently towards sleep he brooded uneasily on the case as a whole. He didn't like these amateur jobs, he thought fretfully. Give him a good professional crime every time. All you had to do then was sit back and wait for some disgruntled villain or other to start singing. Then, when you knew which one of them it was, you just dolled up the evidence a bit and made it point in the right direction. Easy as falling off a tree. 'Strewth, he'd give his right arm for an informer on this case. It wasn't fair to expect him to go round searching for clues and making deductions and God knows what! He sighed deeply. Perhaps the body'd turn up tomorrow. Then they'd have something to go on ... That's what he wanted. A nice solid body ... dripping ... with ... clues ...

*   *   *

Monday morning came, as it always does if you wait long enough, but it didn't bring the body of Juliet Rugg. Dover couldn't understand it. He took her continuing disappearance as a personal insult, and Sergeant MacGregor had a very uncomfortable breakfast in consequence. However, Dover's thwarted fury at least drove him to a bit more action and in sheer desperation he decided to interview all the tenants in the flats at Irlam Old Hall.

'You've got to look as though you're doing *something*,' he explained to MacGregor, 'and you never know, one of the old fools might have seen or heard something.'

'Do you want me to come with you, sir?' asked MacGregor, with his fingers crossed for luck.

Dover glanced balefully at him. 'No,' he decided, 'you'd better go into Creedon and trace that girl's movements on Tuesday afternoon. She may have met somebody somewhere. And you'd better check Pilley's account of what they did, just in case the little rat's trying to pull a fast one. Oh, and go and see his landlady, too. If he's lying about the time he got back, he's the man we're after!'

'But Colonel Bing saw the car drive away, sir,' MacGregor pointed out.

'I know what Colonel Bloody Bing saw!' thundered Dover. 'But he could have driven back again, couldn't he? And how do we know Colonel Bing isn't lying? Have you thought about that, eh?'

Sergeant MacGregor turned the other cheek. 'No, sir,' he admitted, and shrugged his shoulders slightly.

'The whole flaming lot of 'em might be lying like troopers for all we know!' Dover ranted on. 'They're all sitting up there on their backsides not doing a day's work between the lot of 'em. They've all the time in the world to think up any kind of crooked tale. I wouldn't trust any of 'em as far as I could throw 'em! 'Strewth,' he snorted in disgust, 'give me an honest crook any day of the week.'

'Yes, sir.'

'And you, while you're in Creedon go and check with the local boys to see that they really have covered all the railway stations and hospitals and things. You know what I mean. And if they haven't done it properly, make 'em do it again! They're quite capable of overlooking a sixteen-stone body, I'll be bound.'

It was only when MacGregor had already gone beyond recall that Dover realized that he had left himself without transport. Luckily the village possessed a one-man taxi service and thanks to the landlord's good offices (they were brother Elks) the one-man agreed to place himself and his taxi at the chief inspector's disposal for the rest of the day. Dover spent several long and fruitless hours with the elderly, childless and petless tenants in the Irlam Old Hall flats. He emerged a convinced supporter of compulsory euthanasia for the over-seventies, but this was his sole achievement.

It was a fine sunny day and he walked slowly down the drive towards the main gates, wondering what the dickens he was going to do next. He was so wrapped up in his thoughts that he all but fell over Sir John Counter, who was being wheeled out in his bath chair for an airing by his daughter. Her expression was almost as sulky and discontented as Dover's own.

'Well, Mr Policeman,' Sir John greeted him, with a mocking grin, 'have you found the girl yet?'

Dover treated the senile old fool to a blistering look.

'Not yet, sir,' he said with a peculiar intonation which implied, he hoped, that in fact they had but, for reasons best known to themselves, were not yet prepared to divulge this bit of news to the general public.

'Making heavy weather of it, aren't you?' demanded Sir John. 'Been looking for the best part of a week, haven't you?'

'Three and a half days, sir,' Dover corrected him through clenched teeth.

'Humph,' came the reply, 'shouldn't have though it would have taken you three and a half minutes!' He gave a high-pitched snigger. 'Why, even these chaps on the telly don't take longer than half an hour. And' – he shook a bony finger at Dover – 'and their cases are much more complicated. Shouldn't have thought it would have been much of a job to find a wench as fat as Juliet.'

Dover was saved the trouble of a rejoinder by the approach of Colonel Bing and Miss McLintock apparently engaged in exercising the poodle, Peregrine.

'Look out!' exclaimed Sir John in a deliberately penetrating whisper. 'Here come the local Lesbians!'

'Father, really! They'll hear you!' Eve Counter frowned reproachfully at the old man.

'Humph. Do 'em good!' snorted Sir John. 'And, Bingo,' he bellowed to the colonel, 'if that damned dog of your pees on my offside wheel again, so help me, I'll fetch a gun out next time and let him have both barrels in the guts! I'm warning you, now!'

Colonel Bing laughed heartily. It never entered her head that Sir John might not just be having his little joke.

'Good morning, Sir John,' she shouted cheerfully. 'How are you keeping?'

Sir John stared at her. 'What's she say?' he asked his daughter.

'She says, "How are you keeping", father.'

'Well, tell the nosy old devil it's no business of hers who I'm keeping. My private life's my own affair!'

Colonel Bing beamed admiringly and turned to Dover. 'He's a witty old bounder, isn't he?' she boomed. 'Doesn't matter what you say to him, he's always got a snappy answer. Gets me, how he thinks of them. And how's your case going, Inspector, found that girl yet?'

'Not yet!' snapped Dover, keeping a wary eye on Peregrine, who was sniffing around him in an ominous manner.

'Oh,' said Colonel Bing, evidently disappointed, 'it's taking a long time, isn't it?'

'I'm reading a book,' said Miss McLintock, 'about a man who disappeared. He was in M.I.5 and they haven't found out yet what happened to him. Of course,' she added with a kindly smile,

'I've only got up to page twenty-five, so it's a bit early yet, isn't it?'

Dover just looked at her.

Colonel Bing roared into action again. 'Well, Sir John,' she screamed down his ear, 'glad to see you out enjoying the sunshine. Do you a world of good! Eve, why don't you bring him over to tea with us one day? And, by the way,' she added bossily as Eve muttered some polite rejoinder and began to push the bath chair down the drive, 'I'm glad to see you've oiled those damned wheels at last. Can't bear things squeaking when all they want is a drop of oil!'

'The wheels?' Eve Counter looked blank.

'Yes, on the bath chair. I told you about them a fortnight ago at least. They must have been able to hear you coming in Creedon. I've never heard such a row.'

Eve looked down vaguely at the wheels. 'Oh yes,' she said, 'they squeaked, didn't they?'

'They don't now,' said Colonel Bing, bending down to have a look. 'You've oiled 'em, good girl!'

Eve shrugged her shoulders. 'I didn't,' she muttered.

'Well, somebody has,' insisted Colonel Bing. 'Look, there's oil dripping all over the place.'

'Oh, perhaps Bondy did. I suppose he noticed it, too.'

The two groups split up and Dover found himself walking down the drive with Sir John and his daughter. The wheel chair was heavy and awkward to push on the rough surface. Dover let Eve Counter struggle on alone. It never occurred to him to do anything else.

Half-way down the drive they met Mrs Chubb-Smith who was just popping in to see her son and daughter-in-law. Maxine was expertly backing a sleek white Jaguar out of the garage.

'I've got a luncheon engagement, Kitty darling!' she shouted. 'Can you feed the brute? He's inside sulking because he wasn't invited, too.'

She didn't bother to wait for a reply, but shot off down the drive with an impressive scattering of stones and dust. Mrs Chubb-Smith smiled distantly at Sir John and Eve, and treated Dover to a frigid nod before hurrying off to question her son about this latest little rift in the matrimonial lute.

'I'll give 'em six months,' said Sir John to nobody in particular, 'six months at the outside. And then that nubile young madam'll be off with some fellow who's got more of what she wants than that anaemic young husband of hers has – and she'll take her father's money with her, too.' He sighed. 'Wish I were ten years younger! I'd give her a run for her money, by God I would!'

'Hm,' said Dover, and turned round as he heard his name being called.

'Chief Inspector! Chief Inspector!'

It was Amy Freel, waving frantically at him from her upstairs sitting-room. 'I've got those books I was talking to you about, and I've written out a few notes on my theory which I'm sure will be very useful to you. Can you come up a minute?'

'Go on, man!' urged Sir John. 'An invitation's an invitation, wherever it comes from! You can't afford to pick and choose at your age.'

Dover gave him a filthy look. 'I'm not that desperate!' he announced grimly. Raising his voice, he yelled back to Miss Freel, 'I'm sorry, madam, I can't spare the time now. Later perhaps.'

'Oh dear,' wailed Miss Freel, 'well, just wait there and I'll bring them down to you. We can have our little discussion when you've looked through them. Just wait there! I won't be a minute!'

Dover didn't stand on ceremony. Ramming his bowler hat firmly down over his eyes, he made an elephantine charge for the main gates. Sir John screamed encouragement at his retreating back.

The chief inspector pounded manfully down the drive. He reached the gates, his face scarlet with exertion.

'Start up the motor!' he bellowed.

The taxi was waiting for him on the main road. The one-man who found even Dover a pleasant change from the funeral mourners he habitually drove, gunned his massive 1928 Rolls-Royce engine into life. Dover grabbed the door handle and flung himself on to the capacious rear seat.

'The Two Fiddlers,' he gasped, adding, for once in his life, 'and step on it!'

Chapter Ten

'ALL right,' said Dover, dragging in a great lungful of smoke from one of Sergeant MacGregor's cigarettes, 'let's hear what you've been doing with yourself, my lad!'

They were sitting in Dover's bedroom at The Two Fiddlers. The chief inspector, collarless, jacketless and shoeless, was sunk deep in the armchair with his feet propped up on the bed. Sergeant MacGregor, looking as always a credit to the *Tailor and Cutter*, sat near the window on a hard upright chair, his notebook on his knees. Each man had a pint of Long Herbert within easy reach.

Dover closed his eyes the better to concentrate.

If the old bastard starts snoring, Sergeant MacGregor promised himself grimly, so help me, I'll croak him!

Dover opened one eye. 'Well, come on, Sergeant,' he growled crossly, 'we don't want to be here all night! I've had a hard day, if you haven't.'

Sergeant MacGregor, who had got back ten minutes after The Two Fiddlers stopped serving dinner, apologized to his chief inspector, whose after-luncheon 'quiet think' had lasted peacefully till seven o'clock.

'Sorry, sir. I was just wondering where to begin.'

'Begin at the beginning,' suggested Dover pompously, and, rather pleased with this neat bit of repartee, settled himself back even deeper in his chair.

'Well, there's still no sign of Juliet Rugg, sir, dead or alive. I think the local police have done about everything they can, short of searching every house in the country. They've sent out a call to all main-line railway stations and bus termini and they've even had a message put out on the B.B.C. They've organized search parties locally to check all the woods and waste ground where somebody might have dumped her, but they've found nothing at all.'

'Rivers? Canals? Reservoirs?'

'The local river's only two feet deep, the nearest canal is over ten miles from Irlam Old Hall and you can't approach it by road, and the nearest reservoir is twenty miles away. If somebody carted her off in a car or a van, then, of course, she might be anywhere, but I should have thought we'd have heard something by now. What it boils down to is this: nobody has seen or heard of her since Colonel Bing saw her on the drive at eleven o'clock on Tuesday night.'

'Since Colonel Bing *says* she saw her,' corrected Dover. 'Well, I think she's dead !'

Sergeant MacGregor frowned. 'But, there's still the problem of the body, sir,' he pointed out. 'Sixteen stone of a problem ! And it's five days now – surely she'd be stinking to high heaven?'

'Could be buried somewhere,' said Dover vaguely.

'But where, sir?'

'How the hell do I know? Well, what else did you find out?'

'I traced her movements in Creedon on the Tuesday afternoon and evening. They're pretty much what we knew already. She caught the three-fifteen bus from Earlam and got into Creedon at three forty-five. The bus conductor knows her and remembers her quite well. Nothing unusual. She booked a single ticket and I thought we'd got something there, but apparently she often did that, presumably when Mr Pilley was going to bring her back by car. Her first stop was at the newsagents where she bought a couple of magazines – tripey romantic stories about shop girls marrying Ruritanian princes, all told in strip cartoons. The shop-keeper showed me some of them, and from what we've heard, I'd say they were right up Juliet's street.

'Well, her next stop was the chemist's. She must have spent at least half an hour there at the cosmetics counter. The two girls who serve there were at school with her, and from what I can gather they had a good old gossip while Juliet pawed over the pots of cream and what-have-you. Both girls say Juliet was just the same as usual. She told 'em a few hair-raising stories about what old Sir John got up to and a blow-by-blow account of her last evening out with Gordon Pilley. I didn't get the details, of course, but the two girls giggled like fury and it was mutually agreed that Juliet was awful, really, where men were concerned.

'However, she said nothing about any new boy-friend and there wasn't a ghost of a hint that she intended going away. In fact, there was a tentative arrangement that she would call round for one of the girls next Tuesday and go to the pictures with her.

It all depended whether Gordon Pilley was going to be in Creedon and whether the other girl got herself fixed up with a male
date. Apparently, if neither girl could find anything better to do,
they'd spend the evening together. Well, after Juliet had been
hanging around for about half an hour, the owner of the shop
came back and Juliet completed her purchases and left. She
bought some stuff for tinting her hair, a box of mascara and this
green nail-varnish stuff that Gordon Pilley mentioned.

'After the chemist's, she went to the post office and deposited
seven pounds in her Post Office savings-book. We had a bit of
luck there, sir. The post-office assistant also knew her, like everybody else in the place if you ask me, and she remembers that
Juliet's savings-book had to be sent up to the head office – to have
the interest put in or something. Well, Juliet just filled in the
envelope and handed the book over. It's the same old story, isn't
it, sir? Doesn't look like the action of someone who's on the point
of running away, does it?'

There was a long pause. 'Humph,' said Dover at last, still not
opening his eyes. He eased himself slightly in his chair. 'How
much had she got in her savings account?'

'I asked about that, sir,' said MacGregor, not without a modest
satisfaction. 'The assistant couldn't remember exactly, but it was
a fair amount – about one hundred and fifty pounds, she thought.
Of course, we can get the exact figure if you think it worth while.'

'Humph,' said Dover. 'Well, go on.'

'As far as I can gather, Juliet must have gone straight to the
cinema café then. The waitress remembers her quite well, too.
She was a regular customer, always with some man or other,
usually Gordon Pilley, but the waitress described two or three
others as well. While Juliet was waiting for Pilley, she spent the
time undoing her packages and having a look at the things she'd
bought. Then she opened up this green nail varnish and started
doing her nails. The waitress says she'd already got some sort of
silvery-pink varnish on and she just daubed this green stuff on
top. The waitress thought it was a bit off – Juliet painting her
nails at the tea table, but, apparently, she contented herself with
black looks and didn't say anything.

'Then Pilley came and joined her and they had a high tea –
plaice and chips, the waitress thinks.

'I checked with the cinema and the pub too but I couldn't get anything very definite in either place. Still, there was nothing to indicate that Pilley's account of the evening isn't pretty accurate.'

Sergeant MacGregor closed his notebook. 'And that's the lot, sir,' he announced.

Dover's mind crawled back laboriously from wherever it had got to and he groped lethargically for his beer.

'Got another cigarette?' he demanded. 'Well,' he went on with a sigh, 'I reckon that just about leaves us where we were before. Frankly I don't see much point in hanging about down here any longer. We shan't get any further until that body turns up.'

'If she's dead,' MacGregor put in.

'Of course she's dead!' snapped Dover. 'It's the only explanation, so don't start yapping on about kidnapping! I've told you before, kidnapping's completely out of the question! Anyhow, I reckon we'd better go and see that old fool Bartlett tomorrow morning and tell him we're getting nowhere fast. With a bit of luck we should be able to get away after lunch at the latest. You'd better look the trains up. Oh, and there's one other thing I'd like you to check. You can nip up to Irlam Old Hall first thing before we go into Creedon – won't take you a minute. They push Sir John Counter out in a wheel chair. Apparently the wheels used to squeak. Now, somebody's oiled 'em recently, put quite a lot on, too. Eve Counter says she didn't do it, but it's possible that William Bondy might have done. Now, I want you to check whether he did. If he didn't, find out if you can who did and where that wheel chair was on Tuesday night.'

'Oh, I see,' said MacGregor, 'you think somebody might have used this bath chair thing for transporting Juliet?'

'Yes.' Dover didn't sound over enthusiastic even though it was his idea. 'It's all a bit of a long shot, but you never know. Somebody might have killed Juliet on Tuesday night after Colonel Bing saw her, and found himself with this enormous corpse on his hands. She'd be the devil's own weight to move any distance, even for a strong man. Well now, he might have thought about Sir John's wheel chair, got hold of it, oiled the squeaking wheels and loaded Juliet into it.'

'Yes,' agreed MacGregor, rather surprised at the chief inspector's ingenuity, 'on the other hand, the murderer might have oiled those wheels before the murder. That'd make it premeditated, wouldn't it? And in any case, sir,' he pointed out eagerly, 'this

116

would narrow the field down a good bit, wouldn't it? I mean, the murderer would have to know about the bath chair, and about the squeaky wheels, so it looks like somebody up at Irlam Old Hall. And it narrows down the field of the actual murder, too, doesn't it? I mean, you wouldn't go pushing a bath chair for miles in the middle of the night, either empty or with a dead body in it, would you?'

'It looked a pretty rickety old thing to me,' observed Dover thoughtfully, 'I don't think you'd be able to shove it far without it dropping to bits. And, of course, you'd have to keep on level ground, you couldn't push it across a ploughed field or anything. Oh, there's another thing you'd better check – those bloody main gates! See if the bath chair can be got through that little door in the middle. If it can't ... '

'I'll get on to it first thing in the morning, sir,' MacGregor promised excitedly.

'Hey! Don't count too much on it!' warned Dover. 'If it was Bondy who oiled those wheels, it probably doesn't mean anything. Don't let's build too many castles on thin air!'

'No, sir!' The sergeant's enthusiasm was undamped. 'Would you like another pint, sir, before we turn in?'

Dover looked at his empty tankard. 'Might as well,' he accepted ungraciously, 'I think my stomach's got used to this rot-gut now.'

* * *

It had, and Dover slept with the peace which is supposed only to come to innocent little children. Considering he'd already had a good five hours' nap in the afternoon it was amazing that he could close his eyes at all.

However, he came down to breakfast in a benign and smiling mood. He'd had enough sleep, even for him, and there was every likelihood that he'd spend the next night at home in his own bed. Sergeant MacGregor was already hotfoot on the trail of the squeaking bath chair and Dover munched his way through a pretty substantial meal, at peace with the world. As soon as MacGregor got back they would get straight off to Creedon and, with a bit of luck, they should be back in London by early evening.

Then the phone rang. It was Sergeant MacGregor. He wanted to speak to Chief Inspector Dover, urgently.

'I think you'd better come up here straight away, sir,' came MacGregor's voice. 'I'm at Sir John's. Something's happened.'

'What?' demanded Dover, his good humour rapidly ebbing away.

'I don't think we'd better discuss it on the phone, sir, the local exchange is bound to be listening in.'

'Well, of all the blooming cheek!' crackled an outraged female voice, and there was a loud click.

'Oh, all right!' snapped Dover. 'I'll be with you in ten minutes and God help you if you've dragged me up there on a wild goose chase!'

He slammed the phone down and then realized that Mac-Gregor had the police car up at Irlam Old Hall. With a snort of fury he charged out to unearth the village taxi-driver.

He found MacGregor waiting for him in Sir John Counter's bedroom. The old man, wearing, of all things, black silk pyjamas, was sitting up in bed, his eyes sparkling with excitement.

'Here,' he said before MacGregor had the chance to open his mouth, 'read this!'

Dover took the letter which Sir John handed over. 'When did this come?' he asked, morosely eyeing the envelope.

'This morning's post,' said Sir John, 'and be careful how you handle it. Finger-prints!'

Dover scowled at him.

The envelope, a long narrow one, was addressed to Sir John, care of his bank in London. It had been redirected to him at Irlam Old Hall. His name and the London address were neatly printed in pencil in rather large letters, but the redirection was written in a normal hand in ink – obviously the work of some bank clerk. There were two postmarks. One showed that the letter had been originally posted shortly after midday in the West End of London on the previous Saturday, and the second bore a City stamp showing the time of 5.15 p.m. and dated the day before, Monday. It was pretty obvious, even to Dover, what had happened. Someone had posted the letter to Sir John's bank on the Saturday. The letter would arrive on the Monday morning and had been duly readdressed to Irlam Old Hall and posted late on Monday afternoon. Sir John received it on Tuesday morning.

Dover sighed and, mindful of Sir John's watchful eye, carefully extracted the letter with his handkerchief. Fearing the worst, he unfolded the large sheet of paper and read the contents. There was no address or date. The message, like the envelope, was neatly printed in large pencilled letters. It began, with scant regard for Dover's feelings:

We have kidnapped Juliet Rugg, and the ransom is five hundred pounds. She is alive and well but you know what will happen if you don't pay up.

Place five hundred used non-consecutive one-pound notes in an empty tin of Vim or other cleaning powder and place it in the middle lavatory in the ladies' convenience in the Market Square, Creedon. The money must be there by ten o'clock on Wednesday morning next. Place an old dish-cloth on top of the Vim tin.

Don't try any tricks and don't tell the police.

Enclosed please find a signed photograph of Cliff Richard which Juliet always carried in her handbag. You will also find her finger-print in the circle at the bottom of this letter. This is proof that we've got her.

PAY UP OR ELSE.

Not unnaturally, there was no signature.

At the bottom of the letter was a pencilled circle, about the size of a penny. In it was a rather amateurish-looking dab.

' 'Strewth!' said Dover in disgust. He turned to MacGregor. 'Get this photographed and run all the usual checks on it. Where's this picture of Cliff Richard? Oh, it's in the envelope. Is this hers, Sir John?'

'Oh yes, she was very proud of it.' Sir John was thoroughly enjoying the whole thing. 'She always carried it in her handbag. You can see, it's got her name on the back.'

Dover turned the photograph over and sighed. 'I take it, Sir John, that you've no intention of paying the ransom?'

'Not bloody likely!' The old man chuckled. 'Five hundred pounds for Juliet? Oh no, I think not! No, my dear Inspector, it's up to you and your merry men now. Tricky job, too, if the threats are genuine, eh?'

Dover sniffed. 'Does anybody else know about this letter?'

'Only my daughter. I told her to get on the phone to you but luckily she'd seen your assistant just going into the Hall so she fetched him.'

'Well, I don't want you to mention it to anyone else – no one at all, do you understand?'

'My dear Inspector' – Sir John waved a gracious hand – 'I shall be discretion itself. I shall be silent as the' – he sniggered – 'grave.'

'Come on, Sergeant,' growled Dover, 'we shall have to get a move on. We've only got twenty-four hours before the money's due to be collected!'

Eve Counter was waiting for them in the hall.

'Could I speak to you for a moment, Inspector?' she asked hesitantly.

'I haven't time to be bothered with you now!' snapped Dover. 'Oh well, what do you want?'

'Is my father going to pay the ransom money?'

'No.'

'Well, I'm prepared to pay it. Five hundred pounds, wasn't it, in old notes?'

Dover pushed his bowler hat slowly to the back of his head and stood, arms akimbo, staring at Eve Counter.

'You're prepared to pay five hundred pounds for Juliet Rugg?' he asked in utter bewilderment. 'What in God's name for?'

'It's just that I don't like to think of the girl being killed for a measly five hundred pounds.'

'Very noble!' sneered Dover. 'Now, let's have the real reason.'

Eve Counter flashed him an angry look and then shrugged her shoulders helplessly. 'Oh well, I suppose you'll find out some time, whatever happens. I don't want Juliet to get frightened and start talking. She's blackmailing me – oh, it's only the odd pound here and there, I can well afford it. But, if she starts talking to real criminals like these kidnappers, just to save her own skin or buy them off or something – well, then I might find myself facing rather more exacting demands. Five hundred pounds might well be a bargain price in that case.'

'And what,' asked Dover grimly, 'was she blackmailing you about?'

Eve Counter's chin went up but she avoided looking at either Dover or the silent Sergeant MacGregor.

'I had an affair,' she said in a stiff voice. 'He's married, naturally. As a matter of fact, he's my father's doctor and, technically, I'm a patient of his too. You know what that means. If the medical authorities got wind of his – er – misconduct, he'd be thrown out. He's no money and he wouldn't be able to earn his living at anything else – not after all these years – and I, well' – she swallowed hard – 'I haven't got enough money to keep us both. Not while my father is still alive, that is.'

Sergeant MacGregor gazed at her sympathetically. She was very near to tears and very angry with herself for being so.

'Is this liaison still going on?' asked Dover.

'No, we broke it off six months or more ago. We just couldn't stand the strain. It all seemed so underhand and sordid. There didn't seem to be any hope of our ever getting married and, of course, there was always the danger that the whole thing would come out one day and that would mean that Edward would be ruined, his career and everything. He's got two children, you know,' she added miserably, 'we had to think of them too.'

'And how did Juliet get on to it?'

'She found some letters I'd kept. We hadn't been as careful as I thought. I shouldn't have kept Edward's letters, I suppose, but I just couldn't bring myself to burn them.'

'All right,' said Dover, making up his mind quickly, 'how soon can you get the money?'

Eve Counter's face brightened. 'Right away,' she said, 'this morning, if you like. I can get it from the bank.'

'Well, you'd better come into Creedon with us now. We're not going to pay the ransom, mind you, it'd be against the law anyhow, but I'd sooner have the trap baited with the real thing. Now, come on – there's no time to waste!'

There are certain people who really rise to a crisis and it can be fairly said that Chief Inspector Wilfred Dover of New Scotland Yard was one of them. At Christmas-time some children have the distressing habit of blowing up toy balloons to their fullest extent and then releasing them so that the air rushes out of the mouthpiece and the rapidly deflating balloon shoots around dementedly all over the place. This is how Dover habitually rose to a crisis, with the same undignified lack of control and pretty much the same kind of noise.

He reduced the police headquarters in Creedon to a gibbering, panic-stricken shambles within thirty seconds of his right boot crossing the threshold. His unfortunate habit of equating speed with noise produced a screaming pandemonium which the old building had not seen since the Relief of Mafeking when they brought the drunks in. Dover rampaged happily around, bawling his head off.

'I want all your policewomen brought in!' he yelled. 'Right away! There's no time to lose!'

'But –' began the local inspector.

'Don't argue!' roared Dover. 'Get 'em!'

By late afternoon some semblance of order had been achieved and Dover marshalled his troops for their battle briefing.

The kidnapper's plan was quite an ingenious one as the local pessimists were delighted to point out. Wednesday was market-day and along with other establishments in the town the ladies' convenience in the Market Square did a roaring trade. Convention being what it is, Dover had not been able to visit the place, but he had been given a pretty accurate description of what it was like by the Chief Constable's secretary, an intelligent girl who also produced a rough plan of the layout.

The convenience was an underground one, approached by a steep flight of stone steps. Once inside the visitor found herself in a largish, white-tiled dungeon with three cubicles containing lavatories occupying half the available space. All the lavatories had the usual penny-in-the-slot machine fixed on the door. The rest of the furnishings need little description. There was a large bespeckled mirror on one wall and a wash-basin fitted with a cold tap. There was also a machine from which you could buy a nasty little paper towel for twopence and a waste-paper basket in which to throw it when it had disintegrated in your still wet hands. There were a couple of framed notices, one threatening dire penalties to those who misused the place in any way and another fly-blown exhortation on the dangers of concealing venereal disease. Thanks to a completely inadequate ventilation system (one small grille set high in the wall and usually choked with newspapers and old cabbage leaves from the market stalls out-side) the convenience had a highly distinctive and peculiarly unpleasant atmosphere. Nobody lingered there longer than the calls of nature demanded, and there was no attendant.

Surveillance here was going to be more difficult than Dover had at first imagined, though he had recognized immediately that this was a job for the girls, hence his urgent summoning of all the policewomen in the county. He envisaged an elaborate roster system whereby every time a lady came out of the vital centre lavatory, a policewoman would immediately nip in and check whether the ransom money was still there. He could see the snags in this plan as well as anybody. It meant that every customer who used the middle lavatory would have to be followed by another policewoman until her colleague indicated that the money had not yet been taken. But, how was the first policewoman to let the second policewoman know? After all, the second policewoman and her suspect might be half-way across the Market Square while the first policewoman was looking in the Vim tin to see if the five hundred pounds was still there. Well, there'd have to be a third policewoman acting as runner and … Oh, well, they could work out the *details* later.

Now it was later and tricky little points of procedure paled into insignificance as Dover balefully eyed his women colleagues. There were only two of them.

'Where are the others?' he screamed in fury.

'That's all we've got,' said the local inspector. 'I tried to tell you, sir. Recruiting's very bad at the moment.'

'Obviously!' snarled Dover, and raised his eyes eloquently to the unkind heavens.

Woman Police Sergeant Joan Kempton and Woman Police Constable Miriam Alice Smith waited patiently for Scotland Yard's master mind to give them their instructions. Woman Police Sergeant Kempton was an alert, bird-like young woman with a mass of flaming red hair. Miriam Alice Smith stood six feet one inch in her uniform shoes and had a pair of shoulders on her which many a heavyweight boxer would have been glad to own. Both were well-known figures in the town and not perhaps ideally suited for the inconspicuous role in which Dover had cast them.

Grimly the chief inspector explained the problem to them.

'Now, Sergeant,' he concluded, pushing the burden on to the weaker sex without a qualm, 'how do you propose to tackle it?'

Sergeant Kempton rose to the situation like a true-born Englishwoman. 'Quite simply, sir,' she replied firmly, 'it can't be done.'

'God damn and blast it!' stormed Dover. 'It's got to be done!'

'All right! You tell us how, sir, and we'll do it.' Sergeant

Kempton tossed her ginger head, folded her arms and waited. Dover could cheerfully have wrung her neck.

'Well, what about this?' he suggested through clenched teeth. 'One of you waits by the entrance and whenever a woman comes out of the middle toilet you engage her in conversation while the other goes into the toilet and checks if the money's still there?'

Sergeant Kempton laughed, shortly and with contempt.

Dover bridled. 'What's wrong with that?' he snarled viciously.

'Just about everything,' said Sergeant Kempton airily. 'I thought we were supposed to be inconspicuous. What with one of us making polite conversation with every third woman who uses the place and the other popping in and out of the middle lavatory every thirty seconds like a jack-in-the-box, we're likely to be the talk of the town before lunch-time. What are we supposed to talk to 'em about? The weather or the international situation or what? And do you know what that place is like on market-day? It's like Waterloo Station on a bank holiday! There's a queue there nearly all day long. How do you think I can keep popping inconspicuously into the middle lavatory every second turn? Talk about queue-breaking – they'd lynch me!'

Miriam spoke up for the first time. 'Who's going to pay for the pennies?' she asked.

'That's a good point, Smith.' The sergeant nodded her head in approval. 'This lark's going to cost a fortune. Who is going to pay?'

'Police funds,' snapped Dover.

'Well,' said Sergeant Kempton gazing boredly at the ceiling, 'it still won't work.'

'How about putting one of the side toilets out of order?' Dover tried again with a new inspiration. 'Then you could stand in there and peep over the top of the partition?'

'No thank *you*!' snorted Sergeant Kempton. 'What do you think we are? Anyhow,' she added, 'the side walls go right up to the ceiling, so that wouldn't work either.'

'You're a bloody fine help, I must say!' yelped Dover, fast reaching his breaking-point.

'Here! Don't you speak to me like that!' The sergeant was reaching her breaking-point too. 'I've got my rights, you know!'

'Well, I shouldn't count on having 'em much longer, if I were you!'

At this point the briefing degenerated into an exchange of vulgar abuse in which Sergeant Kempton and Chief Inspector Dover both gave as good as they got. Dover threatened disciplinary action and Sergeant Kempton countered by promising a formal complaint to Higher Authority. The problems of supervising the Market Square ladies' convenience in order to thwart the dastardly designs of the kidnappers were rapidly abandoned for more acceptable and fruitful topics such as personal appearance, probable moral and intellectual standards, family background and so forth – on all of which the two protagonists waxed long and eloquent.

When signs of exhaustion at last began to appear, it was Sergeant MacGregor who undertook the delicate and thankless job of acting as peacemaker. Employing all his well-known charm he at last restored some semblance of peace and order to the discussion and it was finally agreed, with a marked lack of enthusiasm all round, that the two policewomen should hang round all the next day in the Market Square ladies' convenience in plain clothes and generally do the best they could. This was not quite the all-embracing, watertight master plan that Dover had envisaged, but, as he pointed out loudly numerous times, if they didn't give him the tools, he couldn't get on with the job.

The supervision which he tried to arrange outside the purely feminine domain of the underground convenience wasn't, he was unhappily aware, very much better. The local police grudgingly agreed to provide an indequate number of police constables, also in plain clothes, to keep an unobtrusive eye on such inhabitants of Irlam Old Hall as might make their way into Creedon on the Wednesday. Gordon Pilley and Mrs Rugg were also included in the list of those whose movements were to be supervised.

'Though, mind you,' said Dover gloomily, 'the odds are they'll use some blasted woman that nobody's ever seen before. I'd give six months' pay to get my hands on the bastard who thought this one up!'

'Where are we going to be stationed, sir?' asked Sergeant MacGregor, wondering if Dover had overlooked this small point. He underestimated the chief inspector.

'Here,' said Dover, jabbing a fat finger at the map. ' "Miss Mathilda's Tea Shoppe" – it's right opposite the ladies' convenience and we'll be able to sit there all day, if needs be, without attracting too much attention. You'll have to park the car as near as you can in one of the side streets, just in case we have to use it.'

With an unerring instinct, fortified by long experience, Dover had picked out for himself the cushiest job in the whole operation. But even the prospect of sitting quietly all day in a Tea Shoppe didn't lift the burden of gnawing anxiety which both he and Sergeant MacGregor were beginning to experience. If things went wrong, somebody's head was going to roll, and Dover recognized resentfully that his neck was already stretched out on the block.

Chapter Eleven

DOVER didn't get much sleep on the Tuesday night. In the quiet of his hotel room, tossing about irritably from one side to the other in bed, he began to think about things which he might have done better to have considered earlier. A telephone call from his superior in Scotland Yard, who had been alerted by the horrified Chief Constable as to what was going on, had not made Dover feel any easier about his hastily-conceived plan. An icy voice had informed him clearly where the responsibility lay in case there was any mishap (squarely on Dover's shoulders, of course) and drew his attention to the fact, in case he had over-looked it, that the safety of the missing girl and of five hundred pounds in untraceable notes was a matter of not inconsiderable importance.

Dover's mind shied uneasily back to the ransom letter itself. He had been so astounded and infuriated by its arrival that he had without thinking assumed that it was genuine. Well, that was fair enough. Juliet Rugg's life might be in danger and he had to take all possible precautions to protect her. If the whole thing turned out to be a hoax, nothing had been lost, except an incredibly large number of police man-hours.

There was nothing particularly significant about the note from a physical point of view. Both the envelope and the paper were mass-produced items which could be bought in every stationer's shop from one end of the country to the other. The minor prob-lem of the large, neatly printed, pencilled lettering had been solved – by Sergeant MacGregor unfortunately, but that couldn't be helped. Whoever had written the note had used one of those celluloid stencils which are, again, on sale everywhere to people who want to do some neat lettering or sign-writing on a do-it-yourself basis. In this case they had been able to identify the actual make of the stencil used – a very small one which was combined with a ruler. Sergeant MacGregor possessed one him-self and had recognized the shape of the letters.

It was, Dover acknowledged, a clever idea. Obviously the writer was well aware of police expertise in identifying handwriting or printing, however well disguised, and the stencil was plainly a good deal less troublesome than the more usual method of cutting words and letters out of old newspapers and sticking them on a sheet of paper. The police had reported that the pencil used was an ordinary HB one and asked if it was worth while trying to identify the actual make. Dover had said yes, just to be awkward. He didn't really expect to get a lead that way.

There were no finger-prints on the letter, except those of Sir John and the ink impression which had indeed been made by Juliet Rugg's right-hand index finger. It had been compared with the prints which were scattered all over her bedroom. The letter had however been sent up to the finger-print laboratories in Scotland Yard in case they could discover something which the much less experienced local men had missed. Dover hadn't much hope of success on this score but he was never one to cut down work and trouble as long as it was somebody else's.

At this stage in his ruminations he climbed resentfully out of bed and rummaged round in his suitcase until he found the crumpled packet of cigarettes which he carried in case of emergency. He lit one and climbed back into bed again, frowning as he sucked the acrid-tasting smoke into his lungs.

Well, it was obviously unlikely that the ransom letter was going to give him any direct physical clues as to the identity of the writer, but there were quite a number of indirect clues which were worth examining. The absence of direct clues was the first one. Somebody with a pretty high level of intelligence had written that note, somebody who was well aware of the obvious pitfalls. Did this mean there was an experienced criminal behind the whole thing, or just somebody who had read widely in detective-story fiction? At any rate he could rub out one vague idea that had nudged at his mind – well endowed with low cunning as she obviously was, Juliet Rugg was hardly likely to have written the note herself. It didn't read like her probable style, and there were no spelling or grammatical mistakes. He could also remove Mrs Rugg from his list of suspects, and possibly the foreigner, Boris Bogolepov, as well.

The next thing to consider, thought Dover, rather pleased with the neat logical way he was dealing with this, was the method of delivery via Sir John Counter's bank. How many people knew the address of Sir John's bank in London? Well, his daughter certainly would, for one, and so would Mrs Chubb-Smith, because Sir John presumably paid his rent by cheque and the cheque would have the bank's address on it. But why bother to send the letter to Sir John's bank at all? Did it mean that the kidnapper didn't know Sir John's address at Irlam Old Hall? No, Dover shook his head firmly, that was quite out of the question. He couldn't believe that anybody, no matter how remotely connected with the case, would not know Sir John's home address. He put this point aside for the moment and moved on to the really vital bit of evidence that the envelope provided – the postmarks.

The letter had been posted in the first instance in the West End of London at midday on Saturday. That meant that the person who posted it was in London at midday on Saturday. Well, Dover sighed hopelessly and scratched his stomach, this either widened the field to something in the neighbourhood of ten million people or narrowed it to one person in Juliet's circle of acquaintances who was away from home all day on Saturday. Say four or five hours' journey up to London in the morning and four or five hours back again – anybody who'd been away that length of time should be easy enough to trace.

With a bit of an effort Dover identified Saturday in his mind. That was the day his stomach was upset, wasn't it? Yes, he'd spent Friday night hopping backwards and forwards to the bathroom and his guts were still queasy the next morning. Now then, who had he interviewed on the Saturday? There was Eulalia Hoppold and Boris Bogolepov for a start – he'd seen them twice, once in the morning and once in the afternoon. Then he'd questioned young Michael Chubb-Smith and his wife, and the caretaker, Bondy, up at the Old Hall itself. And who else? Oh yes, Basil Freel and his sister, Amy. Well, that was seven people straight off who couldn't possibly have posted that letter in London. Right, as soon as tomorrow's little caper in the ladies' convenience was over, providing the whole case wasn't solved – which he very much doubted – young Master MacGregor could get off his elegant backside and do a bit of routine checking on all the rest of the characters. He could find out who was away all day Saturday and who knew the address of Sir John's bank. That might turn up something really useful!

Of course, the thought depressed him, there was more than one way of getting a letter posted in London than physically putting it in the letter-box yourself. Somebody down here might have an accomplice in London who could post the letter, or you could just send it to a friend and say, please post this for me. But that was a bit risky, wasn't it? Friends being what they were might wonder why you couldn't post the letter yourself, might even open the damned thing. After all, Juliet's disappearance had been mentioned pretty widely in the press by Saturday and the friend might recognize the Irlam Old Hall address and ... Hello now, was that why the letter was addressed to Sir John's bank in London? So that somebody wouldn't recognize the Irlam Old Hall address and start wondering? Dover felt a bit more cheerful – he was sure he'd solved one bit of the puzzle, not that it helped all that much.

With a sigh he lit another cigarette and reached for the photostat of the ransom note which MacGregor had got for him. He read it through again, carefully, and frowned. Now that he had time to look at the blasted thing closely, well, he had to admit that it did seem a bit odd. Take the money, for example. Demanding money with menaces was a felony, and anybody found guilty of it was likely to cop a good long stretch of imprisonment from the judge. For a lousy five hundred pounds it didn't really seem worth it, not when you considered all the trouble and expense of kidnapping a grown girl and keeping her in hiding until the ransom was paid. For five thousand pounds, say, the game might be worth the candle, but for five hundred pounds? Of course, perhaps that was all the market would stand. Dover didn't think for one moment that anybody would cough up five thousand pounds just to get Juliet Rugg back safe and well. But, in that case, why kidnap Juliet Rugg? Why not go for someone with a higher price on her head?

Then there was the business of the usual warning, 'Don't try any tricks and don't tell the police.' That was a pretty routine sort of threat but, if the police were not to be informed, why was the main evidence that the kidnapper had really got Juliet one of her finger-prints – the sort of proof that the police, and only the police, could check? It really didn't make sense.

Dover sighed again over the 'don't tell the police' bit. If the kidnapper was one of the Irlam Old Hall lot – or had an accomplice there – they'd probably gathered by now that the police *had* been informed. They wouldn't know exactly which post would bring the letter, but his and Sergeant MacGregor's early-morning arrivals at Sir John's house would surely appear significant to anybody watching – if anybody was watching.

The kidnapper had certainly worked out a pretty foolproof scheme for collecting the money (incidentally, there was obviously a woman involved somewhere, and one who knew the layout of the underground convenience, too), and perhaps he counted on getting away with it, police or no police. And he was probably right at that, thought Dover grimly as he recalled the ludicrously inadequate arrangements which were all he had been able to make.

Dover put the photostat back on his bedside table, stubbed out his cigarette and switched off the light. His thoughts were still chasing erratically round his head like white mice on a miniature treadmill. Why only five hundred pounds? Why the finger-print? Was it somebody at Irlam Old Hall? How was the letter posted in London? What was going to happen tomorrow? Would the money be collected? Would anybody ever see Juliet Rugg again?

Dover turned on to his other side and found himself churning through the older questions which had been bothering him all through the case. How did they get Juliet away from Irlam Old Hall? Where was she now? Why had nobody seen her?

Sleep eventually came but it was shallow and troubled, and Dover awoke on the fateful Wednesday morning very annoyed that his subconscious hadn't come up with any bright suggestions which would have solved everything in one awe-inspiring, Sergeant-MacGregor-rocking explosion of brilliance.

*　　*　　*

When Miss Mathilda, if that's who it was, opened the door of her Tea Shoppe at half-past nine on market-day, she was surprised to find that she had two customers already waiting on the doorstep. They pushed, somewhat unceremoniously, inside.

'Two coffees,' said the fat one, who was wearing a bowler hat.

'I'm afraid we don't start serving coffee until ten o'clock,' said Miss Mathilda.

'In that case,' retorted Dover, barging his way through a tightly-packed jungle of chairs and little tables, 'we'll wait!'

'Oh, I'm afraid you can't sit in the window! That table's reserved.'

'Hard luck,' said Dover, sitting firmly down and drawing back the lace curtain. 'We're from the police, madam – show the old trout your card, Sergeant! – and we shall probably be here all day. Just treat us like a couple of ordinary customers and don't tell anybody else who we are. We shan't get in your way.'

'But Lady Williams always sits at that table on Wednesdays,' protested Miss Mathilda feebly.

Dover peered callously through the window. 'Well, she'll just have to sit somewhere else today. It won't kill her, will it? And don't forget to bring us a couple of coffees when you get round to it.'

Outside it was, much to Dover's satisfaction, pouring with rain. He and Sergeant MacGregor sat snug and dry at their table with its excellent view of the entire Market Square, including both the ladies' and the gentlemen's conveniences.

At ten o'clock two cups of weak, pale coffee arrived just as Eve Counter descended the steps of the ladies' to deposit the money. It had been put, in accordance with the instructions, in an empty tin of Vim, and Eve also had an old dish-cloth to place on top. It was not the sort of thing that any casual patron, however light-fingered, would be likely to pick up and take away. One of the snags of checking whether or not the money had gone lay in the fact that the cylindrical tin had to be opened every time, because there was no guarantee that the kidnapper or his accomplice would make off with both the canister and the money.

Just before Eve Counter emerged into the upper air the two policewomen arrived to take up their stations.

'Oh my God!' howled Sergeant MacGregor, his composure for once deserting him. 'Just look at them!'

Dover's comment was unprintable.

Sergeant Kempton and Woman Police Constable Smith had, of course, been instructed to wear plain clothes, an unhappy phrase when applied to what Sergeant Kempton at least had put on her back. The most striking feature of her ensemble was a huge hairy coat in a scarlet so glowing that you could almost have warmed your hands on it. It was unlikely that anyone who had once seen Sergeant Kempton in her finery would not recognize her again five years, never mind five minutes, later.

'I'll kill her!' snarled Dover. 'I'll kill her with my own bare hands! So help me, I will! What the hell does she think this is? The bloody Chelsea Arts Ball?'

Sergeant MacGregor, dabbing his eyes in a near hysterical condition, could find no words of cheer or consolation.

'Well,' he gasped, choking with irrepressible joy, 'the other one, she ... Oh, God, I haven't laughed so much for years! – she's dressed quietly enough, isn't she, sir?' He took another look at W.P.C. Smith and once again dissolved into bubbles of surging mirth.

W.P.C. Smith was indeed quietly, even soberly, dressed. She had wrapped her enormous broad shoulders in a short off-white riding mac, and below the mac, long, strong, sinewy legs were unconvincingly shrouded in nylon and ended up in a pair of massive regulation shoes. The final macabre touch was a pair of large, white-rimmed sun-glasses worn, with no little pride, on a day which was so gloomy and overcast that all the shops had their lights on. The girl had already been attracting some very peculiar glances as she strode athletically through the market stalls in the Square.

'Dear God,' yelped Sergeant MacGregor, who just couldn't help himself, 'what does she look like?'

'She looks like a bloody female impersonator, that's what she looks like!' growled Dover. 'If I didn't know, I'd run her in soon as look at her!'

The two policewomen, unconscious of the interest they were arousing, disappeared into the underground lavatory. W.P.C. Smith stumbled down blindly and Sergeant Kempton made a great show of taking a deep breath before she too plunged down the grey stone steps.

Dover and MacGregor settled themselves as best they could on their hard upright chairs and began to wait.

At about a quarter past ten they spotted Boris Bogolepov coming out of the chemist's. It was the first time they had seen him not wearing pyjamas and for a moment they didn't recognize him. He turned up his raincoat collar and stuffed a small package in his pocket.

'Been to collect his dope,' said Sergeant MacGregor sourly. 'Makes you wonder what the Health Service is coming to, doesn't it?'

They watched Boris thread his way across the Market Square to join Eulalia Hoppold at one of the vegetable stalls. Two tall, red-faced young men with thick necks and large feet hovered awkwardly near by, pretending to examine a selection of plastic aprons which were selling at the bargain price of 3s. 9½d. each, or two for 6s. 6d.

'That,' Dover pointed out sarcastically, 'is the local police doing a bit of shadowing ! The fat stupid oafs !'

Half an hour later the waiting detectives were rewarded by the sight of Kitty Chubb-Smith and her daughter-in-law loaded down with shopping. For one breathless moment it looked as though they were actually approaching the ladies' convenience, but they turned aside into the George Hotel which, on market-days, served morning coffee at suitably exorbitant prices and stood slightly higher in the social scale than Miss Mathilda's Tea Shoppe.

Dover looked round. 'I can't see the men who're supposed to be following them,' he grumbled.

'They most likely came in by car, sir,' suggested MacGregor; 'your chaps are probably still waiting at the bus station.'

Dover sighed. What could you do?

Time passed slowly. It was all very boring. The number of women visiting the ladies' convenience steadily increased as the market livened up, and more and more people flowed into the town for their weekly shopping, but, in the absence of any indication to the contrary from the two policewomen, it had to be assumed that no one had yet collected the money.

Dover and MacGregor sat on, drinking cup after cup of Miss Mathilda's dreadful coffee. They were naturally a source of considerable interest to the Tea Shoppe's regular clientele. For one thing, they were the only representatives of the stronger sex in the place. For another, they sat over their coffee for such a long time, outlasting even the most persistent of Miss Mathilda's customers. And for a third, they were so obviously the object of Lady Williams's tantrums when she came in and found that her table, at which, as she proclaimed in a piercing voice, she had sat for coffee every Wednesday morning for the last eleven years, had been invaded by strangers, and men at that. Lady Williams, resplendent in a transparent plastic mackintosh and matching pixie hood, had brushed aside Miss Mathilda's mumbled excuses.

She forged her way across the café and seized hold of a vacant chair at the coveted window table.

'Do you mind,' she said in a voice of frigid politeness which rang round the delighted and expectant room, 'do you mind if I join you?'

Dover eyed her slowly up and down as if considering the matter. 'Yes,' he said at last in a loud voice, 'as a matter of fact, I do.'

Lady Williams retreated in shocked disorder and Miss Mathilda lost for ever what had undoubtedly been the Tea Shoppe's most distinguished customer.

Of course, not all the people who came into the café were puzzled as to what two strange men were doing peering through the window. Colonel Bing and Miss McLintock, after a preliminary start of surprised recognition, discussed the matter in loud whispers which even Dover could hear clearly twenty feet away. The ladies were so absorbed in their speculations that Peregrine, the white poodle, was able to spend a penny on the table leg before he was cut off in mid-stream by a hefty belt on the ear from Colonel Bing.

After a few moments Miss Freel joined them and the two detectives were discreetly pointed out to her. Amy Freel, the acknowledged expert after all in this field, summed up the situation immediately.

'Be careful!' she hissed in rebuke as Miss McLintock waved shyly with her library book. 'They're obviously On The Job. We mustn't compromise them. Georgie, for goodness' sake stop staring at them! You'll ruin the whole thing!'

'What whole thing?' demanded Colonel Bing with her usual military bluntness.

'Oh,' Amy Freel laughed airily, 'I'm afraid I'm not in a position to reveal that to outsiders, you know.' Which was as good an example of lying without actually telling an untruth as anyone is likely to achieve with no warning to speak of.

Miss Freel grabbed Georgie's library book, opened it and peered cautiously over the top at Dover and Sergeant MacGregor.

'Oh,' she whispered excitedly, 'they're watching the ladies' lavatory in the Square! How very odd!'

'Odd?' snorted Colonel Bing. 'It's damned disgusting, if you ask me! Somebody ought to tell the police about 'em and get 'em stopped!'

Miss McLintock retrieved her library book and began quietly to hunt through the pages. 'Don't be silly, Bingo dear,' she said mildly.

Sergeant MacGregor looked hopelessly at his chief inspector. 'Well, sir,' he said, 'I reckon that's let the cat out of the bag all right!'

Dover blew crossly down his nose. 'If,' he said bitterly, 'it was ever in.'

At twelve thirty they partook of Miss Mathilda's snack luncheons – baked beans on toast and yet another cup of coffee. Both Dover and MacGregor were feeling increasing uncomfortable and looked wistfully at the sign marked 'Gentlemen' which they could see tantalizingly less than a hundred yards away, but neither wanted to be the first to acknowledge defeat and they hung on with dogged determination.

At one o'clock Sergeant Kempton emerged and propped herself up weakly against the railings. Her face had acquired an unpleasant greenish tinge and she gulped in deep lungfuls of comparatively fresh air. Rather surprisingly she was now dressed in a large hairy green and yellow check coat. It wasn't any less noticeable than her original scarlet, but it was different.

'Hello,' said Dover, 'perhaps something's happened. You stay here, Sergeant!'

Once outside he glanced furtively around him before approaching Sergeant Kempton. He walked past her without a word or look and then stopped, raised his foot on to a convenient wooden box of tomatoes and began fiddling with his bootlace.

'Well?' he growled, being careful to speak out of the side of his mouth.

'Well what?' answered Sergeant Kempton with unconcealed dislike.

'What's happened? Has the money gone?' hissed Dover. 'What the hell have you come up for?'

'To breathe! Do you mind?'

'But suppose the blasted money goes while you're up here?'

'Let it.' Sergeant Kempton was not interested.

'You're supposed to be on duty!'

'Duty?' snorted Sergeant Kempton. 'I've had some pretty lousy jobs in my time but nothing, I repeat, nothing like this! God, it's worse than cleaning up after a post-mortem! Ugh, the stink down there!'

'For God's sake, woman, it's no time to be squeamish! Get back down there and get on with the job!'

Sergeant Kempton sighed. 'All right,' she said, 'but I'm sending Smith up for a break – that is, if she's still conscious.'

'All right,' snapped Dover, 'you can give her a couple of minutes, but no more! By the way,' he added curiously, 'how come you've changed your coat?'

Sergeant Kempton smirked. 'Rather a good idea, don't you think? It's in case anybody pays two visits down there. They're much less likely to recognize me on the second trip if I'm wearing a different coat.'

'Oh yes,' grunted Dover, 'this one makes you practically invisible! But how did you take it in with you? I didn't see you carrying a parcel.'

'It's one of these reversible ones, see?' Sergeant Kempton flung the coat wide open to show the lining to Dover and three-quarters of the Market Square. 'My red's inside. Clever, isn't it?'

'Very,' said Dover without much conviction. 'Well, it's time you got back on the job. Get moving! Just another five hours and you can knock off.'

'Here,' demanded Sergeant Kempton as she saw him preparing to move off, 'where are you going?'

'Not that it's any of your business,' replied Dover pompously, 'but I'm going to the Gents.'

'The Gents?' repeated Sergeant Kempton with a curt and unkind laugh. 'Well, I hope they let you in!' Chuckling merrily to herself she beat a diplomatic retreat back down the stone steps.

At six o'clock Miss Mathilda's Tea Shoppe closed and Dover and MacGregor finished their vigil outside. At five past six a town council employee arrived to lock up both the gentlemen's and the ladies' conveniences for the night. Sergeant Kempton and W.P.C. Smith, their faces ashen white, staggered out.

'What do you want doing about the money?' Sergeant Kempton asked. 'It's still there.'

'Leave it,' said Dover. 'I'll have a man stationed outside all night in case they try to break in and collect it.'

'A Good Idea!' Sergeant Kempton's tone was nasty. 'And what are we supposed to do now?'

'I want everybody back at the station,' announced Dover grandly, 'for a de-briefing session.'

'Woman Police Constable Smith and I,' pointed out Sergeant Kempton, 'haven't had a bite to eat since nine o'clock this morning.'

'Well,' said Dover sweetly, 'that's your fault, isn't it? You should have taken some sandwiches in with you and had a picnic lunch.'

For the next two hours Dover and MacGregor sat in the local police headquarters listening to a stream of reports and trying, without any marked success, to make some sense out of them.

As was to be expected on market-day nearly all the women in the case, if it was a case and if they were in it, had come into Creedon some time during the day. They seemed to have spent their time in suspiciously innocent pursuits.

Eve Counter, after depositing the ransom money in the Vim tin, had done some shopping and then caught a bus back to Irlam Old Hall in time for lunch.

Amy Freel, Colonel Bing and Miss McLintock had come into Creedon by bus and spent the morning there, but none of them had visited the Market Square convenience. They had, as Dover knew, made use of the facilities provided by Miss Mathilda.

Kitty Chubb-Smith and Maxine had come in by car. The two unfortunate constables who were supposed to be keeping an eye on them had spent a boring morning first hanging round the bus station and then aimlessly wandering about the town looking for their prey. Luckily Dover knew from his own observations that neither of the two women had gone down the famous stone steps which led to the ladies' convenience and to five hundred one-pound notes.

Eulalia Hoppold had also driven in by car, accompanied by Boris Bogolepov. Fortunately her shadowing constable was a relatively intelligent fan of hers who knew she had a car and guessed she would use it. By keeping his eyes open he had soon picked her up in the town. She and Boris had spent an uneventful morning and gone nowhere near the ladies' convenience in the Market Square.

Mrs Rugg had been kept under observation too. She had made

use of the public convenience but, unfortunately, it was the one at the bus station, which wasn't really very significant of anything.

Apart from Boris, none of the men at Irlam Old Hall had fancied struggling with the crowds in Creedon and had all remained at home. Gordon Pilley was on his rounds fifty miles away in another town.

As one dreary story of 'nothing to report' followed another Dover grew more and more depressed. As the last nervous, sweating policeman blundered his way out of the room the chief inspector was almost spitting with disgust.

'And the answer,' he snarled, flinging his pencil petulantly across the room, 'is a bloody lemon!'

Sergeant MacGregor looked moodily at his notebook. 'Well,' he agreed, 'we haven't really got anywhere much, have we, sir?'

'Have we hell!' said Dover bitterly. 'What it boils down to is that nobody who's in any way connected with the case made any attempt to collect that money. And, blast it, nobody who's not connected with it did either!'

His subsequent interview with the Chief Constable – 'Just to keep me in the picture, old boy' – was not a particularly happy one.

'Well, Dover,' Mr Bartlett began grimly, 'we've spent eleven shillings and fourpence out of the funds of this police force for the slot machine and received nineteen complaints about suspicious characters hanging around the ladies' convenience in the Market Square. Seven of the ladies spotted that Woman Police Constable Smith was a man, unconvincingly masquerading as a girl, and ten reported that Woman Police Sergeant Kempton was blatantly engaged in luring young girls away to South America for immoral purposes. The remaining two complainants plumped for a Communist spy ring.

'I have further been deprived of the services of fourteen male constables on the busiest day of the week, with the result that my crime figures since nine o'clock this morning have just about doubled. I have also had a complaint from the mayor about two men, posing as police officers, invading private premises and generally behaving with Gestapo-like brutality – I'm using the mayor's own words. The mayor's sister is the proprietress of Miss Mathilda's Tea Shoppe.

'I have also had a telephone call from Miss Eulalia Hoppold, the well-known authoress and explorer, complaining about being followed by two suspicious-looking thugs while she was out shopping this morning in Creedon. She would, she said, have reported the matter to a policeman at the time, but,' the Chief Constable paused deliberately, 'but she couldn't find one!'

There was a pregnant silence.

'Well,' Mr Bartlett went on, 'those are my results! What are yours?'

'None,' said Dover sullenly. 'There was no attempt to touch the money!'

'And where does that leave us?'

'Just about where we were before.'

'And what do you deduce from the fact that they didn't try to collect the ransom money?'

'Well, either the whole thing was a hoax, somebody's idea of a practical joke or … ' Dover's nose twitched.

'Or?' prompted the Chief Constable.

'Or,' repeated Dover, who always believed that attack was the best means of defence, 'thanks to the unbelievable incompetence and lack of co-operation of the members of your force, the whole operation was bungled from beginning to end and the kidnappers were scared off!'

'Now look here!' roared the Chief Constable slamming his fist down on his desk rather more painfully than he had meant. 'Don't you try to leave me holding the baby! The whole operation was your idea and if it didn't work, then it's because the overall plan was at fault. I thought it sounded pretty bloody disastrous when I heard about it, but you're supposed to be the expert in charge of the case and I've never believed in interfering with the man on the spot. The whole affair's been bungled from beginning to end! You've spent six days here, and what have you discovered? That Juliet Rugg is missing – and we damned well knew that before you came! You've no more idea now of what's happened to her or where she is than when you first arrived! Well, if this is an example of how Scotland Yard works, you can keep it! I'm not satisfied with your handling – if that's the word for it – of the case and I'm telling you here and now I'm going to ring up the Yard first thing tomorrow morning and get you taken off!'

Dover's piggy little eyes narrowed and his nostrils flared out ominously as he took a deep breath preparatory to launching himself into the battle. It wasn't the first time this sort of thing had happened to him and it probably wouldn't be the last. He had managed to wriggle out of worse situations with a fairly whole skin and he wasn't going to go down this time without a fight. He'd pin Mr High-and-Mighty Bartlett's ears back for him with a few home truths about the collection of mental deficients posing as a police force and then he'd ...

Luckily the phone rang.

'It's for you.' The Chief Constable almost flung the receiver at Dover. 'Finger-print division at the Yard.'

Dover listened silently with a set, heavy face. Once or twice he said, 'I see', thoughtfully, and then he sighed.

'Right! Thanks very much.' He put the receiver down.

'Well,' demanded the Chief Constable, who'd calmed down a bit, 'anything new?'

Dover gaped vacantly at him for a second and then pulled himself together. 'They've given the ransom letter a good going over,' he explained, 'no clues as to who wrote it, naturally. I didn't expect there would be.'

The Chief Constable waited for him to go on.

'They examined the finger-print too – you know the one Juliet Rugg was supposed to have made.'

'Do you mean it isn't hers?'

'Oh yes,' said Dover slowly, 'it's hers all right, but, apparently she was dead when she made it!'

Chapter Twelve

WHATEVER might be Dover's failings as a detective, he had one most important, even essential, attribute – luck. As he and the Chief Constable sat staring dumbly at each other they both realized that, once again, by a miracle, Dover's bacon had been saved.

In the face of the knowledge that Juliet Rugg was dead, and had been for some days, the howling fiasco of the unsprung trap for the kidnappers oozed gently away. It would be unfair to say that Dover was delighted at the gruesome news which he had just received over the telephone, but he was certainly relieved. With an unconscious gesture he mopped his brow with his handkerchief and relaxed back comfortably in his chair.

'Well,' he said benignly, 'this certainly changes the picture, doesn't it?'

'I suppose it does.' The Chief Constable was wary. 'Were you expecting it?'

Dover smiled smugly. 'I'm not entirely surprised,' he admitted with becoming modesty; 'I've been pretty certain for some time that she was dead. I've never paid much attention to this kidnapping theory.' With a little shock he realized that, for once, he was telling the truth. For a brief second it quite put him off his stride.

'What are you going to do now?'

Dover pulled himself to his feet and began to fasten up his overcoat. 'Well, there are one or two small points I want to get tidied up first,' he said, 'then I think I should be able to see my way more clearly.'

Mr Bartlett was impressed. Much against his better judgment he was beginning to feel that Dover couldn't be such a fool as he looked. After all he *was* a chief inspector at New Scotland Yard and the Assistant Commissioner *had* said he was just the man for the job.

'Are you pressing on tonight, then?' he asked in a rather awed voice.

Dover quickly wiped a look of outrage and horror off his face. 'Well, not exactly,' he hedged, 'can't really do anything at this time of night. These – er – little points I want to check, they'll have to wait till morning. But,' he added hastily, 'I imagine I'll be up most of the night – thinking things over, you know.'

'Ah, yes,' sighed Mr Bartlett, nodding his head wisely, 'I find I think best late at night too.' He sighed. 'Only time you get, really, on this job.'

'That's very true,' said Dover, 'very true.'

Both men sighed as they contemplated their unhappy, un-appreciated, burdensome lot and parted, each to a warm and comfortable bed, with something approaching mutual good-will.

When Dover came down to breakfast at The Two Fiddlers the following morning his mood was definitely chirpy. Now that Juliet Rugg was really dead the pressure had eased. There was no longer the danger that one false step in the police investigation might endanger the girl's life, and if, by some vague mischance, Chief Inspector Dover didn't manage to solve the case – well, it didn't do much harm to anyone, did it? There were lots of unsolved murder cases (quite a number of them Dover's) and one more wouldn't make all that amount of difference.

Dover beamed at the waitress. 'Porridge, bacon, eggs and saus-ages, and a pot of tea, dear,' he ordered.

The waitress relayed his wishes to Mrs Jelly who did the cooking.

'He called me "dear",' she commented in astonishment.

'Cor, you'd better look out! He's got real bedroom eyes, he has.'

'Not *him*!' retorted the girl as she took the proffered plate of porridge. 'It was that fat old bastard! Must be going off his rocker or something.'

'Well,' said Dover as he scattered the best part of half a pound of sugar on his porridge, 'what's the matter with you this morn-ing, Sergeant? Cat got your tongue or something?'

'No, sir,' replied MacGregor dully, 'I had rather a heavy night of it last night.'

'Hm,' said Dover, ladling his food down in huge spoonfuls, 'now you mention it, you do look a bit seedy. You should keep off this Long Herbert, you know. I reckon it's laced with methylated spirits.'

'I wasn't drinking, sir,' Sergeant MacGregor pointed out stiffly, 'I was working.'

'Oh,' said Dover.

He started on his next course.

'What were you, er, doing?'

'Well, I thought I'd better get this oil thing cleared up. You know, find out who oiled the wheels on Sir John's invalid carriage. So after I'd brought you back here last night I nipped up to Irlam Old Hall again to see if I could find anything out.'

Dover took a mouthful of tea and reached for the toast.

'Very commendable. And did you?'

'A bit.' MacGregor rubbed his hand wearily across his face. 'I saw the caretaker chap, Bondy. He was quite certain he hadn't oiled them. Eve Counter never even mentioned it to him, and he couldn't think of anybody else who would be likely to have done it. He does all the odd jobs around the place.'

'Interesting,' said Dover. 'Just pass me the butter, there's a good chap.'

'Then I went round to the Counters' again. Eve, Miss Counter, said quite definitely that she hadn't oiled the wheels. She vaguely remembered Colonel Bing commenting on the fact that they squeaked, but she'd not really paid much attention and she certainly hadn't asked Bondy or anyone else to fix them.'

'Hm,' said Dover, and poured himself out another cup of tea.

'She's got something, that girl, you know,' announced MacGregor suddenly. 'I had a drink and a chat with her last night and, really, you wouldn't think it was the same person.'

'No doubt,' commented Dover spitefully, 'her father's doctor would agree with you.'

'Oh, she explained all about that.'

'Did she, indeed? Well, you'd better watch it, my lad. It doesn't do for a detective to get emotionally involved with a possible murder suspect.'

Sergeant MacGregor, surprisingly, turned quite pink.

'I hope,' pursued Dover, 'that you didn't tell her that the fair Juliet is dead?'

'Of course not, sir! I didn't tell her anything. By the way, she's going to pick up her five hundred pounds from the police station in Creedon this morning. They were going to ring us if anybody'd tried to collect it and, since they haven't, I suppose it's still there.

Anyhow, I got a sample of the oil used on the wheel chair and I took it back into Creedon last night for a lab. report. I'm pretty certain it's not the same kind as the Counters have. Eve found me their tin and it looked quite different to me. Incidentally, sir, you can't push the wheel chair through that little door in the main gates – it's at least four inches too wide. And at night they keep it in a little shed, just at the side of the house. They never lock the shed door.'

'So anybody could have got at it on Tuesday night?'

'Anybody who knew it was there, sir.'

'Precisely,' said Dover. 'Got a cigarette?'

'Well, now,' he went on, puffing happily away, 'you seem to have had a very busy time. Find anything else out?'

'There is one thing, sir' – MacGregor frowned a little – 'it may be nothing but it is a discrepancy. I read through all my notes again last night and for some reason or another, well, it struck me as a bit odd. I don't know whether you think it's worth following up but it just ... '

'Well, what is it?' snapped Dover with a lightning return to his habitual manner.

MacGregor got his notebook out and thumbed through until he found a marked passage. 'Well, sir, you remember, early on, when Eve Counter was talking about Juliet, she mentioned her nail varnish. I've got her exact words here. She was talking about what a dirty slut Juliet was, and she said that her nails were thick with grime and looked as though they'd been dipped in blood.'

'So what?'

'Well, "dipped in blood" – that means *red* nail varnish, doesn't it?'

Dover snorted fretfully. 'For God's sake, get on with it, Sergent! We're not a pair of blasted cross-talk comedians!'

'No, sir. Well, sir, somebody else just casually mentioned her red nail varnish. It was the waitress in the Regal café. Well, actually, she said Juliet was wearing a silvery-pink colour when she first came in and then she painted the green stuff on while she was waiting for Pilley.

'Now, we know she bought a bottle of green nail varnish on Tuesday afternoon when she was shopping in Creedon at the chemist's. She didn't start painting her nails green until she was

145

in the cinema café at the Regal – the evidence of Gordon Pilley and the waitress shows that.

'But, according to the other evidence we've been given, nobody, except Colonel Bing, at Irlam Old Hall saw her again at all. In other words, before Juliet disappeared she always wore red nail varnish, or pink, but not green. Now, Colonel Bing never said a word about Juliet's nail varnish, and at that distance, late at night, I don't see how she can have seen what colour it was anyhow. But somebody else at Irlam Old Hall *did* talk about Juliet wearing green nail varnish, although they denied having seen her after Tuesday lunch-time at the very latest. Now, Juliet couldn't have been wearing green nail varnish then, because she didn't even buy it until the middle of Tuesday afternoon.'

'Here, hold on a minute, lad!' protested Dover. 'You're jumping to a few too many conclusions, aren't you? All right, Juliet bought a bottle of green nail varnish on Tuesday afternoon and then painted her nails with the disgusting stuff. But that doesn't mean that she'd never used green nail varnish before. She might have bought a bottle weeks or months ago and this one was just a replacement.'

'Oh, I'd thought of that, sir,' Sergeant MacGregor pointed out smugly, much to his chief inspector's irritation, 'but there are a couple of points which seem to indicate that green nail varnish was a novelty for Juliet. First of all, she was in such a hurry to daub it on her nails in the Regal café – Gordon Pilley said ... ' MacGregor hunted through his notebook again ' ... he said, "she'd just bought the stuff and couldn't wait to try it". Now, that seems to indicate that she'd never had green nail varnish before, doesn't it?'

'Hm,' grunted Dover reluctantly.

'And then you remember when we searched her room at the Counters' and found all that money? She'd got lots of old bottles of nail varnish littered all over her dressing-table, but none of them was green. I checked that last night.'

'Ah, but' – the chief inspector thought quickly – 'if she had had green nail varnish before, she wouldn't have bought a new bottle until the old one was finished, would she? And then she'd have thrown the empty bottle away. That's why we didn't see any green nail varnish in her room!'

'Well, yes' – Sergeant MacGregor sounded disappointed – 'that might be the explanation, but it's worth checking up with the girls at the chemist's shop, isn't it, sir? I mean, they'd probably know whether or not Juliet had bought any before, or she might have said something which'd give us a clue to whether or not it was her first bottle.'

'Hm.' Dover regarded MacGregor pensively. He was always complaining about the stupidity and bone-headedness of present-day detective sergeants, but, God knows, he didn't want one of the clever-devil types working with him. If MacGregor was going to develop into a real smart alec, life was going to get very uncomfortable. Still, the lad had obviously got something here. It was a very neat bit of deduction, and Dover would be the last one to admit it.

'All right,' he went on, pretending not to be very interested, 'might be worth checking. We'll do it later today.'

This was one occasion when Dover wasn't anxious to push all the work off on to someone else. If this was going to lead to anything, he, Dover, had every intention of being in on it, right from the beginning.

'By the way,' he asked elaborately off-hand, 'who was it who mentioned seeing Juliet with green nail varnish?'

'It was Eulalia Hoppold, sir. You remember she talked about telling Eve Counter to get rid of Juliet, no matter what her father thought, and she talked about black babies, green nail varnish and stiletto heels.'

'Oh,' said Dover doubtfully, 'Eulalia Hoppold?'

'You see what this means, sir? If my theory's correct and Juliet wasn't wearing green nail varnish until, say, after five o'clock on the Tuesday afternoon, then Eulalia Hoppold must have seen her *after* she got back to Irlam Old Hall at eleven o'clock that night.'

'The Hoppold woman might have been in Creedon too on Tuesday afternoon and seen Juliet then.'

'Well, in that case, sir, why didn't she tell us about it? There'd be nothing suspicious about that, would there? And, don't forget, we've already caught her out once in a lie – about spending Tuesday night with Bogolepov in his bungalow. This'd be the second time she's given us the wrong story, and why should she if she's nothing to hide?'

'Hm,' said Dover, and sighed. 'But if she had anything to do with Juliet's death – and, let's face it, it sounds a bit far-fetched, doesn't it? – what about her alibi? She spent the night with Bogo-lepov. They both say that and we've got Maxine Chubb-Smith as an independent witness.'

'Well, obviously, they're both in it together!'

'Oh, 'strewth,' said Dover wearily, 'I don't like the sound of that. What's the motive? And the same old bloody question – what did they do with the body?'

'Well, there's a motive of sorts, sir. Maybe Juliet found out about Eulalia's affair with Boris and threatened to tell her hus-band. Just Juliet's line of country, if you ask me.'

'Hell!' groaned Dover. 'It sounds a bit thin, doesn't it? By the look of her I shouldn't think it's the first time Miss Hoppold has indulged in a little extra-marital activity, and I shouldn't think it'll be the last either. D'you see her, a woman like that, com-mitting an elaborate murder, just to stop her husband finding out? Because, frankly, I don't. And what about Bogolepov? I'm damned if I see him risking his neck just to protect the fair Eulalia's good name, if any. And anyhow, let's get down to a few brass tacks! How did they do it, and where's the body?'

'How about this, sir? They know roughly what time Juliet gets back most Tuesday evenings – that was common knowledge at Irlam Old Hall. They waylay her on the drive and kill her. Then they get Sir John's wheel chair out of the shed and use it to cart the body off in.'

'Brilliant!' snorted Dover down his nose. 'And where's the corpse now?'

'I don't know, but it must be somewhere.'

'And what about all this kidnapping palaver?'

'Well, they organized that too – that was just to put us off the scent. Whatever else that scheme was, it was clever. You've got to admit that. And there's no denying that both Bogolepov and Miss Hoppold are clever people – they're just the type to think up a kidnapping ploy like that. As I see it, it was just a red herring – they never intended to collect that money. And you've got to admit, sir, there must be a woman in it somewhere. No man would know the layout of the ladies' convenience in the Market Square, and he wouldn't be able to collect it, even if they ever meant to.'

'Well, you may be right there,' admitted Dover grudgingly, 'but what about the ransom letter? It was originally posted in

London at lunch-time on Saturday, right? Well, neither Eulalia Hoppold nor Bogolepov could have posted that letter personally, because, if you remember, we saw both of 'em, just before lunch, and after. Of all the people in the case who couldn't possibly have been in London at the vital time, they're the outstanding ones.'

'Perhaps the kidnapping note had nothing to do with the murder at all?' suggested MacGregor, clinging valiantly to his theory. 'Maybe it was somebody who just wanted an easy five hundred quid or a good laugh, or something. After all, people have tried to pull phoney tricks like that before, haven't they?'

Dover shook his head. 'The finger-print,' he reminded MacGregor, 'that was Juliet Rugg's and she was dead when it was taken. I don't see how anybody else except the murderer could have sent that letter.'

'Maybe the finger-print boys were wrong? Perhaps she wasn't dead when it was made? That would change everything, wouldn't it? There'd be hundreds of ways of getting hold of her finger-print while she was still alive. I mean, I know they're experts and all that, but how can they be sure?'

'I dunno,' admitted Dover, 'it's something to do with sweat, I think. When a living person makes a dab there are traces of sweat. Well, apparently, when you're dead you stop sweating, which seems reasonable enough. The chaps in London analysed the ink that was used to make Juliet's finger-print and they just ran a routine check on the sweat as well. There wasn't any. In any case, if she isn't dead, we're right back where we started from, aren't we?'

'All right' – Sergeant MacGregor was not to be put off for long – 'how about this for getting the letter posted – you just send it to an accomplice or even an innocent friend and ask him to put it in the box for you. Why, Eulalia Hoppold might have got her husband to do it.'

'I've been thinking about that,' said Dover, gloomily taking MacGregor's last cigarette, 'but I reckon it's too risky. Sir John Counter's name's been in the newspapers and so's Irlam Old Hall. Now, I know the letter was sent to his bank, but what would you think if one of your pals sent you a letter to post to a man who lives practically next door to him? Course, there could be a whole gang of 'em, with associates in London and what-have-you – but why on earth should a gang be involved in the killing of someone as insignificant as Juliet Rugg?'

'God only knows!' agreed MacGregor morosely. 'I must admit, I think it's a local crime, don't you? Juliet doesn't seem to have any significance outside Irlam Old Hall, and Creedon, and the village.'

Dover rose unwillingly to his feet. 'These chairs are damned hard,' he grumbled, 'let's go into the bar parlour. They've got armchairs in there.'

MacGregor got some more cigarettes and joined Dover, who was sprawled out comfortably and looked as though he was settled for the rest of the day.

'What's the programme now, sir?'

Dover sighed resentfully. A policeman's work is never done.

'I think you'd better get back to Irlam Old Hall and see if you can find out whether any of 'em did, or could have, nipped up to London to post that letter. Shouldn't take you long. You'd better check all the people who live in the flats too. Oh, and Mrs Rugg. And Gordon Pilley and his wife – you can get the local boys to check them. We might as well cover the lot while we're at it.

'You can ask about this celluloid stencil thing at the same time – you know, the one the ransom letter was written with. You never know, we might be lucky and find somebody who owns one.

'When you've finished you can come back here and pick me up and we'll go into Creedon and see the girls in the chemist's shop about this green nail varnish.'

'I could ask Eve whether she ever saw Juliet wearing the stuff.'

Dover gave him a sharp look. 'You could,' he admitted, 'but tell her to keep her trap shut! If there is anything in this green and red nail-varnish idea, it's a very delicate thread. And it won't take much to snap it, so just you watch out where you put your big flat feet!'

'But if we can prove that Juliet never wore green nail varnish before late on Tuesday afternoon, we've got our man, haven't we? Eulalia Hoppold, I mean?'

'Look, MacGregor,' said Dover with heavy patience, 'if you go yapping your head off about green nail varnish all over Irlam Old Hall, Eulalia Hoppold may get wind of it and start thinking.

Once she realizes she's made a slip, if she has made one, she'll cover up immediately and we'll be up against a blank wall.'

'But how can she cover up, sir? We know what she said at the time.'

Dover sighed fretfully. 'My God, I can think of a dozen things she could say. She could deny she ever said it in the first place – after all it's her word against a bit of your private shorthand scribble, isn't it? Or she could say it was a slip of the tongue and she didn't mean green at all. Or she could say she's colour-blind and can't tell the difference anyhow.

'Just you take a hold on yourself, my lad! Even if all the castles you're building on a bottle of green nail varnish are true, you couldn't hang a cat on that sort of evidence, much less drag anyone into a court of law. It's just, at best, a teeny weeny pointer, and don't you forget it!'

'Very good, sir,' said MacGregor huffily. 'Do you want me to do any more checking on the oil? I could find out which of the tenants have got cans of this type of oil and … '

'No,' said Dover, 'we'll leave that one for a bit. We don't want to show our hand too much at this stage. You might tell your girl-friend and this Bondy fellow not to go around discussing it.'

'I've already done that, sir.'

'Good! Well, get moving!'

'Are you going to stay here, sir?'

'I am.'

'Perhaps you wouldn't mind taking a message if the lab. people come through with a report on the exact make of the oil used on Sir John's wheel chair?'

'Oh, all right,' grumbled the chief inspector, putting on his 'I-don't-know-why-everything-is-left-to-me' expression. 'And you just remember, Sergeant, don't start trying to clap a pair of hand-cuffs on Eulalia Hoppold if she looks sideways at you.'

'But you do think she's got something to do with it, don't you, sir?'

'If I were a betting man,' said Dover pompously, leaning back in his chair and closing his eyes, 'which I'm not, I'd give you shorter odds on a few of the others. There's your fancy bit' – he opened his eyes to see how this was received – 'for one. She's no alibi. She's the one who says Juliet never entered the house on

Tuesday night. She, better than anyone, knows all about the wheel chair, where it's kept and that the wheels were squeaking. And' – he waggled a fat finger – 'she's got not one but two motives, and damned strong ones at that. Juliet could have got this doctor-lover struck off the Register and she was trying to drag Eve Counter's father to the altar. Sex and money, my lad – the basis for most crimes, as you well know! And then there's the question of this ransom letter. We may not know how that letter was posted but we do know that whoever sent it knew the address of Sir John's bank. Who better than his one and only daughter? Then there was all this business of rushing forward to pay the ransom money. Very fishy, that! But, of course, if she knew the kidnapping was all a red herring anyhow, she'd be the first one to offer to pay the money – just to put us off the scent. I mean, she wasn't risking anything, was she? She'd know her five hundred pounds would be perfectly safe.' He thought moodily for a moment. 'I think you'd better get the name and address of this doctor chap. If we can't pick up a lead anywhere else we'll have to have a word with him.'

'Oh, sir!' Reproach was written in every line of MacGregor's handsome face.

'Well, dammit!' yelped Dover. 'You don't expect me to turn a blind eye to murder, do you? Just because you've taken a passing fancy to one of the birds in the case! I'm telling you again, Eve Counter's quite high on my list. And if you're going to bump somebody off, I can't imagine a better accomplice than a doctor, can you? We still haven't found the body – well, I can think of plenty of ways in which a doctor would help there!'

'Yes, sir.'

'Anyhow, you don't have to ask the girl herself. You can get the name and address from Sir John. You don't need to tell him why you want 'em.'

'No, sir. But, surely, you're not serious about this, sir?'

'For God's sake, Sergeant, she's a possible, same as the others! There's Mrs Chubb-Smith, for example, either with or without that shiftless son of hers. They've got a motive – Juliet was blackmailing them and likely to start again. Sir John must have had business transactions with Mrs Chubb-Smith over that house. She's bound to know the address of his bank. Neither she nor her son's got an alibi – although, if you remember, he tried to make us believe at first that he had. Both of 'em would know where the wheel chair was kept and my guess is that Michael Chubb-Smith might well have enough intelligence, and cheek, to cope with that false kidnapping set-up – and find somewhere clever to hide Juliet's body as well.

'Then there's William Bondy. We know nothing about his relationship with Juliet Rugg except what he's told us. He says he wouldn't touch her with a barge-pole, but he's a man and she's a woman, or was, and we all know what that can lead to! He's no fool – he's bright enough to have done this job. There's a good chance he knows the address of Sir John's bank and he certainly knows all about that wheel chair. And when it comes to the actual killing, he'd probably be the most capable one of the lot. After all, he's been trained and he's no doubt had a bit of practice in his time. Whichever way you look at it, he's been a professional killer all his life. He'd most likely have less scruples than anybody about removing Juliet from the scene.'

Dover paused for breath and scratched his stomach vigorously.

'Anybody else, sir?' asked MacGregor, a trifle overwhelmed with all this.

'Well,' said Dover, 'apart from your favourites, Hoppold and Bogolepov, I've still got my eye on Mrs Rugg and Gordon Pilley. And what about Amy Freel? She let it out that she was a keen student of detective stories – and she tried to "collaborate" with us, remember? And if there's one thing that stands out a mile in this whole damned case it's the' – he groped for the word – 'bloody ingenuity of the thing!' He smirked triumphantly. 'It's got cleverness written all over it – typical amateur stuff. Oh, I know your professional villain sometimes thinks up a fancy scheme, but you've got to admit, generally he goes in with a crowbar and a cosh – straightforward like. No real crook'd produce anything as elaborate as this lot, but somebody like Amy Freel might. You can get lots of smart ideas from detective stories – most of 'em won't work for a minute in real life, but they might, with a bit of luck, give people like us a minor headache or two to begin with. Let's face it, there are one or two details in this case we haven't got cleared up yet.'

MacGregor's jaw dropped fractionally at this majestic understatement of the extent of their difficulties. 'But, sir,' he said, 'you don't really think Amy Freel had anything to do with murdering

Juliet Rugg, do you? Why, she's no motive and, good heavens, physically it's surely quite beyond her.'

'She's as likely a suspect as your Eulalia Hoppold anyhow!' snapped Dover, losing patience with the whole thing. 'And if you're going to give the Hoppold woman an accomplice, well – how about Amy in conjunction with her brother, Basil? He looks capable of anything! Or what about three of 'em – Amy Freel, Colonel Bing and Miss McLintock, banding together to rid Irlam Old Hall of one who has brought shame and disgrace on her sex?' Dover chuckled richly at this thought. 'It's not a bad idea, you know! Working together, I reckon that trio could manage anything they set their minds on!'

'Yes, sir,' said MacGregor, who disapproved of this sort of frivolity – after all, it was a murder case. 'Well, I'll be getting off to Irlam Old Hall now, shall I, sir?'

Dover's lower lip stuck out sulkily. 'Yes, you do that,' he growled.

As MacGregor strode out of the room, the chief inspector pulled another chair up, put his feet on it and let his head drop back comfortably. Then he gently closed his eyes.

'Toffee-nosed young bugger!' he murmured softly to himself.

Chapter Thirteen

IT was nearly twelve o'clock when Sergeant MacGregor got back to The Two Fiddlers. He found Dover wide awake and ensconced in the bar, tucking into the Long Herbert again. The landlord had offered him a drink on the house and Dover, not surprisingly, had accepted it. Sergeant MacGregor arrived just in time to pay for the next round.

'Get anything?' asked Dover, toying idly with a tin ash-tray.

MacGregor grimly took the hint and pulled out his cigarette-case. 'Not a damned thing,' he said. 'I'm sorry I've been such a long time but I thought it was worth counterchecking to be absolutely sure. There's nobody up at Irlam Old Hall who could possibly have been in London on Saturday. You can take my word for that! Mrs Rugg wasn't there either. Nor was Gordon Pilley nor was his wife. I've just checked with the local police.'

'Hm,' said Dover, and turned for consolation to his fresh pint. 'What about this celluloid stencil thing?'

'Most of 'em had never even heard of one and none of 'em could remember seeing one.'

'Hm.' Dover thoughtfully took a long drink and belched gently. 'What about the green nail varnish? Did you ask your girl-friend about it?'

'She wasn't there!' snapped MacGregor. 'I'd forgotten she was going into Creedon to collect the ransom money. But I did ask Sir John. He was pretty certain she'd never worn green nail varnish, but I think we'll want something a bit stronger than that. Incidentally, he was asking when we were going to get some results. Said the Lord Lieutenant of the county was an old friend of his. Sort of hinted he might mention we didn't seem to be getting on very quickly.'

'Oh,' said Dover with a sneer, 'and what's the Lord Lieutenant of the county going to do about it, for God's sake?'

'He's an old friend of the Assistant Commissioner.'

'Oh,' said Dover, 'well, we'll try this green nail-varnish theory and see if that gets us anywhere. We'll have lunch here first and then go into Creedon. Oh, they rang through about the oil on the wheel chair. Apparently it's some stuff called "Lubrykate". Just ordinary household oil, as you might say. Anybody might have it.'

'They probably all have,' agreed MacGregor glumly. This, he thought, with not unjustified pessimism, was going to be another typical 'Dover' case. Magnificent inaction and no results. He didn't give a damn about the chief inspector, but it just didn't do a young, enthusiastic and rising detective sergeant any good at all to be associated with a seemingly unending stream of failures. Perhaps if he put another request in to the Assistant Commissioner, tactful but a bit stronger than the last time ...

* * *

At half-past two the police car ambled carefully into Creedon and stopped right outside the chemist's shop. There was no trouble about parking. The Market Square was empty.

Dover gazed around him at the vacant scene.

'You bloody fool!' he snarled at Sergeant MacGregor in disgust. 'It's early closing day!'

The chemist's shop was shut.

'Perhaps he lives in the flat over the shop,' suggested MacGregor sheepishly – he'd forgotten it was Thursday. 'Shall I try?'

'You can do what you bloody well like!' Dover's tone was heavy with implied menace.

Sergeant MacGregor was lucky. The chemist was in and Dover, still sulkily fuming, stumped upstairs to interview him.

'We really wanted to speak to your girl assistants,' he began, with his usual charm of manner, 'but I suppose you'll do.'

'Oh dear,' said the chemist anxiously, 'I do hope they haven't done anything silly again. They're very nice girls, you know, good-natured, willing, generous to a fault, but they are a little bit casual at times.'

'Indeed?' sniffed Dover with raised eyebrows. 'I should have thought that was very dangerous where poisons and drugs are concerned.'

'Good heavens!' The chemist threw up his hands in mild horror. 'I don't let them get near the dispensing side of the business! I wouldn't have a customer left alive by the end of the week, if I did. They're only supposed to deal with the cosmetic trade and a few harmless things like hot-water bottles and rolls of sticking plaster. Even so, you wouldn't believe the mess-ups they get into.'

'Wouldn't I?' said Dover.

'Do you know what one of them did? Dawn it was – just about a month ago – and she's the reliable one of the pair. It lost me a very good customer, I don't mind telling you. It was very careless of her, very careless, but I don't think it was anything more than that because as far as I know she'd never even seen Lady Williams before. And after all, when you come to think of it, it was as much her fault as anyone else's. She's one of these people who doesn't think medicine does you any good unless it's got a nasty taste. You see, what happened was this. Lady W. came in and asked Dawn for some throat pastilles. Well, Dawn got the boxes mixed up and instead of throat pastilles she gave her ... '

'Now just a minute, Mr What's-your-name!' Dover broke in impatiently.

'Simkins, Walter William Simkins.'

'Well, Mr Simkins, we're really in rather a hurry so if you wouldn't mind just answering a few straight questions as briefly and directly as you can ... Now then, green nail varnish! I understand your shop-girls sold a bottle of green nail varnish to Juliet Rugg last Tuesday week, on the afternoon of the day she disappeared.'

'Well, I believe they did but, of course, I didn't come back into the shop until just before Miss Rugg left, so I don't know myself exactly what she bought.'

'What we really want to find out,' the chief inspector went on, 'is whether or not it was the first time she'd bought green nail varnish. Do you know if she purchased any from you before?'

Mr Simkins thought for a moment. 'Well, I'm pretty certain she hadn't bought any from me because, if I remember correctly, that order had only come in that morning. A traveller had called on – yes, that's right – on Monday, the day before, and the girls made me order a dozen bottles. I wasn't too keen because I couldn't think who was going to buy green nail varnish in Creedon, but Dawn and Shirley said it was the latest teenager rage and, well, business is business. We got the dozen bottles first post the next morning and I can't say I was surprised to hear that Juliet Rugg had bought one.'

'Did you know Miss Rugg then?'

'Oh lord, yes! And her mother, too. I've known 'em both as customers for years – and some very revealing things they've bought in my shop, too, I can tell you. And Juliet often used to pop in to get things for old Sir John as well as herself.'

'You didn't by any chance speak to her, did you?' asked Dover, who felt that any straw was worth clutching at at this stage.

'Well, of course I did,' said Mr Simkins in surprise. 'I asked her to give a message to Mr Bogolepov when she got back to Irlam Old Hall.'

Dover and MacGregor exchanged glances. Dover swallowed hard. 'You asked her to give a message to Mr Bogolepov?' he repeated tensely. 'What about?'

Mr Simkins looked a bit embarrassed. 'Well, I make up a weekly prescription for Mr Bogolepov – it's all above board and properly authorized, you know – and he usually comes in and collects it on Wednesday mornings. Well, now, last week the stuff hadn't arrived from my suppliers and I didn't want to give Mr Bogolepov the trouble of coming in all this way for nothing. He's rather an awkward sort of chap and of course he's a bit anxious to have the stuff on time ... '

'It's all right,' said Dover, 'we know he's a drug addict. He got his supplies from you, did he?'

'Yes, but only those he was entitled to on prescription,' Mr Simkins hastened to point out. 'He was properly registered and all that. Well, I was wondering how to get a message to him – he's not on the phone – when I saw Miss Rugg. I asked her if she'd pop in and tell him to come in on Friday instead of Wednesday as his prescription wouldn't be ready until then. Of course I didn't tell her what it was.'

'And what did she say?'

'Well, she just said, all right, she would.'

There was a pause while Dover summoned up enough courage to ask the vital question. He cleared his throat nervously.

'And did Mr Bogolepov come in on Friday?' he croaked casually.

Mr Simkins thought for a minute again. 'Well, yes, now you

mention it, he did. I remember handing the packet over to him. I always have it made up ready and I always serve him myself. It was Friday morning all right. No doubt about it. The supplier didn't deliver it until quite late on Thursday afternoon anyhow, and I was beginning to wonder if it was ever coming.'

'Did you say anything to him?'

'Oh, I just apologized for the hold-up and he was quite nice about it, said he had to come into Creedon that day to post a parcel or something anyhow. He was quite pleasant about the whole thing.'

'But why on earth,' asked Sergeant MacGregor, 'didn't you tell us about this before?'

Mr Simkins looked surprised and even hurt. He produced the classic answer. 'Well,' he said, 'you never asked me.'

Dover and MacGregor climbed thoughtfully back into the waiting police car. Both were a little dazed.

'We've got him, sir, haven't we?' asked MacGregor in breathless excitement. 'I felt all along he was mixed up in it somewhere.'

'Yes,' agreed Dover with a deep sigh, 'it certainly looks as though we're on to something, at last. But, just sit tight a minute while we sort out what we have got.'

'Well, first of all,' MacGregor pointed out, 'we've cleared up the green nail varnish. Eulalia Hoppold described Juliet as wearing green nail varnish. Now we know for certain she could only have seen the green nail varnish if she saw Juliet *after* her return to Irlam Old Hall on Tuesday night.'

'Always remembering that even the fact that she did see her doesn't make Eulalia guilty of murder,' grumbled Dover.

'No,' agreed MacGregor, 'but it's significant that in spite of having been found out in one lie – about where she was that night – she is still persisting in another.'

Dover nodded his head. 'Let's have another cigarette, my lad,' he said, and waited patiently while MacGregor dug out his case and lighter. 'Now then,' he went on, not going to be outdone in constructive analysis by a blooming sergeant, 'if Eulalia Hoppold is concerned in any way in Juliet Rugg's disappearance and death, then Boris Bogolepov is involved too, because they provide an alibi for each other. 'Strewth!' said Dover crossly. 'I wonder if they let us drag that alibi out of 'em deliberately? It made it seem much more effective than if they'd nearly broken their necks trying to tell us about it.'

'I wouldn't be surprised,' agreed MacGregor. 'In any case, it was a nice little ace to keep tucked up their sleeves.'

'Mind you, Boris Bogolepov mucked things up a bit. He was so keen to impress us that his vices were dope and drink not women, so that we wouldn't connect him up with Juliet, that it looked a bit odd when he had to claim he was Eulalia's lover. Now, he's lost out both ways. If Eulalia's his girl-friend, so might Juliet have been, and there may be a motive there. And if he's not interested in women, what the hell were he and Eulalia doing together all night?'

'And, thanks to Mr Simkins, we can now tie Boris in with Juliet independently of his connection with Eulalia.'

'We can, indeed,' said Dover, 'let's try and reconstruct what happened. Simkins asks Juliet to call and give a message to Bogolepov when she gets back to Irlam Old Hall. She's to tell him not to come into Creedon on the following, Wednesday, morning – his usual day – but to call on Friday because his dope is going to arrive late from the wholesalers or whoever's supposed to send it to Simkins.'

'And we know from Simkins that Bogolepov got the message because that week, instead of coming in on the Wednesday, he came, as requested, on the Friday!' Sergeant MacGregor was getting quite excited.

'Yes,' said Dover sourly, 'and we don't only know it from Simkins either. Damn and blast it! We knew it right from the beginning if only' – he sighed moodily – 'we'd recognized its significance.'

'I don't follow you, sir,' said MacGregor.

'Well, get your blasted notebook out!' snapped Dover. 'It's all in there! I should have thought you'd have picked it up when you were supposed to be studying all hours of the night. Remember when I interviewed Bogolepov the first time and we had to listen to all that drivel about what a rotten life he'd had? Well, he told us then he was a dope addict and that he collected the stuff under the National Health once a week from Creedon. And, if my memory serves me correctly, he actually said he went in on Wednesday mornings.'

'Yes, that's right, sir,' said MacGregor, hunting through the pages like fury. 'Yes, I've got it here. We saw him on the Saturday morning, but we didn't know that he'd collected the stuff on Friday that particular week.'

'Oh yes, we did,' said Dover flatly, 'Miss McLintock told us.'

'Miss McLintock?'

'Yes. When we were talking to Colonel Bing in her sitting-room on Friday morning, the day we arrived down here, Miss McLintock came in. Remember where she'd been?'

'Oh, yes! She'd just got back from Creedon. All that rigmarole about library books and posting a parcel.'

'That's it,' said Dover, 'and you remember who she'd seen in the post office?'

'Boris Bogolepov!' MacGregor's excitement grew. 'He was posting a parcel, too. That must be the one he mentioned to Mr Simkins. Miss McLintock read the address, didn't she? He was sending it to some refugee organization.'

'My God!' exclaimed Dover, his jaw dropping in astonishment. 'I've had an idea!'

There didn't seem any appropriate or tactful rejoinder to this statement, so MacGregor observed a respectful silence.

'My God!' said Dover again in a voice of awe. 'I believe I've got it!'

'Got what, sir?'

'The ransom note, you fool! How they could have got it posted in London without ever leaving Irlam Old Hall! That silly old cow, Miss McLintock, and the parcel! It's so simple and with that address to Sir John's bank on it, it's nearly a hundred per cent safe!'

'Miss McLintock and the parcel, sir? You don't mean she's involved in it, too?'

'Oh, wake up, MacGregor!' barked Dover irritably. 'Of course, she's not involved in it. It was just thinking of her that gave me the idea. You remember all that drivel she talked about her hobby? Saving the damned fool things she found in her blasted library books?'

'Yes, she had a little "museum", didn't she?'

'That's right. Now, MacGregor, use your brains for once! Suppose you found a stamped and addressed envelope in a library book – what would you do with it?'

'Well, I'd post it, sir. Anybody would, wouldn't they? But Miss

McLintock wasn't in London on Saturday, so how could she have posted the ransom note?'

'She didn't!' yelped Dover. 'The letter was in the bloody parcel, don't you see?'

'Er, no, sir!' admitted MacGregor, privately thinking that this was not entirely his fault.

'Look,' said Dover, trying to be patient about it, 'let's suppose Boris Bogolepov croaked Juliet Rugg. How and why, we don't know, but he's killed her. Now, just to put everybody off the scent, he thinks up this kidnapping idea. Right? He writes out the ransom letter and sticks the dead girl's finger-print on it. Then he addresses the envelope to Sir John Counter, care of his bank. Then he bundles up a parcel of old clothes ... 'Strewth! They probably were Juliet's! It'd be a much safer way of getting rid of them than trying to burn them, besides, he hadn't got a boiler in that bungalow, had he? I'm pretty certain it was all electric central heating – probably hadn't even got a fireplace. Well, that doesn't matter now. He bundles up a parcel of old clothes and sticks the letter inside. When he goes into Creedon on the Friday morning, he posts the parcel to this refugee organization – in London. Now, with a bit of luck the parcel would arrive in London on Saturday morning. Somebody opens it, finds the letter, thinks it's been packed by accident and, like any decent citizen, when they go off to lunch they slip it in the nearest pillar-box. There's no Irlam Old Hall address on it to catch their eye – just Sir John Counter's name – and the odds are they'd never link that up with some fat girl who was missing from home a couple of hundred miles away. The bank would get the letter Monday morning, readdress it and send it on Monday afternoon.' Dover paused and mopped his brow. 'How about that for a piece of reconstruction, my lad?'

'It was brilliant!' said MacGregor, who'd hardly been able to believe his ears. 'It was just brilliant, sir!'

'Yes, not bad, I reckon,' agreed Dover with great self-satisfaction. 'You need imagination to be a successful detective, you know, Sergeant! And a good logical brain, of course.'

'Well, that's that, isn't it, sir?' MacGregor closed his notebook. 'What are you going to do now? Get a warrant?'

Dover frowned horribly and began to gnaw at a bit of loose skin near his thumb-nail. 'I'm sure we've got the answer,' he said doubtfully, 'but we haven't got an ounce of proof. Supposing Bogolepov and the Hoppold woman both saw Juliet Rugg on Tuesday night – it still doesn't prove they killed her! There may be some quite normal explanation. And this letter business, it's only a theory.' He chewed his thumb a bit more.

'Well, we can easily check the ransom letter bit, sir,' proffered Sergeant MacGregor. 'Miss McLintock may even remember the name and address, but, even if she doesn't, there won't be all that many refugee places that get bundles of old clothes. We can get the London boys to go round the lot and ask whether anybody remembers posting a letter.'

'All right,' said Dover grudgingly, 'you'd better try that straight away. Be very useful if we could tie up that letter definitely with Bogolepov – but I'd be surprised if he's been such a fool as to put his name and address on the parcel.'

'Well, you never know your luck,' said MacGregor with the unquenchable optimism of youth.

'Hm,' grunted Dover, 'I know mine, all right!' He sighed. 'Well, we'll wait and see what results you get from the refugee organization side of things. It may give us the whole case in a nutshell and we'll have something to go on that'll stand up to examination in court. If it doesn't – well, I dunno what we can do, other than poke around a bit more. At least we know where to look now.'

'We could go and see Bogolepov,' suggested MacGregor.

'Yes,' agreed Dover, 'I don't think he'll be a very tough nut to crack, all things considered. If the worst comes to the worst, we can always try thumping the truth out of him. I've been itching to get my boot up his backside ever since I first clapped eyes on him.'

'You don't mean that we should go and beat him up, do you, sir?' MacGregor had heard some horrifying stories about Dover's rather unorthodox methods but this was going a bit too far. He began to sweat gently at the prospect of standing up in court to justify a confession obtained by the toe of Dover's boot.

'Why not?' asked Dover in surprise. 'He's a murderer, isn't he? You can't be too squeamish in this job, MacGregor. You've got to use your fists as well as your brains, you know! As long,' he added piously, 'as you're careful not to leave any marks.'

Chapter Fourteen

UNFORTUNATELY, the worst nearly came to the worst. Chief Inspector Dover retired to the local police headquarters in Creedon to wait while Sergeant MacGregor got on with the work. His unexpected arrival struck fear and horror into the hearts of the entire staff, not excluding the Chief Constable himself, who paled at the thought that the episode of the ladies' convenience in the Market Square might be re-created in some even more devastating form.

Dover's brooding, scowling face did little to restore morale. For want of somewhere better to go he descended on the local C.I.D. inspector and caught that unfortunate man, once again, in the process of filling in his football pools.

Dover sniffed. 'Glad to see you can spare the time,' he commented nastily, and installing himself in the leather armchair, the only comfortable one in the room, he propped his feet up on the radiator, tipped his bowler hat over his eyes and promptly fell asleep.

The local inspector gazed miserably at him and then, with a guilty movement, slipped his football pools out of sight under the blotter. He took one of the official files out of his in-tray and, after another sidelong glance at the sleeping Dover, he began, rather hopelessly, to read it.

An hour later the Chief Constable popped his head round the door. Dover was still well away and snoring valiantly through his open mouth. Mr Bartlett tiptoed into the room.

'What's he doing here?' he whispered.

The local inspector shrugged his shoulders.

The Chief Constable leaned closer. 'Damned funny way to conduct a murder case, if you ask me,' he breathed. 'I thought they were supposed to have got a lead somewhere. Has he said anything to you?'

The inspector silently shook his head. Both men stared at Dover.

'Oh well, none of our business, I suppose,' said the Chief Constable, his words barely audible. 'What I really came in for was to ask you about Tottenham. How about them for a draw this week?'

The local inspector shook his head again – it was a respectful reproof.

'Oh?' said Mr Bartlett, and with a sigh tiptoed out of the room, closing the door noiselessly behind him.

When five o'clock came the local inspector began to get worried. It was his time for knocking off but he didn't like leaving Dover fast asleep in his chair without so much as a word. He didn't fancy waking him up to wish him good night, either. Fortunately the arrival of Sergeant MacGregor delivered him from his dilemma.

'Excuse me, sir,' the sergeant began courteously, 'have you seen ... Oh, there he is.'

Dover choked on a final snore, coughed unpleasantly and woke up.

'And about time, too!' he snarled at his sergeant. 'What did you do? Walk to London and back again?'

He caught sight of the local inspector, who was hovering uncertainly by his desk.

'What the hell are you doing here?' Dover demanded.

The inspector jumped. 'Oh, nothing, nothing at all, sir!' he gabbled, grabbing his hat and coat. 'I was just going!'

'Good!' snapped Dover. 'Don't forget your football pools!'

The local inspector made a confused exit.

Dover rose unwillingly from his easy-chair and went to sit behind the desk. 'Well,' he remarked in passing, with a contemptuous nod at the door through which the inspector had gone, 'looks as though there's hope for you yet, doesn't it, Sergeant?'

Sergeant MacGregor smiled, faintly.

'Well, we've had a bit of joy from London, sir,' he announced, 'but not enough to solve all our difficulties. Luckily Miss McLintock remembered the name of the refugee organization – apparently she's sent a few things there herself from time to time. I phoned through to the Yard and they sent a chap round right away. Most of the staff there are voluntary part-timers but the appeals organizer, or whoever it is, is a regular full-time person and she remembers the letter being found by one of the women who were unpacking the parcels on Saturday morning.

The woman just handed it in to the office – they quite often find things which have been packed by mistake and this is the normal procedure – and the organizer woman posted it herself. She remembered the pencilled address. So we can tie that letter up quite definitely with a parcel posted to the refugee organization, but I'm afraid that's about all.'

'What about the parcel itself?'

'No joy there I'm afraid, sir. Apparently this is what happens. When the parcels come in they unpack them and sort out the clothes into big sacks – one for trousers, one for overcoats, one for children's clothes and so on. If the sender's included his name and address, they write it down in a book and he gets a printed thank-you letter in due course. The Yard chap checked the book. No sign of Bogolepov's name.'

'What about the paper the parcel was wrapped in?'

'They save all the paper and string and sell it for what it's worth to the pulp merchants. It's collected monthly. Unfortunately last Monday was the day for collecting it, so there's no hope in that direction.'

'Well, how about the clothes themselves? Don't tell me they've been shipped out to darkest Africa already.'

MacGregor grinned. 'No, sir. There's just a faint hope that we might be able to get our hands on them. Everything they get is sorted out again into sizes and things like that and then they examine it all to see if it wants washing or mending or anything. I gave the Yard a list of what Juliet was wearing and they're going to search all through the stuff and see if they can find it. Mr Pilley provided us with an excellent description, if you remember, so they shouldn't have any difficulty in picking it out – not in those sizes. I suggested they put a couple of policewomen on the job. They'll be better at it than the men.'

Dover grunted. 'Well, it all helps, I suppose, but I'd feel much happier if we'd something a bit firmer to go on.'

'Surely this is enough, sir?'

The chief inspector blew disgustedly down his nose. 'It's all very circumstantial,' he grumbled, as though it was MacGregor's fault. 'We can prove that whoever wrote that ransom letter had, at least, access to Juliet Rugg's dead body. We can prove that the letter was sent in a parcel to this refugee place. We can probably prove that her clothes were sent there, too.'

'And we can prove that Boris Bogolepov sent the parcel,' MacGregor chipped in. 'What more do you want?'

'We can prove that Bogolepov sent *a* parcel,' corrected Dover, 'we can establish a strong possibility that his parcel was the one containing the ransom letter and Juliet's clothes, but we haven't actually got proof that it was.'

'But what about the message he got via Juliet from the chemist?'

'Proves that he saw Juliet after she got back to Irlam Old Hall on that Tuesday night. Very suspicious, I grant you, but it's a damned long way from proving he killed her. No, there's no doubt about it, what we've got is a bit on the thin side. I'd be much happier if I knew why he'd done it and what he did with the body after he'd done it. We still don't know a blind thing about that.'

There was a depressing silence.

'Oh, there's one other minor point, sir,' said MacGregor, 'I think we can prove Bogolepov knew the address of Sir John's bank. Do you remember he said he'd sold Sir John a six-speed electric razor? We can easily find out if the old man paid by cheque – if he did, well, that's how our friend Boris got the bank's address in London.'

'Yes,' said Dover with a shrug, 'well, every little helps, doesn't it? Even if it's not much.'

'I suppose the crux of the matter is, sir,' began MacGregor, frowning in concentration, 'Juliet's dead body. If we could find out where that is, or what's happened to it … '

'Well, I'm damned if I can see how he's disposed of it. He hasn't even got a car.'

'No, but Miss Hoppold has.'

'A two-seater sports!' snorted Dover. 'And Juliet Rugg weighed sixteen stone! Can you imagine anybody humping that much dead meat around in a tiny car? Besides, Miss What's-her-name – Amy Freel – said that nobody took a car out on the Wednesday. Of course,' he added with a sigh, 'she may be wrong, but even if they got it away from Irlam Old Hall, where the devil is it now?'

'How about getting a search warrant for Bogolepov's house, and for Miss Hoppold's for that matter?'

Dover sighed crossly. 'I suppose we'll have to, though where on earth you can hide a dead body in an all-electric bungalow,

I'm damned if I know! Of course, they might just have stuck it in a cupboard – that's been done before, heaven knows – but it's a terrible risk and those two have kept their heads pretty well so far. And what about the smell? Juliet's been dead – how long? – nine days? And all that fat! Gawd, it doesn't bear thinking about!'

He sighed again. 'Oh well, we shall have to do something. We'd better go and pay a call on Mister Bogolepov and see if we can get anything out of him, one way or another. We'll get a search warrant as well. Can't do any harm.'

It was well after seven o'clock when the two detectives, armed with their search warrants, arrived once again at Irlam Old Hall. For some reason known only to himself Dover decided to go to the back door of Bogolepov's bungalow. There was a light on in the kitchen and a radio was playing softly.

Dover thumped morosely on the door. After quite a long delay – Dover's fist was already raised for the second assault – it was opened and Boris Bogolepov's drawn, handsome face peered out into the darkness.

'Good evening, sir,' said Dover, very formal. 'May we come in?'

Boris frowned. 'We are just about to have dinner. It is not very convenient. Perhaps you will come back later, yes?'

Dover inserted his boot in the closing door.

'And perhaps we won't,' he growled. 'We want to have a word with you now, if you don't mind, sir.'

Boris shrugged his shoulders. 'Very well,' he said, and turned back into the room.

Dover and MacGregor followed him into the kitchen.

'Well, well! How very romantic!' Dover, bowler hat still on his head, leisurely surveyed the scene. It was not quite what he had come to expect from the Bogolepov menage, though he was not surprised to find Eulalia Hoppold forming part of the decor. She was standing by the electric cooker and, as Dover and MacGregor came in, she pushed a casserole back in the oven and impatiently slammed the door shut.

'Well, well!' said Dover again. 'We seem to have interrupted a little celebration.'

The kitchen table, rather incongruously, was formally laid out with a white linen cloth, long-stemmed wine glasses, silver knives and forks, a bowl of spring flowers and even a six-branched candelabra. Obviously an elegant little dinner party for two was about to take place.

Boris, looking quite respectable and even more handsome than usual in a clean white shirt and black jeans, silently sat down on one of the chairs at the table, and, lounging nonchalantly, waited for what was going to happen next.

Eulalia took off her apron with resolution. 'Well?' she demanded in a hostile manner. 'And what do you two want?'

Dover stared thoughtfully at her. He spoke, without turning his head, to MacGregor. 'Switch off that bloody row!' he barked, and waited grimly while the radio was silenced.

'An Englishman's home is his castle,' drawled Boris to nobody in particular.

'I hope you know what you are doing, Chief Inspector.' Eulalia Hoppold's voice was icy. 'I am not without influence in certain quarters.'

'Shut up!' snapped Dover. 'I'll deal with you in a minute. Right now I want to have a chat with Mister' – the word was a sneer – 'with Mister Bogolepov.'

He swung a chair up to the table and sat down facing Boris.

'But, please, don't let me stop you getting on with your dinner,' he said with mock consideration, 'I should hate to cause you any inconvenience.'

'Perhaps, my dear sir, you will join us?' Boris was not to be outdone in the exchange of politenesses. 'I am sure there will be enough for all – that is, if you do not mind taking pot luck.' He gave a rather disagreeable snigger.

For a second Dover hesitated. He was, he realized, extremely hungry. He'd not had a bite to eat since lunch, except for two cups of tea and a pork pie in the police canteen, and the stew or whatever it was in the cooker was sending out a most delicious aroma. Then, with a manful effort, he put the temptation aside. After all he was, he hoped, practically on the point of arresting Bogolepov for murder and it might be going a bit too far to start sharing his dinner with him. Besides, he didn't want the blooming business dragging on all night. No, better not.

'No, thank you, sir,' he said at last, and there was an audible sigh of relief from Sergeant MacGregor who, using the deep freeze as a rest for his notebook, had been anxiously awaiting his chief inspector's answer.

'A glass of wine, perhaps?' tempted Boris.

'All right,' said Dover, and quite unperturbed watched Boris remove the bottle from its bucket of ice and pour him out a glass of a cool, yellow-white liquid.

Dover sipped it cautiously. It wasn't at all bad.

'A glass for you, Sergeant?' asked Boris with a grin.

'No, thank you, sir,' replied MacGregor as frigidly as he dared.

'Well now, my dear Inspector,' said Boris, running his hand carelessly through his black hair, 'what can we do for you?'

'Just one or two little points we want to clear up, sir,' said Dover blandly.

Eulalia moved away from the cooker. 'Perhaps you'd like me to go?' she asked.

'No, I'd like you to stay, too, madam. There are one or two little points you might be able to clear up for us as well.'

Eulalia glared at him and then sat down at the table.

'Now, sir' – Dover turned back to Boris – 'can you remember selling a six-speed electric razor to Sir John Counter some little time ago?'

Boris frowned. 'Yes,' he said, looking puzzled.

'How much did Sir John pay you for it?'

Boris's frown deepened. He flashed a quick glance at Eulalia whose eyes, however, were riveted on Dover's face.

'Ten pounds.'

'I see. Did he pay for it by cash or by cheque?'

'He gave me a cheque.'

'I see, sir. And how long ago was this?'

Boris shrugged. 'About a month, five weeks, perhaps.'

'A month or five weeks,' repeated Dover slowly. 'I see, sir. Now, this business of you being a registered drug addict, sir, could you give me the name and address of the doctor who's dealing with your case, the one who authorizes your prescription?'

Boris's face became more guarded, but he still looked puzzled. He shrugged his shoulders again and gave the address of a doctor in London.

'And how do you actually get these drugs, Mr Bogolepov? Are they sent to you by post or what?' Dover was playing it very kid glove.

'No, I collect them from Simkins the chemist in Creedon.'

'How often, sir, once a month or once a week?'

Boris's eyes narrowed swiftly. 'Once a week.'

'Which day, sir?'

Boris picked up his wine glass. 'Oh, it varies. Sometimes one day, sometimes another.'

Dover sighed, more in sorrow than in anger. 'We can check with the chemist, sir,' he said wearily.

Boris rose angrily to his feet. 'Are you calling me a liar?' he shouted. 'I have told you, I do not have a special day! I go when I feel like it.'

'Boris!' Eulalia's voice rapped out in an authoritative warning.

The German hesitated a moment and then sat down again.

'Mr Bogolepov,' Dover pointed out mildly, 'no *genuine* drug addict could be quite so casual about getting hold of a "fix" as you appear to be. He'd want it as soon as the chemist would let him have it, wouldn't he? Now, which day was it?'

'Wednesday,' mumbled Boris sulkily.

'You go into Creedon to the chemist's every Wednesday?'

'Yes.'

'Without exception?' probed Dover relentlessly.

Boris grabbed a knife off the table and began to bend the blade between his strong, nervous fingers. From under lowered brows he shot another glance at Eulalia. This time she stared back at him.

'No,' he muttered at last through clenched teeth, 'last week I went on Friday.' He waited tensely for the next question. Eulalia seemed to be holding her breath.

Dover didn't oblige. He always enjoyed a bit of the old cat-and-mouse business.

'Oh, so you were in Creedon last Friday, were you? Did you go anywhere else except the chemist's?'

'No,' snapped Boris.

'Mr Bogolepov!' Dover waggled a reproving finger.

'Oh, I … I went to the post office, I think.'

'What for?'

'To post a parcel!' Boris almost shouted his answer.

'Who to?'

'It is none of your damned business! I want to know by what right you are asking these questions. I do not answer any more!' He leapt up from the table again and MacGregor got ready to stop him if he attempted to dash for the door.

Dover looked at him in surprise. 'Was there anything wrong about that parcel, sir?' he asked innocently.

'Of course not!' Eulalia took charge. 'Boris, sit down and don't be such a damned fool!' She swung back to the inspector, her eyes boring watchfully into his. 'You must forgive him, Chief Inspector. As you've probably noticed, he's a rather unstable character. He likes to pretend he's very tough and detached, a misanthrope in fact, but underneath he's as much humanity as most of us. The parcel he posted on Friday contained some old clothes – some of them mine, incidentally – for the refugee appeal. Boris is rather ashamed of his good action. That's why he got so excited.'

'Thank you, madam,' said Dover, not without a certain admiration for such quick-thinking composure. 'By the way,' he added casually, 'I wonder if you can help me on one minor point? Ladies notice these things more than we men do. Can you remember, by any chance, what colour nail varnish Juliet Rugg used to wear?'

It was Eulalia's turn to frown as she carefully examined the implications of this question. She decided to play it safe.

'I'm sorry, Inspector,' she smiled, not without a flicker of triumph, 'I'm afraid I can't remember.'

'Pity,' said Dover slowly. 'Oh well, it can't be helped.'

He put his bowler hat straight on his head and got up with a sigh from his chair.

'Is that all?' asked Eulalia suspiciously.

'I think so, madam, unless of course you've got anything you want to tell me.'

Eulalia relaxed almost imperceptibly and shook her head. Boris lolled back in his chair, grinning widely.

Suddenly Dover turned on him, dragged him to his feet by a fistful of his whiter-than-white shirt and slammed him up against the kitchen wall. Bogolepov's head cracked painfully as it came into contact with the unyielding surface.

'What happened,' bawled Dover ferociously, his face not more than an inch from Bogolepov's, 'what happened when Juliet Rugg called here on Tuesday night at eleven o'clock?' He underlined the importance of the question by giving his victim a good shaking.

Boris blinked. 'Don't hit me!' he screamed suddenly in a high, terrified voice. 'Don't hit me!'

'What happened?' roared Dover.

Boris opened his mouth and let out a stream of German. He struggled ineffectively to free himself from Dover's grip. The chief inspector bunched an enormous meaty fist menacingly under his victim's nose. In the background Sergeant MacGregor groaned inwardly.

'What happened?' snarled Dover again.

'Nothing! Nothing happened!' sobbed the young man.

'Nothing happened when she called?'

'No, nothing! Nothing!'

'Oh, so she *did* call, did she? You did see her on the Tuesday night?'

Boris tried to pull himself together and collect his thoughts.

'No, I haven't seen her at all.'

'Don't – lie – to – me!' shouted Dover, punctuating each word with a bone-jarring shake. 'I know you saw her.'

Eulalia had jumped to her feet. 'Don't answer, Boris!' she screamed. 'They're only trying to trap you. Don't answer!'

But the German wasn't listening to her. He cringed, whimpering and blubbering, back against the wall. 'Don't hit me,' he begged, 'don't hit me!'

'If you don't tell me the truth,' promised Dover, 'I'll break every bone in your body, one by one.'

'Don't hit me! It wasn't me! She killed her! She did it! It wasn't me. Don't hit me!'

'Shut up, you blabbing fool!' shouted Eulalia from the other side of the table. 'For God's sake keep your damned mouth shut!'

'What did you do with the body?' demanded Dover. 'D'you hear me? What did you do with the body?'

'No!' Eulalia's scream cut through the air. With a tremendous leap she flung herself on Dover's back, her hands clawing desperately for his face. As Dover released his hold to protect his eyes, Boris slipped out of his grasp and laughing in a shrieking hysteria, tears and sweat streaming down his face, he dashed across the room towards MacGregor.

'The body?' he screeched dementedly. 'The body? You wish to know where the body is?' He broke into a spine-chilling giggle which racked his whole body.

Dover flung Eulalia to one side. 'Get him, Sergeant!' he

shouted to MacGregor, who was still hovering uncertainly on the outskirts of the fracas.

The two detectives came at Boris with a rush but he side-stepped them smartly. Giggling uncontrollably and dancing about on his toes he went on shouting his refrain.

'You want the body? You want the body? Well, you are getting quite warm! Do you understand? You are getting quite warm!'

Dover made another clumsy grab at him, but Boris tore himself away and went crashing into the kitchen table. The whole lot toppled over; glasses, cutlery, flowers and wine shattered on to the floor.

''Strewth!' ejaculated Dover, gesticulating ludicrously as he tried to free his feet from the clinging folds of the table-cloth.

'Look out, sir!' yelled MacGregor.

Dover did and, much to his annoyance, found Boris charging at him, his eyes wild and a nasty-looking table knife in his hand. The chief inspector parried the savage knife-thrust with his left arm and sank his clenched fist into the pit of Bogolepov's stomach. His assailant doubled forward, choking and spitting, just as Dover's right knee jerked upwards. Boris received the blow right on the point of his chin.

With a sigh Dover tugged his handcuffs out of his hip pocket, snapped one end round Boris's wrist and dragged his unconscious body across the kitchen floor. With a grunt he bent down and clipped the other end of the handcuffs to the leg of the electric cooker. Boris groaned and began to show feeble signs of reviving. Dover thoughtfully gave him a kick where it would do most good and turned to see how his sergeant was getting on.

MacGregor, inhibited by a gentle upbringing and the mistaken idea that women are the weaker sex, wasn't doing any too well. Eulalia had already managed to drag her finger-nails effectively down the side of his face while the sergeant tried manfully to restrain her without actually doing anything which might cause annoyance or offence. No such delicacy of feeling deterred Dover. He grabbed one of Eulalia's arms and twisted it painfully behind her back. She lashed out with her feet at Dover's shins but he merely increased the pressure. Eulalia may have picked up a few pointers about hand-to-hand fighting from the noble savages with whom she had spent so much of her time, but Dover had learned

174

his methods from free-born Englishmen and modestly reckoned, when it came to slashing and gouging, that he could hold his own with anyone. Once again the arts of civilization triumphed.

'Get your handcuffs out, you fool!' he shouted at MacGregor.

They managed to get one handcuff on Eulalia's wrist and then Dover picked her up bodily, still kicking and biting and cursing, and carted her across the room. He dumped her heavily and unceremoniously on the floor beside Boris and clipped the handcuff to the other leg of the cooker.

'Hell's teeth!' he exclaimed as he looked round the room, his bowler hat still resting squarely on his head. 'What a mess!'

MacGregor mopped the blood off his face. 'Whew!' he said. 'I never expected 'em to run amuck like that, did you, sir?'

'No, and that's not the only thing I didn't expect either. What was it he said about the body? "You're getting warm" or something, wasn't it?' Dover looked grimly round the room again. 'Just have a look in that deep freeze thing, MacGregor,' he said casually.

MacGregor threw his chief inspector an inquiring glance and then went obediently across to the deep freeze and opened the lid.

'Seems to be full of food or something, sir,' he said, pulling out a fair-sized, Cellophane-wrapped package.

He wiped some of the frost off one end of it and peered through the transparent paper. For a second he didn't get it. Then the significance of the object he was holding penetrated. It was a human arm, frozen solid and ending in five green-painted finger-nails.

'Oh my God!' he said in a horrified voice. 'It's ... ' His eyes bulged and he gulped ominously. Dropping the parcel on to the floor he stuffed his blood-bespattered handkerchief into his mouth and made an ignominious dash for the back door. From the pitch blackness outside came a distressing, choking sound. Detective Sergeant Charles Edward MacGregor was being sick in the garden.

Dover, sneering complacently to himself over the squeamishness of present-day policemen, strolled over to the deep freeze and pulled out another tidily wrapped bundle. It was large and round, like a football. His own stomach gave a sympathetic heave. He slammed the lid down and hurried, rather shakily but with an unerring instinct, across the room to one of the kitchen cupboards. Inside was Boris's supply of whisky.

'I reckon poor old MacGregor could do with a shot of this,' he muttered as he poured out a tumblerful and then tossed it, with one tremendous gulp, down his own throat.

It was at this somewhat inopportune moment that Colonel Bing arrived.

'Hello!' she called inanely. 'Anybody home?'

With Peregrine in her arms she stepped through the open back door into the kitchen.

'I've come for Peregrine's bone. He did so enjoy the last one, the greedy little ...' her voice trailed off.

She gaped at Dover, still clutching his bottle of whisky, and stared in blank astonishment at the prostrate bodies handcuffed to the legs of the electric stove. Eulalia was cursing horribly and Boris had started to giggle feebly again. Finally her eyes wandered to the mess of plates and broken glass on the kitchen floor.

'Dear God!' she exclaimed, almost inaudibly. 'What on earth's going on?'

'I'm just in the process of making an arrest,' announced Dover loftily. 'I think it would be as well if you didn't stay here.'

Colonel Bing ignored him. 'Eulalia!' she cried. 'What have they done to you?'

She dropped Peregrine and hurried across to her neighbour.

The dog, pausing only briefly to cock his leg up against one of the overturned chairs, headed straight for the grisly parcel MacGregor had dropped on the floor. He grabbed it and started proudly for the back door.

'Hey!' yelled Dover with visions of his evidence disappearing before his eyes. 'Drop that, you filthy brute!'

The chief inspector had never played Rugby in his life, but, with a valiant lunge, he got Peregrine round the back legs in a superb flying tackle. The poodle squealed in outrage, dropped his trophy and bit Dover.

Just as Sergeant MacGregor, his face tinged unpleasantly with an obscene yellow hue, appeared sheepishly in the doorway, the electric cooker suddenly began belching out an inordinate quantity of black, greasy smoke. Colonel Bing, Boris and Eulalia practically disappeared from view. The stew was burning.

'For God's sake,' bawled Dover, still fighting it out with Pere-grine on the floor, 'why doesn't somebody do something?'

MacGregor seized a towel and flung himself heroically at the oven door. He grabbed the casserole, burnt black and still smoking furiously, and rushed outside with it. Colonel Bing switched the cooker off and opened a window. Dover managed to struggle to his feet and Peregrine, his rear end a couple of inches ahead of Dover's boot, fled to the safety of his mistress's arms.

'What on earth's happening?' demanded Colonel Bing, cough-ing, black-faced, dishevelled and not at all impressed by Scotland Yard's detection methods.

'Never you mind!' rasped Dover. 'None of your business.'

'I'm a tax-payer,' snapped Colonel Bing, 'I have a right to know what's going on.'

MacGregor staggered in again.

'Sergeant,' roared Dover hoarsely, 'get this blasted woman out of here! And that damned dog too!'

While MacGregor, always a miracle of tact, was carrying out his instructions, Dover helped himself to another shot of whisky. It made him feel better, but not all that much.

After a bit the sergeant came back, somewhat unenthusiastic-ally, into the kitchen.

'She's going to write to her M.P., sir,' he said, squeamishly keeping his eyes away from the deep freeze, 'and the Ministry of Defence.'

'Silly old bitch,' said Dover. He helped himself to yet another glass of whisky. 'That foreign swine come round yet?'

'I think so, sir.'

'Good. Well, I'm going to have another little chat with Mr Bloody Bogolepov and see if I can get a bit more information out of him. The woman obviously isn't going to say anything, but I think, with a little persuasion, I can make him open his mouth and sing.'

Dover flexed his muscles. They creaked a bit.

'Now, you nip off and phone the local police in Creedon and tell 'em to send the lot over here pronto. Finger-print men, photo-graphers, a doctor and the police wagon for these two. Oh, and they'd better get hold of a Home Office pathologist as well. We shall no doubt want him.'

'Where shall I phone from, sir?' asked MacGregor.

'How the hell do I know?' snorted Dover crossly. 'There isn't one here. Try next door — no, better still, try the Hoppold woman's house. She's probably got one.'

'Very good, sir,' said MacGregor, and moved over to Eulalia who was still handcuffed to her leg of the cooker. MacGregor knelt down beside her. She kicked and screamed at him as he stretched out his hands towards her.

'MacGregor,' said Dover with diminishing patience, 'are you attempting assault on that woman?'

MacGregor looked up. 'Of course not, sir, I was just looking for her keys.'

'Never mind about the blasted keys!' The chief inspector's control broke. 'Kick the bloody door down if it isn't open. And for God's sake get a move on!'

When MacGregor returned half an hour later he found Boris, calm and relaxed, sitting up on one of the kitchen chairs. Most of the smoke had dispersed and Dover was just putting a hypodermic syringe back on the shelf.

'Well, the bugger's talked all right,' he announced casually.

'You haven't doped him, have you, sir?' asked the sergeant, unwilling to believe that even Dover would go quite so far.

'I gave him a shot' — Dover dusted his hands fastidiously on his handkerchief — '*after* he'd made a free and voluntary statement. Now both of us have got what we want.'

Chapter Fifteen

FRIDAY morning dawned at last, bright and sunny but distinctly chilly. The police were still hard at it in Bogolepov's bungalow. Boris and Eulalia had been carted off – Eulalia protesting, fighting and screaming the whole way – in a police van and the experts had moved in. The Home Office pathologist had rushed through the night to get his hands on what promised to be the most interesting corpse of his entire, none too distinguished, medical career. With little whimpers of admiration for the surgery, 'very good, very good indeed for an amateur,' he lovingly unloaded the deep freeze. All the bits and pieces of Juliet, now frozen solid, had been neatly wrapped up in transparent paper. 'Just like the supermarket,' remarked one youthful uniformed policeman with a silly giggle.

By six o'clock everything was finished and Dover and MacGregor returned wearily to The Two Fiddlers for breakfast. Neither had much of an appetite.

A couple of hours later, rather haggard and drawn but washed and shaved, they were ushered into the Chief Constable's office to make their final report.

'Jolly good show, chaps!' said Mr Bartlett, sounding and feeling just like Montgomery after Alamein. 'I understand you've done a really fine bit of work. Well up to the traditions of the Yard, eh? Now, I'd like to have the whole story from you, step by step, just so that I can get the picture clear in my mind. I suppose you have got it completely tied up all right? Aren't going to be any loose ends or' – he glanced doubtfully at Dover – 'or any repercussions?'

Dover shook his head. 'There'll be no slip-up on this one, sir,' he promised smugly. 'Bogolepov's turning Queen's Evidence, but we've got enough circumstantial evidence to put a rope round both their necks.'

'It's not capital murder, sir,' MacGregor pointed out.

Dover frowned. 'Blast it!' he snorted in disgust. 'No more it is. Pity.'

'Well, never mind,' said the Chief Constable encouragingly, 'we've caught the murderers and that's what really matters, isn't it? Now come on, let's have the whole story. My inspector just told me that you'd made the arrests but he didn't give me any details.'

'Well,' said Dover, leaning back in his chair and closing his eyes, 'what happened was this. Boris Bogolepov and Eulalia Hoppold decided one fine day to murder Juliet Rugg.' He opened his eyes suddenly. 'They may try to wriggle out of it, but there's no doubt the murder was premeditated. They'd planned out all the details months before they actually pulled the job.' He shut his eyes again. 'Now, Juliet Rugg's regular afternoon off was Tuesday. Most weeks she used to clear off after lunch and not return to Irlam Old Hall until round about eleven at night. Usually she'd been out on the tiles with her current gentleman friend, Gordon Pilley. He used to drop her outside the main gates and she used to walk alone up the drive to the Counters' house. Anybody at Irlam Old Hall could have found this out if they'd taken the trouble to keep their eyes open. Well, the plan was this. Eulalia was the one who was going to do the actual killing. I think she's been the instigator all the way through. Bogolepov's not a very forceful character, what with drink and drugs, but the Hoppold woman's got nerves of steel, if you ask me. Now then, just before eleven o'clock she was going to go out and hide in the bushes at the bottom of Sir John's garden. The drive bends round to the left there and, as Juliet walked along, for a brief moment she would be facing the exact spot where Eulalia was concealed, and only ten yards or so away. It would be very dark but Eulalia's done a lot of hunting under much worse conditions and at that range she was hardly likely to miss.'

'What about the noise?' asked the Chief Constable, 'had she got a silencer?'

'Bow and arrow,' said Dover laconically, 'believe it or believe it not! She'd got several that she'd brought back as souvenirs from her travels. She's a crack shot with 'em, too. Well, after Juliet had bitten the dust, Boris was to come out of his house and help load the body into Sir John's wheel chair. Oh, I forgot to mention, Eulalia had got it out of the shed ready before she took up her position. She knew the wheels squeaked so she gave 'em a good oiling first. We found a can of the oil that was used in her kitchen. Nothing very exciting, but corroborative evidence all the same.

'Now, it was Boris's job to wheel the body back to his house while Eulalia cleared up any traces of the murder which might remain – spots of blood, Juliet's handbag which no doubt she would drop and so on. Then Eulalia was to give Boris a hand with lugging the dead girl – don't forget she weighed sixteen stone – into the bathroom. Bogolepov's place is a bungalow, so they wouldn't have to carry the body upstairs. Then they were to strip the body and while Eulalia got to work, Boris would take Sir John's wheel chair back to its shed and have another look round to make quite sure they hadn't left any clues. All very efficient, you see, and well thought out.

'In fact' – Dover scratched his head thoughtfully – 'if it had gone strictly according to plan, there's a fair chance we might never have got our hands on 'em – well, we mightn't have been able to bring it home to 'em, anyhow. But the unexpected happened. Eulalia was out waiting in the bushes with her bow and arrow, the wheel chair was standing ready and Boris was peering through his front-room window, ready to rush out and give a hand when the time came. They probably heard Gordon Pilley's car drive off, and here was Juliet, walking, as they'd expected, up the drive. But, most unexpectedly, when she got level with the gate of Bogolepov's garden, she turned in, marched up his path and rang the front-door bell. I reckon Boris, who was pretty keyed up with dope and excitement, just about dropped down dead himself with shock. However he managed to keep his head and opened the door. Juliet had just called with a message from Simkins, the chemist, in Creedon. Boris's prescription, which he collected once a week on Wednesdays – and this was Tuesday night, remember – wouldn't be ready this week until Friday morning. The prescription was actually Bogolepov's supply of drugs which he got under the N.H.S., but of course Juliet wouldn't know this. Boris wasn't on the phone and Simkins had asked Juliet to give him the message so that he wouldn't make an unnecessary trip the following morning.

'Well, presumably, Boris thanked her for her kindness and said good night. Juliet went back down the path, out of the garden gate and then started up the drive again towards Sir John's house. Eulalia, who must have been wondering what the hell was going on, remained as cool as a cucumber and when the girl came level with her, calmly shot her, as planned, clean through the heart with a genuine Australian aborigine bow and arrow.'

'Weren't they taking a terrible risk that somebody might see them?'

'A bit, sir, but murder's a risky business, when all's said and done. Actually there wasn't all that much danger. It's very quiet up there and I think they'd have heard if anybody was knocking about. And then all the houses stand pretty far back from the drive and the trees provide a fair amount of cover. I don't think anybody, looking casually out of a window at the wrong time, would actually have seen anything.

'Anyhow, where was I? Oh yes, Eulalia gets a bull's-eye on poor old Juliet and, right on cue, out pops Boris. They load the dead girl into the wheel chair and the whole thing goes off like clockwork.

'Now, while Boris is returning the wheel chair to its shed and having a last look round, Eulalia sets to work with a carving knife. She's apparently quite experienced in cutting up the dead bodies of animals for the pot and, as the pathologist fellow remarked, she did quite a good job on Juliet. Bogolepov's bathroom was the ideal place, all pink tiles, covering the floor as well. There's a little drain thing in the middle for the shower water to run down so it didn't matter how much mess Eulalia made, really, because you could just swill the whole place down, walls and all. Very nice, that bathroom was,' said Dover with envious reminiscence, 'wouldn't mind one like that myself. All pink and black – very artistic. Shower as well and a little foot-bath thing – continental idea that, you know. Oh well,' he sighed, 'where was I?'

'Miss Hoppold was dismembering Juliet Rugg in the pink and black bathroom,' the Chief Constable prompted.

'Oh yes. Well, that's really all there is to it. She cut Juliet up into handy-sized joints, wrapped the pieces up neatly in that transparent paper stuff and packed them away in the deep freeze cabinet in Bogolepov's kitchen. No wonder we couldn't find the flaming body!'

'And are you going to be able to prove all this?' demanded the Chief Constable.

'Oh, I reckon so,' said Dover easily. 'We've got Bogolepov's statement first of all and, even if he tries to retract it in court, which he won't, he'll never get away with it. Then we can prove that Eulalia Hoppold has a tin of the same kind of oil as was used on the wheel chair. Your boys have been working on the bathroom and I'm pretty certain they'll find traces of human blood somewhere – in a crack or something. It's difficult stuff to get rid of, you know. Same with the bow and arrow. Eulalia hung 'em back on the wall with her other trophies when she'd finished with 'em – well cleaned, of course. Even if the lab. doesn't find traces of blood on the arrow-head, the fact that it has been cleaned thoroughly is significant in itself. None of the other weapons had been.'

'But, how did you get on to all this?' asked the Chief Constable.

'Well, it was pretty difficult,' said Dover, anxious not to have his achievement played down. 'Actually, they both slipped up and like all these flipping amateurs they couldn't leave well alone. Silly fools tried to be clever and get a rise out of the police. Well' – Dover sniffed triumphantly – 'now they know better.'

'All right,' said the Chief Constable, who knew his wife would be furious if he didn't give her all the details at lunch-time so that she was well primed for her bridge afternoon, 'how did they slip up?'

'Well, first of all there was the green nail varnish,' said Dover, making a mental note to write up the final report himself instead of leaving it to Sergeant MacGregor – just to keep things in perspective. 'We found that Juliet couldn't have been wearing green nail varnish until tea-time on the day she disappeared. Red nail varnish, yes – but not green. So when Eulalia Hoppold talked about Juliet having *green* nail varnish on we knew she must have seen her *after* the girl returned to Irlam Old Hall – as, of course she did, when she cut the body up.

'But much more important was the slip Bogolepov made. The damned fool actually acted on the message that Juliet had brought from the chemist. Instead of going into Creedon to collect his drugs on the Wednesday, as he normally did, he waited and didn't go in until the Friday. That was a bad mistake because, of course, it showed that he, too, had seen Juliet round about eleven o'clock on the Tuesday night. Obviously no junky would casually wait a couple of days before getting hold of his supplies.

Mind you, I reckon Boris was getting dope illegally somehow in any case, but when I challenged him about going into Creedon on the Friday he just hadn't got any answer.'

'And what about this kidnapping note to Sir John Counter?'

'Oh, that was Eulalia and Boris being a bit too damned clever. It was meant, as I suspected at the time, just as a red herring. They'd no intention of collecting the money. Boris bundled up a parcel of Juliet's clothes and sent them to a refugee organization in London. The ransom letter, addressed to Sir John's bank, you remember, was inside. One of the helpers unpacking the parcels found it, handed it on to the woman in charge and, quite naturally, she posted it. The whole thing was planned to make us think that somebody in London had kidnapped Juliet because everybody at Irlam Old Hall could prove that they hadn't been in London at the time the letter was posted. Unfortunately, they hadn't realized that the finger-print was a complete give-away. It showed Juliet was already dead.'

'Well' – Dover reached for his bowler hat – 'if there's nothing else we'll be getting back to town, sir. I'll let you have my report as soon as I can get it done. Might be useful to let some of your chaps have a look at it – just to give 'em some idea of how we tackle a job at the Yard. Meticulous attention to detail, you know, studying and restudying every tiny point and then the flash of inspiration ... ' Dover smiled complacently.

'I still don't understand quite,' said the Chief Constable, 'what the motive was. I mean, why did they bother to kill this perfectly harmless girl?'

Dover avoided MacGregor's eye. 'Well, I don't know that you could call Juliet a perfectly harmless girl, sir,' he said. 'We know she'd been trying a bit of the old blackmail game on at least two other people at Irlam Old Hall. My guess is that she'd spotted that Bogolepov and Hoppold were having an affair and she started trying to put the pressure on there too. Unfortunately, La Hoppold wasn't the one to submit to that sort of thing quietly – hence the murder.'

The Chief Constable didn't look very satisfied. 'Sounds a bit thin,' he objected.

The fact that this was the opinion Dover himself had held only a few hours before didn't make it any more palatable.

'Well, there it is!' he snapped impatiently. 'You can take it or leave it! And anyhow, we don't have to prove motive – not with the blooming body there in the deep freeze.'

'I know we don't have to prove motive,' retorted Mr Bartlett testily, 'but it makes a case more convincing if you do, doesn't it? Besides, I've had quite a lot to do with dope addicts in my time and I'm blowed if I can remember one of them who was really hooked, as you say Bogolepov was, who ever bothered over much with women. And Miss Hoppold's not exactly what you'd call a sex kitten, is she?'

Dover snorted crossly down his nose. He didn't relish having all his own arguments tossed back at him like this, especially with Big-Ears MacGregor greedily drinking in every word.

'I know it's a bit unusual,' he admitted grudgingly, 'but there it is. Damn it, there's no law about it, is there? Eulalia Hoppold was Bogolepov's mistress and she didn't want her husband to find out and she didn't want to be blackmailed by Juliet. That's all there is to it.'

'Well, I don't know,' said the Chief Constable doubtfully. He hesitated for a moment and then picked up a bright green envelope from his desk. 'I got this this morning. Of course,' he added hastily, 'I'm not saying there's anything in it, but perhaps you'd like to have a look at it – just to see what you think.'

With an irate sigh Dover took the envelope and removed several sheets of bright green paper. He raised his eyebrows pityingly at the Chief Constable and began to read.

The letter was written in purple ink and bore the address of Irlam Old Hall. It began in a neat, old-fashioned hand:

Dear Chief Constable,
I don't think we have actually ever met but I know your cousin Nancy Sells *very* well so perhaps that will serve as an introduction(!).

I don't know whether they've told you but a young girl called Juliet Rugg has been missing from Irlam Old Hall for over a week now. She worked for Sir John Counter, of whom you may have heard.

Naturally everybody is very worried about her and I myself have spent a long time trying to solve the riddle of her disappearance. I have tried once or twice to talk the matter over with Chief Inspector Lover (such an *unusual* name) from New Scotland Yard, but he has been so busy that we haven't really had time to discuss my theory in detail so I thought I would write to you and then you can bring all the weight of your high office (!) to bear on the investigation.

It was really Sir John Counter who sowed the *first* seed of the idea in my head – purely by accident, you understand. You may know that he is a great sweet eater (much better than cigarettes, as we all know, but unfortunately he smokes as well). Usually he has special sweets sent to him from London but from time to time he buys half a pound (or even a pound) of jelly-babies. Not long ago in the drive I met him and he offered me the bag, saying 'Let me give you a baby, Miss Frail!' He always says this and it is his idea of a joke. (Sir John, in spite of coming from a *very* old family, is unnecessarily coarse at times, but I never let on that I know his words have a *secondary* meaning.) (He always calls me Miss Frail though, of course, he knows quite well what my real name is.)

On this occasion I refused his offer of a jelly-baby, saying with a laugh, 'No, thank you, Sir John, they always make me feel like a *cannibal* ! ! !'

When Juliet Rugg disappeared everybody seemed to be worried about the whereabouts of the *body* and I thought – remembering the jelly-babies – that a good way to get rid of a dead body (always a difficulty, I understand) would be to *eat* it ! !

Purely by chance I had been reading one of my brother's books on this very subject. It was written by a missionary to the Fiji Islands and naturally the cannibalism of those dreadful heathens played a large part in his memoirs. (I still have the book and would be pleased to lend it to you should you so desire.) (There is no need to let my brother know about it.) Now, this missionary, the Reverend Dr Augustine Browne, said that once people started eating human flesh, they came to prefer it *above all other*.

Well, you will appreciate, this gave me furiously to think!

I began looking at my neighbours with a critical eye. 'Has this one,' I asked myself, 'ever eaten another human being?'

To my surprise, and horror (because Irlam Old Hall is really very select and well thought of in the district) I found that the answer in *two* cases was, YES! Two people had been in circumstances when, at the very least, they had the opportunity to eat human flesh.

And who are these people? You may well ask! They are Miss Eulalia Hoppold and Sergeant-Major Bondy!!

I will take the member of the fair sex first. Miss Hoppold is a noted woman explorer and has even appeared on television, though I have not seen her, and she has spent many years living with savage tribes and studying their habits. She has written at least *three* books about her adventures with tribes who practise cannibalism! Miss Hoppold is a very *whole-hearted* person and one who is eager for new and exciting experiences. Can we believe that she could resist the temptation to try a morsel of human flesh herself??

Then there is Sergeant-Major Bondy. Did you know that during the war a troopship on which he happened to be travelling was *sunk* (by the Japanese, I believe)? He and fourteen other of our Brave Boys were adrift for twenty-three days on an open raft. Only Sergeant-Major Bondy and one other survived!!! I have questioned Mr Bondy several times about his experiences and his *extreme* reticence about how he survived this shipwreck strikes me, under the circumstances, as very suspicious! He admits they had no food, and only rainwater to drink. What other explanation can there be, except that to preserve his own life he ate *some*, or all, of his companions??

That is my theory!! These two people have already tasted and enjoyed (!!) human flesh. The longing to repeat this terrible experience grew on them. Together they killed poor Juliet Rugg to satisfy their vile desires! I have, of course, no proof but I feel sure that you can convince Chief Inspector Lover that it is worth investigating further. Since formulating my theory I have kept a careful eye on my two suspects. In my opinion they are studiously avoiding any contact with each other – a well-known habit of malefactors hoping to avoid suspicion until the *heat* dies down! Miss Hoppold and Mr Bondy have not, to the best of my knowledge, exchanged *one word* since the disappearance of the unfortunate Juliet Rugg. What do you think of that??

Only this afternoon Miss Hoppold told Colonel Bing (one

of my neighbours up here) that she had a *nice large bone* which might be suitable for Peregrine (Colonel Bing's white miniature poodle – a charming little chap). Colonel Bing asked if it was the kind that splintered and Miss Hoppold said, NO!!

As a single woman living (for all practical purposes) alone, my suspicions were aroused *immediately*! Single women just do not buy large joints of meat containing unsplinterable bones, and Miss Hoppold (although I know for a fact she is a married woman) is living *alone*. This is a clue which Chief Inspector Lover as a *man* may well have overlooked! It is true Miss Hoppold from time to time takes her meals with Mr Bogolepov (another of my neighbours), but that young man appears to obtain most of his nourishment out of bottles (!) and I am sure has never sat down to what I call a *square* meal for years.

I shall endeavour, tactfully, to obtain this bone from Colonel Bing (or Peregrine!) and, if I am successful, I will send it to you for analysis. I should myself like to pursue my investigations further but fear that I may inadvertently arouse the suspicions of Miss Hoppold and Mr Bondy. Having killed once, they will not hesitate to kill *again*, and my brother is not the kind of man who would be able to offer me much protection in the event of an attack on *me* because I know *too much*!

So I feel I shall now have to leave the matter in your capable hands! And I look forward to hearing from you in the near future.

Please give my kind regards to Nancy when next you see her and tell her that I still have a wee chuckle to myself about our amusing little misunderstanding at the Annual General Meeting of the W.I.!

With all best wishes,

Yours sincerely,

AMY FREEL (MISS)

P.S. Please treat this letter as *highly confidential*!

As Dover finished reading each sheet of the letter he passed it with a broad wink to Sergeant MacGregor. As he handed over the last page, the Chief Constable, who had been fidgeting rest-lessly in the background, spoke.

'Well?' he asked.

'Well, what?' replied Dover with a grin.

'Well, is there anything in it?'

'In that?' Dover's grin widened. 'You must be barmy, sir! Load of rubbish from beginning to end.'

'She got Eulalia Hoppold right,' the Chief Constable pointed out stiffly.

'Yes, and she got this Bondy fellow wrong, didn't she?' retorted Dover. 'Bondy'd nothing to do with it at all. He's never even come remotely into the picture. Though mind you, if we'd known he hadn't spoken to Eulalia for a week we might have had our suspicions about him, eh, Sergeant?'

The two Scotland Yard men exchanged condescending smiles.

'Yes' – the Chief Constable's face was red with embarrassment but he ploughed resolutely on – 'but what about the motive?'

'Well, what about it?' snapped Dover impatiently. 'Cannibal-ism? At Irlam Old Hall? Don't make me laugh!'

'I don't see why.' The Chief Constable was now scarlet to the top of his ears. 'It seems to fit the known facts better than the motive you've suggested.'

'Now look here, sir.' Dover assumed the air of a man who's just about had enough. 'You've had a letter from some old girl up at Irlam Old Hall who's read a few too many of these detective story things and gone a bit off the old rocker. By pure chance she guesses one thing right – Eulalia Hoppold. Everything else is wrong! Cannibalism is wrong. William Bondy is wrong. The dog's blasted bone is wrong.'

'Oh, I agree Bondy is wrong, but what about Bogolepov?'

'Oh dear me, sir, you're not suggesting he was a cannibal too, are you?' Dover's ample stomach wobbled with mirth. 'D'you hear that, MacGregor? Mr Bartlett thinks Bogolepov's a cannibal now!'

'He spent years in that concentration camp. Some of the poor devils had to eat human flesh to survive. It's a well-known fact. Strikes me he's an even better candidate than Bondy. And look at the way the body was carved up and stored in the deep freeze!'

Dover liked a good laugh at somebody else's expense, but this was going on too long. He looked pointedly at his watch and settled his bowler hat more firmly on his head.

'Well, it's up to you, sir. If you want to put your faith in the potty theories of crack-brained old biddies who write to you on green paper, you go ahead and do it! If you really believe that Hoppold and Bogolepov killed Juliet Rugg because they wanted to *eat* her, you can send a special report to the Director of Public Prosecutions yourself because, I can assure you, it won't appear in my report!'

'Yes, I suppose it is a bit far-fetched,' the Chief Constable agreed doubtfully, 'but ... '

'Far-fetched? Gawd, it's enough to make a cat laugh! Look here, sir, I've investigated this case, and I've bloody well solved it. Juliet Rugg was killed because she was a blackmailer, and if I were you, sir, I'd burn that letter before anybody else gets wind of it. You don't want to be the laughing-stock of the county, do you, eh? 'Strewth, can you imagine what the newspapers'd do to you if they ever found out you thought you'd caught a couple of cannibals?' Dover laughed heartily. 'You'd never live it down, sir, straight you wouldn't!'

The Chief Constable didn't like being laughed at and his manner as he shook hands with Dover was rather cool.

The chief inspector was still chuckling as he took his leave. 'We'll be up for the trial I expect, sir,' he said. 'Perhaps you'd better warn 'em at the prison that Bogolepov and Hoppold'll need a special diet! Long pig they call it, don't they? Oh well, come on, Sergeant, or we'll be missing our train.'

As he reached the door he couldn't resist a final crack.

'I don't suppose you'll be calling the Yard in again if you get another murder, will you, sir? Not when you've got your own "private eye" up at Irlam Old Hall, eh? Miss Sherlock Holmes Freel, the wonder woman detective. Cannibals? That's a ripe one that is!'

Now Back in Print

Margot Arnold

The first four adventures of Margot Arnold's beloved pair of peripatetic sleuths, Penny Spring and Sir Toby Glendower:

The Cape Cod Caper	192 pages	$4.95
Death on the Dragon's Tongue	224 pages	$4.95
Death of a Voodoo Doll	220 pages	$4.95
Exit Actors, Dying	176 pages	$4.95
Lament for a Lady Laird	224 pages	$4.95
Zadok's Treasure	192 pages	$4.95

"The British archaelogist and American anthropologist are cut in the classic mold of Christie's Poirot...." — *Sunday Cape Cod Times*

"A new Margot Arnold mystery is always a pleasure...She should be better known, particularly since her mysteries are often compared to those of the late Ngaio March." — *Chicago Sun Times*

Joyce Porter

American readers, having faced several lean years deprived of the company of Chief Inspector Wilfred Dover, will rejoice (so to speak) in the reappearance of "the most idle and avaricious policeman in the United Kingdom (and, possibly, the world)." Here is the trilogy that introduced the bane of Scotland Yard and his hapless assistant, Sergeant MacGregor, to international acclaim.

Dover One	192 pages	$4.95
Dover Two	222 pages	$4.95
Dover Three	192 pages	$4.95

"Meet Detective Chief Inspector Wilfred Dover. He's fat, lazy, a scrounger and the worst detective at Scotland Yard. But you will love him." — *Manchester Evening News*